MARK ELLIS

THE FALCON™
RESURRECTED

Published by Millennial Concepts
www.millennialconcepts.com
Cover art by Rob Moran
Book & cover design by Melissa Martin Ellis

THE FALCON LEGEND

HE EXISTS as a whisper, a myth, a shadow that crosses between fable and reality.

The only thing really known about the man called The Falcon is that nothing is truly known—it's rumored he adopts and discards names and identities almost on a whim.

Although The Falcon has been suspected and accused of being a professional thief, freelance adventurer, private detective and even a spy, his actual movements could no more be tracked than those of a ghost. There were reports he fought as a mercenary in several wars and revolutions, that he held degrees from Cambridge and served as an intelligence officer in the American military.

But those who preyed on the weak and defenseless knew The Falcon was far more substantial than a spirit—the bodies of those he made his own prey were found in all countries, in every corner of the globe…marked with a small card imprinted with the image of a fierce hunting bird, with backswept wings and outstretched talons.

The legend of The Falcon lived on—expanding, taking on a new a frightening resonance as the symbol for a vengeance that struck swiftly and mercilessly.

When The Falcon at last decided to fold his wings and give up the hunt, he was offered legal sanction to continue his work by The Eyrie—a very small, very secret organization that accepted assignments considered too risky or too extreme to be undertaken by government intelligence or judicial agencies.

The Falcon accepted the offer and became known as Michael Waring—whether this was his real name or yet another identity he assumed, no one knew and no one asked. All he required of The Eyrie was the freedom to accept or reject the missions offered to him. As he said: "Men and falcons are born to fly free."

PROLOGUE
May 10th, the Zittertal Alpen, Austria

THE STEADY sound of steel driving into ice stopped. The setting sun threw shadows across the frozen surface of the titanic glacier which crept down from the Hochfeiler peak.

Three men shivered at the foot of the frozen flow. Their breaths plumed before their faces. Although they were bundled up in heavy overcoats, they were still cold. Winter stayed a very long time at 9000 feet above sea level.

The three men represented three generations of age, divided by time and experience, but united for the moment by a single purpose.

Julius Eicke was of medium height, his silver-streaked hair stirred by the chill wind. Thick of feature and body, his grey eyes were masked by dark sunglasses. His top-coat was expensive and stylish. He was seventy-six years old and president of Hauser and Hochbach, a prestigious brokerage firm based in Berlin, with branch offices in nine European metropolitan centers.

Ulrich Schreck's thin, ancient body sat hunched over in a wheelchair, his lower face protected from the cold by a woolen scarf. His naked, blue-veined head trembled slightly. His face was withered and criss-crossed with a network of wrinkles, seams and lines, but his eyes burned as hot and as blue as the sky high above the Alps.

Lieutenant Colonel Avery Simmons, U.S. Army, stood slightly behind Schreck's wheelchair. His dark blonde hair was cut in a severe military style. He was forty-five, and his unlined face was all sharp angles and planes. His brown eyes squinted against the sun-glitter from the ice field.

The three watched two men, a hundred yards into the base of the glacier, hack and chopped at the ice with axes and hammers. They were young, barely out of their teens. Their heads were shaven. One had removed his heavy gloves and blue tattoos stood out sharply against his pale skin. His right hand bore a crude likeness of a swastika, and the other a stylized iron cross.

His companion took off his scarf and wiped bits of ice from his face. The word *Herrenvolk* was stenciled in crude Gothic script across his acne-spotted forehead. A close inspection of the word would have revealed a successful, if painful, experiment with a red- hot needle.

The gloveless man inserted two fingers into his mouth and whistled.

He shouted, "Almost have it, Herr Eicke!"

Schreck grimaced and said, "Does that animal think he's on a street corner in Dusseldorf?"

Eicke shrugged. "They are useful, Standartenfuhrer."

Schreck spat onto the snow. "Don't call me by rank, you idiot. Hitler's war is long over."

He squinted at the pair of young men as they bent over the hole chopped in the ice and struggled with something within it.

"They can be trusted?" he asked.

"Of course not," Eicke replied. "They believe with all their hearts in the Aryan struggle—this week. Next week, they could be just as passionate about cross-country skiing."

After a long moment of grunting and cursing, the two men dragged a long, rectangular box out of the hole. Made of lead, it was shaped like a casket. Schreck leaned forward, his fierce eyes gazing raptorially at the dark, metallic surface of the thing. Over half-a-century of ice clung to it.

The pair of youths carried it, sliding and stumbling across the base of the glacier to Eicke, and they dropped it carelessly at his feet. They panted, and despite the cold, they were perspiring.

"Hard fucking work," said the one with Herrenvolk stenciled across his forehead. "I think you owe us another hundred Euros."

The man with the tattooed hands gestured to the casket. "You want us to open it for you, Herr Eicke?"

Schreck's toothless mouth opened. Spittle strings clung between his gums. "What lies within is not for the eyes of swine," he snarled.

Herrenvolk glared at the old man. "Fuck off, you old prick. We don't work for you."

He turned to Eicke. "When do we get paid?"

Before Eicke could respond, Schreck said, "Immediately."

One claw-like hand dove inside his coat. It came out gripping a Walther P-38, the official service pistol of the German forces during the war. Schreck didn't seem to aim—he squeezed the double-action trigger and two flat cracks shattered the still, frosty air.

The first nine millimeter slug took the youth with the tattooed hands directly through the heart. The second bullet inscribed a blue-edged umlaut over the "O" of Herrenvolk on the other man's forehead. The two shots had come so fast they sounded like a single report.

Eicke and Simmons regarded the two corpses lying in the snow with dispassionate eyes. Steam arose from the blood streaming from their bodies.

"Your eye is as keen as my father told me," Eicke said wryly.

Schreck shoved the pistol back inside his coat. "Before we leave, you must plant that trash in the hole they've dug. Maybe in another seventy years someone may wait for them to surface. I can't imagine who."

He laughed, a dry, crackling sound. One gnarled finger pointed to the casket. "Open it, Julius."

Eicke's eyebrows rose. "Here?"

"Why not?"

"I assumed you would wish a ceremony of some sort—"

Schreck laughed again and this time it held a bitter, humorless edge. "You engage two street pigs to dig it out of the ice, and you think I want a ceremony? Rituals can wait, Julius."

Eicke thought it over a moment, then shrugged. "As you wish, sir."

Taking a chisel from the tool belt around Herrenvolk's waist, Eicke attacked the solder holding the lid in place. As he worked, Schreck glanced up into Simmons's expressionless face.

"You stand in the presence of history, Colonel," he said in sardonic English. "Does that not send a chill up your spine?"

"I am honored, sir," was Simmons's flat reply.

"I thought as much."

Eicke removed the old solder in sections, chunks and the occasional strip. On his knees, he worked his way around the casket. Far from being offended that Schreck had assigned him this manual labor rather than the American, he trembled with awe. His father had never told him exactly what lay within the leaden container. He only said that the contents were treasures beyond compare.

Eicke was the only child of Oberfuhrer Helmut Eicke, a man who had distinguished himself in the service of the Brandenberg Division, the Third Reich's elite commando force. The elder Eicke had been one of the less notorious Schutzstaffel alumni, and he had never been invited to testify at the Nuremburg War Crimes Tribunal. Helmut Eicke had died in Bavaria nineteen years before, his excesses with his former fraternity known to only a few.

One of the few was Ulrich Schreck. Standartenfuhrer Schreck, like Oberfuhrer Eicke, had served the Reich faithfully as Fortress Commandant of Schloss Wewelsburg, the S.S. monastery and repository of artifacts.

Schreck, Helmut Eicke and one other had met for the last time in the Schloss in the pre-dawn hours of May 10th, 1945 and sworn an oath. Later that day, the three men had stood on the Hochfeiler glacier and watched, as with great ceremony, S.S. troopers buried a three-by-four leaden casket in the ice.

All the troopers knew was that the contents of the casket must not fall into the hands of the Allies. Hitler had died a little over a week before and the war, for all intents and purposes, was over.

Helmut Eicke had performed mathematical measurements and calculated that the casket would be in position for recovery seventy years hence. Eicke, Schreck and one other promised to meet at the glacier on that day, more than half-a-century in the future.

Of the three only, Schreck had kept the promise. Julius Eicke represented his father, and the third member of the triad had not appeared. Lieutenant Colonel Avery Simmons had stepped into the vacancy.

Whether the casket held gold bars or priceless art objects looted from European museums, Julius Eicke did not care. The casket and its contents were legacies from a glorious era of blood, honor and iron resolve.

The final piece of solder came away in his hands. He rose stiffly to his feet and stood at attention beside the casket. On impulse, he raised his right arm and slashed the cold air with the flat of his hand. "It is done. Seig Heil."

"Oh, shut up," growled Schreck. "Don't befoul the atmosphere with memories of that maniac. He has nothing to do with this."

Eicke dropped his arm, feeling humbled and foolish.

Schreck wheeled his chair close to the box and bent over, his long-nailed fingers gripping the edge of the lid. Taking a deep breath, he closed his eyes. A thin smile touched his lips and he heaved the lid up and over onto the red-streaked snow. Eicke leaned forward, eyes wide. Simmons moved closer, inclining his head a fraction of an inch.

Eicke wasn't sure what he was looking at. Oilcloth wrapped objects of varying shapes and sizes were packed tightly and neatly into the casket. For all the awe the contents evoked in Eicke, he might as well have peered into the hope chest of a spinster.

"Sir," Eicke asked softly. "Do you know what these things are?"

"Of course I do," snapped Schreck. "I inventoried them myself in a crypt beneath Schloss Wewelsburg. Goetz was responsible for the actual packing, and he packed them in the order I listed."

Mouth open, lips shining wetly, Schreck began to remove items from the casket, unwrapping the oilcloth coverings reverentially. Eicke and Simmons stood by silently and watched as Schreck identified each piece in a breathless voice.

The first object was a brown, grinning human skull, the cranium encircled by a discolored golden diadem. "The skull of Ulrich der Vogler, the fuhrer of the First Reich, a thousand years ago...I was named after him, you know."

Next came a large package containing a battered shield and a pair of three-foot long swords. The hilts were inlaid with gems.

"The shield and swords of Emperor Charlemagne, one of the greatest of Aryan monarchs..."

A small package held the head of an ancient-looking spear, the metal dull and notched. Leather thongs affixed it to a broken wooden haft.

"The Holy Lance, with which the German centurion Longinus pierced Christ's side as he hung on the cross..."

After Schreck unwrapped the items and inspected them briefly, he placed them on the snow beside his wheelchair. He reached into the casket for a fourth time, then he paused. His eyes slitted.

"Something is wrong," he hissed. "It should be the next piece. It's not here."

Schreck pawed through the casket, pushing the contents from one end to the other. He kept up a steady refrain of "It's not here, it's not here!"

His frantic breath clouded before his face like steam escaping from a cracked boiler.

Eicke laid a hesitant hand on Schreck's boney shoulder. "Sir, what is missing?"

Schreck flung the hand off. His raging blue eyes bored into lenses of Eicke's sunglasses with such ferocity that Eicke took an involuntary step backward.

Crooking his fingers like the talons of a hawk, Schreck snarled, "The Dag! Goetz stole the Dag!" Spittle flecked his lips.

Eicke cleared his throat and asked calmly, "You mean a knife, sir?"

Schreck struck at Eicke's arm. "Don't speak to me like I'm one of your senile investors!"

Straightening up in the wheelchair, Schreck mimicked, " 'You mean a knife, sir?'," adopting the tone of an imbecilic child. He took several deep breaths.

"The Dag," he said in an even voice, "is an emblem of my office in the Brotherhood. It dates back to 772 A.D. It was ceded to me by Himmler himself, in the Great Hall of the Schloss. It represents the number of original knights who formed the Brotherhood. It is a holy object. Sacred not only to myself, but to our Brotherhood."

Hesitantly, Eicke said, "But surely the lack of this... artifact cannot cause us harm. After all, it has been buried for over seventy years, and we have only grown stronger."

Schreck's lips compressed in a tight, white line. His voice was low, deadly, and as cold as the glacier looming over them. "The Brotherhood can survive without it. But it cannot survive thieves and traitors."

Eyeing the butt of the Walther protruding from the old man's coat, Eicke asked, "To whom do you refer, sir?"

Schreck's fingers dug into the wooden arms of the wheelchair. "Himmler assigned three of us tasks for the burial detail. Your father saw to the construction of the container. I collected and inventoried all the artifacts. Goetz packed them and sealed the container. Of the three, Goetz is not represented here."

"So you suspect that Goetz stole the Dag?" The note of outrage in Eicke's voice was not forced. "For what purpose?"

"The Dag represents an important link in the chain of a tradition dating back a thousand years. Without that link, our chain is broken. And there is very little you can do with a broken chain."

Eicke cast a fearful glance into Simmons's expressionless face. "But our undertaking...it is too late to abort it. The Colonel has been prepared, the timetable is set, and the window of opportunity is narrow—"

Schreck interrupted Eicke with a savage gesture. "Stop babbling. The undertaking will continue on schedule. I will concern myself with finding Goetz. He has violated the most fundamental pledge of the Brotherhood: Honor Is Loyalty."

Schreck's voice dropped to a gloating croon. "He has had seventy years to forget that pledge. I will take a great deal of pleasure in jogging his memory."

ONE
May 30, The Upper Amazon Basin, Brazil

IN THE village, only shadows moved.

The grass-roofed huts were empty, and the cook fires long extinguished, but the Tupi-Gurani people were still there. The thirty-seven inhabitants—men, women and children—lay scattered on the ground where merciless autofire had hammered them. The bare earth had soaked up their blood like a sponge, turning the ground into crimson-stained sludge.

Mike Waring emerged from the bushes at the perimeter of the village and watched and listened. A half moon shone down on the jungle like a brightly polished medal, and the only sounds he heard were the calls of night birds.

He moved through the brush in a wide circle. A big, dark-haired man with a lean and agile build, his black T shirt and twill pants helped him blend with the shifting pattern of moonlight and shadows. A faint hairline scar stretched like a length of white thread across the sun-bronzed skin of his right cheek. His deep blue eyes held the color of a sharp steel blade.

Waring kept the Ruger SR1911 leathered snugly in the shoulder rig, but he used the foot-long combat knife in his right hand to push aside hanging lianas and foliage in his path.

Waring peered closely at the ground. He saw the marks of many booted feet, and where twigs had been stepped on and broken. Once he bent and picked up a small brass object. More by feel than sight, he identified it as a cartridge case from an assault rifle, a 7.62 millimeter.

In the heavy jungle growth on the north side of the village, his silent circuit completed, he stopped and bent down again. He studied a small residue of viscous liquid on the grass. He touched it, smelled it, and then stood up. It was gun oil, and judging by the three widely separated indentations in the grass, the oil had dripped from a tripod-mounted machine gun. Whoever who had attacked the villagers had intended nothing less than a massacre. The attackers had been fairly efficient in policing the killzone, but they had neglected to collect a few calling cards. This had been a military style operation from start to finish, with an emphasis on anonymity.

Waring froze and sank down on one knee, the Ruger slipping quietly into his hand. Two men moved fast through the village. They wore khaki, with shapeless green Aussi slouch hats on their heads. They carried Gewehr 3-A3 West German army assault rifles slung over their shoulders by straps. Although they passed too far away to see their faces, Waring heard them.

One of them said, "Wie wiele mehr zeit machen wir haben zu kommen ruckwarts hierher?"

The other responded gruffly, "Bis wir finden seiner die Bruderschaft sein leiche."

The pair moved on around and vanished into the jungle on the southward edge of the village. Waring returned the pistol to its holster and glided through the brush again. He re-evaluated his first suspicion that he had stumbled onto one of Brazil's indigenous tragedies.

It was no secret that the Indian inhabitants of the Amazon basin were being methodically exterminated on orders of the military junta. No one bothered to negotiate with the Indians for the lumber rights to their land—they were simply shot on sight and had no choice but to retreat further into the rapidly shrinking forest.

This massacre did not seem to be the work of the Brazilian military or hired mercenaries. Though Waring wasn't as fluent in the German language as he was others, he had understood the two men well enough.

The first had asked, "How many times do we have to keep coming back here?"

His companion had replied, "Until the Brotherhood finds him or his corpse."

The pair of Germans were searching for someone, and Waring felt sure he knew who it was.

He approached the hospital and research station at the edge of the village. The building was much larger than the huts and had a covered veranda. The veranda leaned, and a palm frond wall lay fallen-in, toppled by the fury of automatic weapons fire. Waring crept up the sagging steps and entered the main room.

By the light of a pencil flash, he saw chairs had been smashed, the walls themselves torn down, tables broken, bottles and vials of medicine shattered on the floor. Waring found the small radio transceiver in a far corner. It had been blasted into a twisted mass of metal, plastic and broken glass.

The examination room and laboratory looked as though grenades had been lobbed into them. Everything had been shot, smashed or torn, until there was nowhere for anyone to hide.

Waring returned to the examination room. By the narrow beam of the small flashlight, he saw a small trace of blood on the littered floor. It was dark, but it still felt tacky to the touch.

Placing the pencil-flash between his teeth, Waring covered the room inch by inch on his hands and knees. He saw nothing but debris. At the far corner, he turned to retrace his steps, then he stopped. He detected a faint difference of sound when he moved into the corner. Bending low, he lightly rapped the floorboards, and he heard an unmistakable hollow sound.

Waring cleared away the debris from the corner as quietly as he could. He saw nothing but bare floorboards at first, then the light of the flash showed him the thread-thin outline of the trap-door.

Jamming the long steel blade of his combat knife into the tiny space between the edge of the door and the floor, Waring tried prying it open. It refused to budge, held fast by a catch on the underside. Waring put his back against the wall and launched a straight-leg kick at the knife's handle. There was a sharp snap of metal as the catch was broken, and a three-by-three square of flooring popped up.

Waring returned the knife to its ankle sheath, unholstered the Ruger and swung down onto a narrow ladder. He dropped into a small, dark room only ten feet below.

The walls were dirt, reinforced by plywood panels. He saw signs of feet on the hard-packed dirt floor and spots of blood. The signs led to an earth wall, the only one not shored up by wooden paneling.

Waring's fingers found a break low down near the floor. At a tug, a small section of the wall came away and revealed a passage, just big enough for a medium-sized man to crawl through. The passageway was hidden by sheet metal covered with dark paint and glued-on dirt to match the wall and floor.

Waring squeezed into the small opening. It was an exceptionally tight fit. He struggled for twenty feet, then he saw a dim light and heard a low roaring sound—the rush of the Madeira River, a tributary of the Amazon.

The passage opened into a chamber ten feet wide by seven high. Diffused moonlight peeped through another opening on the far side of the room.

Over the rush of the river, Waring barely heard the rasp of labored breathing and the faint rustle of cloth. Waring shone the pen-flash around. The man leaning against the wall stared into the light without blinking.

"Ehre Ist Treue...Ehre Ist Treue..."

The man repeated it, staring at the light without really seeing it. His blue eyes shone bright. His bush clothing was black with sweat and caked blood. Long, thin, white hair topped an equally thin and deeply creased face. His eyes were surrounded by dark rings of suffering, sunk deep back in their sockets.

His exposed left leg was covered by dark-purple patches that shone moistly in the gloom. Waring saw a small bullet-hole midway on his thigh. The exit wound was further down on the inside of his leg, a raw crater surrounded by a discolored ring of proud flesh. A length of rubber hose was knotted tightly around his leg above the wounds.

Waring smelled the odor of putrefaction. The man had tied on the tourniquet to stop the bleeding, but had evidently neglected to loosen it. Gangrene had settled in the leg, and only amputation would save his life.

Waring kneeled beside him. "Doctor Grimminger?"

The man muttered, *"Ehre Ist Treue...Ehre Ist Treue."*

Waring realized he said, "Honor Is Loyalty" like a mantra. He pressed a hand against the man's seamed forehead. He was burning up with fever.

The man shrieked at the touch. Glassy eyes gleaming, his mouth convulsed, starting another scream. Waring clamped a hand over his mouth, and holstered his automatic. With his free hand, he quickly unsnapped a pouch on his web belt and took from it a small squeeze hypodermic. It contained a stimulant developed by the medics at the Eyrie. Whether it would reverse Grimminger's delirium, Waring had no way of knowing, but he injected the ampoule's contents into the man's inner arm just the same.

Grimminger's scream turned into a moan and Waring released him. The man's head lolled, and he banged it back against the wall. His eyes closed and his body sagged.

Waring shone the flash around the room. He saw nothing in it but a padlocked metal strongbox. It bore a curious symbol on the lid, both familiar and strange at the same time—a jet-black disk against a blood-red background. Nine thin lines, stylized representations of sun beams radiated out from equidistant points around the disk.

Looking at it, Waring couldn't help but wonder if Aladar Herne had any idea of the hellzone he had asked him to investigate as a personal favor.

The day before, Herne had contacted Waring in his Manhattan

apartment from the Eyrie via a secured line. Herne told him that a conduit in Interpol had passed along a radio message to a contact the State Department, who in turn had passed it along to him. He passed it along to Waring.

"You ever heard of Doctor Gerald Grimminger, Michael?"

"Should I have?" Being addressed by his first name rather than "Falcon" made him instantly suspicious.

"Not unless you keep up with advances in biochemistry. He's a German-born scientist, but a naturalized American citizen. He's on the board of the World Health Organization."

Herne described Grimminger as a dedicated medical man who had spent most of his life trying to help the less fortunate of the world both spiritually and with more practical aid. For the past fifty years he had operated a research center and hospital in a small Indian village in the Upper Amazon Basin.

That very morning, a voice message had been transmitted from Grimminger's village to an Interpol office in Sao Paulo.

"It was only a few words," said Herne. "Evidently he didn't have time for more. He said, 'Village under attack. die Bruderschaft—'."

"Sounds more like a concern for the local authorities or the United Nations, Aladar."

"That's what I said. But the State Department was very clear on this. They want someone with no traceable governmental agency ties to go down there and look around."

"What's Interpol's interest in this?" asked Waring. "Why don't they send an investigator?"

"That's all I'm at liberty to divulge. What do you say, Michael?"

Waring had hesitated. His arm's length relationship with the Eyrie was uncertain even when he had chosen to accept missions, but after his last assignment he had planned to retire. Still, Herne and the Eyrie acted as a buffer between him and law enforcement agencies when he was forced to circumvent due process. After a few moments of thinking it over, Waring, as usual, had said yes. And as usual, he regretted it.

Grimminger's eyes flew open. They were no longer so bright and wild. He said in slightly accented English, "I expected you yesterday. After I made the call."

"I'm not from Interpol," Waring said. "Who did this to you, to the people here?"

Grimminger focused on something behind Waring, as though he

were trying to view the past. "Should've known. I missed the reunion. I knew Eicke had died. Didn't figure after seventy years anyone would be there. I mean, I was only a boy when I took the oath. A frightened boy whose entire world was in flames."

Grimminger shifted position and grunted in pain. "They came on us suddenly at dawn. Killed everyone."

"Who did?"

Grimminger covered his face with his hands and a great, shuddery sob broke from his chest. "Killed them all. The children—"

"Doctor Grimminger—" Waring began.

The man dropped his hands. His face was contorted in such a mask of self-loathing and rage, Waring nearly recoiled.

"Don't call me that!," he man shouted. "Not any more! My name is Goetz! Karl Gustav Goetz! Lieutenant Goetz of the Reichssicherheitshouptampt!"

It took Waring a moment to recognize that ear-filling conglomeration of consonants. When he did, he knew disgust showed on his face.

The man referred to the Reich Main Security Office, the foreign espionage bureau of the S.S. Now he knew why Herne had hedged about giving him the full picture, and why Interpol was involved. For decades, Interpol's administrators had favored veterans of the Reich Main Security Office as both field men and contract agents. The Nazis had filled most of that agency's staff positions with party members from the early 30s through the end of the war.

Grimminger/Goetz had obviously used Interpol's influence to acquire a new identity and a new citizenship. Though Waring bore the average German soldier of that conflict no particular animosity, S.S. and Gestapo members were a different breed. They had pledged their loyalty to their organization, not to their country.

Waring shook Goetz by the shoulder. "Turn off the waterworks. Who attacked the village?"

Goetz took a great breath. *"Die Bruderschaft..."*

"Die Bruderschaft? The Brotherhood?"

"Ja."

"The Brotherhood of what?"

"Of Schwarze Sonne."

That was a new one on Waring. He repeated the words aloud sounding them out. "Black Sun? What's the Brotherhood of the Black Sun?"

Licking his lips, Goetz said, "The very source of Nazism, the fundamental well-spring of the National Socialist Party, the true power behind the rise of Adolf Hitler."

"I never heard of it."

"That is its greatest defense. A political party can be smashed, but not the power behind it. The Third Reich was shattered into a hundred pieces. But the Brotherhood exists unchanged and unchanging to this day, as it has for nearly a thousand years."

Afraid the old man was ranting in delirium again, Waring changed the subject. "What did they want?"

Goetz gestured to the strongbox. "That. It was supposed to have been buried with the other sacred relics. I kept it back. I didn't think they would ever know it was missing. I didn't want the chain to be forged again."

Goetz slapped himself in the face, snarling, "*Dumbkopf! Mein glaubensbekenntis schandlich! Schutzing schlanges—!*"

Waring was gaining interest in the topic, but losing interest in the circumstances in which it was discussed. There was no time for a tantrum, and he reached out to shake Goetz. "Knock it off, old man."

A coughing fit halted Goetz's diatribe. When he recovered, he spoke English again. Fixing his eyes on Waring's, he said tersely, "We buried the most sacred relics of the Brotherhood in a glacier at the very end of the war. The three of us vowed to return to the glacier this month on a prescribed day. Or, if we were unable to attend, we were to arrange for representatives to attend in our place."

"And you," said Waring, "broke the vow."

"Eicke is dead. Ulrich is at least a hundred ...I've had no contact with them for over a half a century. I have a new identity, a new life. How could they have found me after all this time?"

Grimly, Waring said, "Through the same agency that arranged for your new identity and new life."

Goetz's eyes widened in horrified realization. "Ach."

"The old firm never lets you retire," Waring said. "Especially if they think you owe them something. Tell me, if you didn't expect them to track you down, why the escape tunnels?"

"I successfully appealed to the Ministry of the Interior to stop a logging operation nearby." Goetz's voice was hoarse and weak. "I had the tunnels constructed in case the junta or mercenaries came after me."

Waring looked around quickly. "I've got transportation not too far away. We can make it while it's still dark, but we've got to move fast.

Patrols are looking for you."

"Ja," murmured Goetz. "I have heard them. And a *hubschrauber.*"

"A helicopter?"

Goetz nodded. When Waring went to pick him up, he struggled, pushing his hands away. "Leave me. I'm dying. You know it and I know it."

Waring hesitated, looking into the man's face, then at the discolored, suppurating leg. Goetz was right.

The old man gestured weakly to the strongbox. "Take that *ubel* thing with you. Sink it into the Madeira. Make sure the Brotherhood never gets their hands on it again."

Goetz's eyelids drooped down, his head fell forward. Waring watched as his entire body was racked by terrible shudders. Then, as if his bones were suddenly liquid, he flowed down to the floor. His final exhalation was a prolonged hiss.

Waring arranged the man's body, folding his hands on his chest. Though the smell of necrotic tissue was strong, he doubted that blood poisoning or blood loss had killed him. Goetz had simply given up.

Waring picked up the strongbox. It weighed less than twenty pounds. Tucking it under one arm, he went through the far passageway. Emerging from a screen of thick-leaved bushes, he saw the river less than a hundred feet away. A narrow path led from the concealed opening to the river bank.

He followed it, deciding to walk the river's edge rather than backtrack around the village. He had parked his Land Rover downriver a mile to the south.

Muffled by the sound of the rushing current, Waring didn't hear the boat until it had slid from the shadowed overhang of a heavy-boughed hardwood tree. The boat was sharp keeled, outfitted with a diesel outboard motor and a mounted searchlight. A brilliant blade of light stabbed out and impaled Waring.

TWO

"EUCH DORT! Bleiben wo ihr seit!"

The voice, distorted by the electronic amplifier, carried an unearthly echo. Waring dropped flat, beneath the light, and he rolled to one side. The searchlight swung to follow him. He saw three khaki-clad men aboard the boat, all armed with HK-94 auto carbines. Two of the three men fired.

Staccato bursts shattered the stillness of the jungle. Birds screeched as a steel-jacketed barrage ripped through the foliage.

Waring rolled back into the underbrush. Though the men's aim was high, bullet-sheared leaves and twigs showered him. The brilliant beam of light swung back and forth, probing the darkness for him.

Bullets pounded into the riverbank, fragments of rock and clods of earth flying in all directions. Ricochets buzzed into the night. Behind it all was the steady double-hammer of the carbines.

The autofire suddenly ceased, the 12-round magazines of the weapons exhausted. Waring heard metallic clickings as the empty magazines were ejected and new ones inserted.

Swiftly, Waring came to his knees, the Ruger gripped in both hands. He brought the searchlight into the pistol's sights and squeezed the trigger only once. As the heavy, deep-throated boom! of the big gun sounded, a .45 caliber round shattered the searchlight in an eye-dazzling blaze of blue sparks.

The men on the boat cursed viciously and all three opened up with their weapons. Phosphorescent tracer slugs cut threads of fire through the night. Waring knew better than to dig in and return triple streams of autofire. He belly-crawled through the underbrush, changing direction twice, heedless of the thorns that scratched him and the vines that tried to snare him.

The men continued to fire wildly into the darkness. If they were angry or dedicated or stupid enough to come ashore and try to track him, they would receive the final surprise of their lives.

Though the rain forests of South America were far removed by time and distance from the tangled green hell of Rwanda, Waring hadn't forgotten a single trick of jungle warfare .He figured the men on the boat would stay put and radio the patrol he'd seen in the village. Even if they heard the gunfire and were racing to its source, he doubted he would encounter them.

A little over a mile downriver, Waring emerged from the jungle onto a narrow dirt road. Parked in a copse of parana pines, covered by camouflage netting was his open-topped Land Rover. It was an old model, and somewhat battered, but it was the best Herne could arrange on short notice.

Yanking the net away, Waring got in and started the engine. Although the sound of the motor turning over and catching wasn't particularly loud, in the quiet of the night it sounded like a band striking up a fanfare.

Putting the strongbox on the passenger seat, Waring pressed the accelerator and the front-wheel drive vehicle moved fast along the road. He didn't turn on the headlights, relying on his memory to guide him around obstacles and curves. He kept checking his backtrack in the rearview mirror.

One of those checks showed a small flash of reflected light, bright against the sky. Waring glanced over his shoulder.

A helicopter dove down from the sky, silhouetted against the glow of the moon. Safety lights flashed red and green.

Waring's hands tightened on the steering wheel and he floored the gas pedal. Rather than radio the jungle patrol, the men on the boat had called in their aerial reconnaissance.

The Land Rover roared at an appallingly unsafe speed along the road twisting between tall jungle walls. Waring hadn't been able to identify the make of the chopper, but he was positive if it wasn't armed, the men aboard were.

Waring heard the vanes whipping the air and the engine sounds growing louder with every passing second. He risked another backward glance. The helicopter dove in barely a hundred feet behind him, perhaps only twenty-five feet above the treetops. Fortunately, the road cut through the jungle was too narrow to allow the aircraft to descend to a lower altitude.

Flickering spear points of yellow flame danced briefly just beneath the chopper's undercarriage. He heard a rattling roar, and .50 caliber bullets knocked up great gouts of earth behind the Land Rover. Waring jerked the wheel and swerved in a left-to-right zigzag.

Bullets slammed into the tailgate, and one shattered the windshield to the left of Waring's shoulder. He steered the vehicle beneath an arch formed by the intertwining boughs of tall evergreen trees, and he was temporarily hidden from the crew of the chopper. He listened to the strong thrum of the engines and whirling blades as the helicopter hovered over the arch, then moved on.

Waring eased off on the gas and braked. He put the Land Rover in neutral while he weighed his options. He knew he would run out of road in another mile or so. The dirt path opened up into a vast, treeless tract where the logging operation Goetz mentioned had been underway only a few months before.

Although the timber company was gone, they left behind barren ground and an almost limitless sea of tree-stumps. The loggers had built this road through the jungle to the river, and though Waring was grateful for that, he damned them for removing all spots of cover for five square miles.

He figured if he drove slowly and carefully, it was possible to navigate around and sometimes over the tree-stumps, as he done on his arrival. Now, slowly and carefully would be tantamount to painting a bull's-eye on his ass.

Ditching the Land Rover and hiding out in the jungle would buy him some time, but it would also give his pursuers the time to call in reinforcements. They would cover the river, the village and every way out of the jungle. Waring did not have the inclination to play a prolonged game of hide n' seek.

He came to a snap, almost insane, decision—snap because it was such a big risk, and insane because it would leave him without transportation, nearly twenty miles from the nearest outpost of civilization. Even the satphone in his war bag was useless.

Still, he had made longer hikes through more treacherous zones than this one. Waring grabbed his war bag from the back of the Land Rover and shoved the strongbox into it. He got out, and after a brief search, found a heavy lump of sandstone on the roadside, weighing about twenty pounds.

From his bag he removed a coil of thin, nylon rope with a collapsible grappling hook attached to one end. He measured out a three-foot length, cut it with his combat knife and looped the remainder over his right shoulder.

He wrapped the rope around the steering wheel and the column, but he didn't tie it. He put the Land Rover into gear and drove down the road at barely ten miles an hour, holding both ends of the rope in his left hand.

At the demarcation point between the jungle and the tract, Waring saw the helicopter waiting for him. It hovered some eighty feet over the treeless expanse, and he recognized the two counter-revolving sets of blades of a Messerschmitt. He guessed the chopper to be at least twenty years old, but it appeared in excellent condition. A red cross was emblazoned on the fuselage.

Waring's lips quirked in a mirthless smile. It was a good disguise, since the aircraft of medical aid organizations constantly buzzed to and fro over the Amazon Basin.

A long gun pod was mounted beneath the craft. It looked like a Swedish Uni-Pod 0127, containing a .50 caliber M-3 with a 200 round magazine. Though the gun-pod packed devastating firepower, Waring knew it was a bolt-on weapon, and therefore less accurate than an internal gun.

Its operation required a separate gunner, and he would be forced to rely on the pilot to bring a target into the proper acquisition.

Waring put the Land Rover in neutral and lashed the wheel tight to the column so it would follow a straight course. He slid out of the driver's seat, slinging his war bag over his right shoulder.

With the door open, he stood beside the vehicle, hefted the stone and jammed it down over the gas pedal. As the engine roared, Waring carefully pressed down on the clutch and engaged the first gear.

The Land Rover leaped forward, and Waring flung himself away from it, the rear tires barely missing the toes of his boots. He crouched down in the shadows bordering the edge of the jungle.

He watched as the pilot of the Messerschmitt caught sight of the Land Rover emerging from beneath the tree-arch. Plumes of dust spurted from the tires.

The helicopter whirled, descended and zoomed in, its landing gear barely ten feet above the barren ground. The snout of the M-3 protruding from the end of the pod flickered with fire. .50 caliber slugs punched a cross-stitch pattern in the dirt in front of and to the left of the vehicle.

The Land Rover kept going, avoiding direct hits. The lines of impact scampered across the dirt, chewing up a tree-stump and flinging wood chips and splinters in all directions.

With the rear of the chopper facing him, Waring began running, skirting the edge of the tract. He went in the opposite direction of the pursuit, hoping to put considerable distance between himself and the helicopter before its crew realized no one was driving the vehicle.

With the amount of dust swirling in the air, churned up by the chopper's rotors, the Land Rover's tires and the bullets pounding the ground, he felt there was at least a 50/50 chance the diversion would work long enough for him to disappear into the shadows.

At the sound of the crash, Waring sourly adjusted the odds. He looked behind him, then stopped and went to one knee.

The Land Rover had plowed into a tree-stump, one wheel going over its smoothly-sawn top. It tipped to the right. Its momentum might have carried it on over, but a storm of bullets striking the bodywork caused it to list, tilt, then crash over on its side, wheels spinning.

The helicopter hung over it like a bird of prey, strafing the body with steady bursts. One burst punctured the gas tank, and its contents went up in a brilliant fireball.

The Messerschmitt heeled away from the licking flames, and for an instant the entire area was illuminated by the orange-yellow flare. In that instant, the tinted, bubble-enclosed cockpit of the helicopter faced Waring.

Caught in the glare, Waring unleathered the Ruger and began running again, along the jungle's edge.

The Messerschmitt executed a figure eight from east to west and made a roaring pass, driving down from the rear. Bullets exploded dirt all around him.

Waring dug in his heels and skidded to a sudden stop. He dropped flat just as the chopper soared over his head. It came so close to the jungle perimeter that when it banked sharply to port, the vanes slashed through the tips of tree-limbs.

Rolling over onto his back, Waring squeezed off three shots as the chopper ascended, correcting for the decreasing range. Either the helicopter was armored, or the motion of the aircraft threw his aim off, because his shots seemed to have no effect.

Leaping to his feet, Waring ran broken-field style across the tract. He changed direction and raced away from the jungle, crossing a flat, bare space, heading for a drainage ditch dug by the loggers.

The helicopter's pilot managed to straighten out and level off, but by then Waring had nearly reached the ditch. The gun-pod spat lead and noise and flame again. Bullets kicked up dirt in waist-high fountains two yards behind him.

Waring dove headlong into the ditch, unmindful of the foul-smelling mud or what might live in it.

The Messerschmitt roared overhead, the landing rails scraping the edges of the ditch and causing several shovel-loads of dirt to collapse onto Waring. Springing to his feet, the Ruger in his hands, he squeezed off three rounds.

Two the bullets drilled through the rear tail assembly and the third twisted the struts of the right landing rail out of shape.

The helicopter veered wildly up and away. The pilot maneuvered the craft in a high, wide circle above the stump-dotted tract. Standing knee-deep in mud, Waring watched it describe a circle, then hang in the sky, well out of the 200 meter range of his handgun.

He knew what would happen next—the crew of the chopper would call for ground support. They would hover and report on his movements and position and cut off any attempt to return to the jungle until more troops arrived. They would make no more passes at him unless he tried to escape the killzone. He was bottled up in a muddy ditch, with no adequate cover to make a stand, and they could afford to be patient.

The sudden surge of anger stimulated Waring's imagination. From his war bag he removed an apple-sized and shaped grenade. He unslung the coil of rope and attached the grappling hook to the triggering ring of the grenade.

Holstering the Ruger, he climbed out of the ditch, holding the grenade in one hand and the rope's slack in the other. He didn't move. He stood at the edge of the ditch and stared up at the hovering chopper, a direct challenge.

The grenade was an M68 fragmentation type, equipped with an impact fuse. The detonation mechanism was armed electrically three seconds after making a hard contact.

Objectively, three seconds was a very fast fuse, but subjectively was another matter. Three seconds was an eternity in which Waring would be completely vulnerable to .50 caliber autofire.

Waring and the helicopter faced off. The aircraft didn't move, except to list slightly from side-to-side. The crew obviously suspected he was luring them in. So, Waring turned his back on the chopper and began to deliberately walk toward the edge of the jungle.

Senses alert for any change in sound from the chopper's position, Waring kept walking. When he heard a whining, high-pitched roar, he spun around.

The Messerschmitt dropped suddenly from where it had hung poised in the sky. It swooped down, head-on. The pilot kicked it into a steep dive, and then banked so the gun-pod would be aligned with Waring's right side.

Waring stood his ground, a dark and mud-streaked figure. He whirled the rope with its grenade-weighted end over his head. He gauged distance vertically and horizontally.

When the helicopter was only twenty feet away, and less than that in altitude, he gave the lariat a final, humming spin and launched it at the chopping vanes of the aircraft. At the same time, the machine gun opened up. Autofire sowed the ground with .50 caliber seeds.

Waring flung himself ahead of the dancing eruptions of dirt in a frantic somersault back toward the ditch. He kept rolling until he felt solid ground give way beneath him and he splatted down into the ditch's muddy bottom. The stream of bullets did not intersect with his body, but they chewed up the edge of the ditch.

Even as he rolled, the rope wrapped itself around the main rotor shaft of the Messerschmitt. The grenade banged loudly on the canopy, and the pilot pulled back on the stick.

The helicopter reared, seeming to stand on its tail.

Face-down in the ditch, Waring heard the heavy bass note of the explosion. Flame, smoke and shrapnel bloomed in a hellfire flower atop the Messerschmitt.

The rotor blades went pinwheeling off in opposite directions. The helicopter keeled over, and the bubble-enclosed cockpit cannonaded into the ground.

The fuel tank ruptured, then went up in an eardrum-slamming, fire-spurting explosion.

Waring got to his feet. Black smoke rolled over him in low clouds. The Messerschmitt had made its one-point landing barely forty feet away. It lay crumpled and burning on its starboard side. There was no movement from behind the shattered plexi-glass canopy.

The billowing smoke made him cough, so Waring climbed out of the ditch and put more distance between him and the wreckage. He surveyed the scene.

It was like an impressionistic painting of Hell. Two blackened shapes burned steadily in a barren expanse of dirt and tree-stumps, and the licking flames cast an eerie, shifting light.

By that light, Waring glimpsed movement at the end of the road leading out to the tract. A burst of autofire sounded. Bullets kicked up dirt several dozen yards in front of him.

The two man patrol he had seen in the village were racing toward him, firing their weapons as they did so. One screamed to his partner, *"Schiessen! Schiessen der swine!"*

They were too angry to take their time to aim properly, and too far away for a stray shot to tag him. They were also too stupid to know better than to run side-by-side.

Waring unleathered the Ruger, checked it to make sure the slide mechanism wasn't fouled by mud or dirt, squinted along the fore blade and rear combat sights, adjusted for elevation and windage and squeezed the trigger twice, shifting the barrel slightly from left to right.

It was a long shot for a handgun, but the two men went down. One rocked to an arm-flailing halt and went over onto his back. The other jackknifed at the waist, and his head reversed positions with his feet.

Waring didn't bother to check the accuracy of his shots. He knew he'd hit them, and even if they were still alive, they were in no condition to crawl after him.

Shouldering the war bag, Waring began walking across the tract. He wasn't concerned about the hike in front of him—he figured he would sooner rather than later come across a vehicle used by the gunmen. He focused his thoughts on Goetz and the murdered Indians. He didn't know why anyone thought an elderly ex-German intelligence officer was worth slaughtering a village or sacrificing manpower and ordnance for, but he knew where he should start looking for the answers.

And when he found those answers, he knew what he would do next—what he always did, planned retirement be damned.

The Falcon would spread out his wings and run his prey to ground.

THREE
May 31, The Federal Republic of Germany

FOR OVER thirty years, a concrete wall topped with rolls of barbed and razor wire divided west and east Germany and dominated that country's character.

In central Berlin, nearly all traces of the Wall have been removed. Even Checkpoint Charlie is no more than a nondescript kiosk in need of a fresh coat of paint. Nonetheless, to travel from the former West Germany to former East Germany is to cross a wide chasm not measured in miles.

The West possesses the memory of nearly a century of relative prosperity. The East still suffers the wounds inflicted by many decades of brutal dictatorship.

Reunification was conceived as a way to heal the wounds. The concrete wall and barricades are down, but *Die Mauer im Kopf,* "The Wall in the Head" is as strong as ever. The principal effect of reunification has been insecurity. As insecurity grew, so did intolerance toward foreigners, especially refugees.

The Republic of Germany's constitution mandates that anyone seeking asylum be allowed to stay, pending an immigration hearing. There are well over a million refugees in Germany, fleeing from Afghanistan, Iran and Bosnia.

In the reunited Germany, refugees and foreigners became the scapegoats of the nation's traumas.

According to Germany's secret service, the Verfassungsschutz, there are about 40,000 extremists belonging to at least eighty neo-Nazi organizations. For the most part, the extremists are young men who call themselves skinheads. They brandish the emblems and shout the slogans of the Fascist regime that had ruled most of Europe seventy years before. Some of them carry baseball bats studded with nails, they listen to blaring heavy metal rock music with racist lyrics and greet each other with the straight-arm Nazi salute and shouts of "Seig Heil!"

They also tend to get hog-piss drunk, then storm into the streets to attack anyone who doesn't meet their standards of racial purity, American servicemen included. They have proudly claimed responsibility for scores of arsons, assaults and murders. Only a handful of the perpetrators have ever been prosecuted, and fewer still have been sentenced to jail terms longer than three years.

The deficit between crimes and convictions has been noticed by human rights groups in Europe. They have argued convincingly that the republic's failure to forcefully prosecute members of neo-Nazi organizations only encourages more outbreaks of violence. Some civil rights advocates in the government have made graver charges—they have accused some of their fellow members of deliberately looking the other way.

Though there is no sign of a new fuhrer, the time is ripe for one. Followers are already in place, waiting for him to appear and make a Germany for Germans.

Other countries are also contending with the problems posed by a unified Germany, the least of which are geo-economic. The end of the Cold War placed the spectrum of old politics and loyalties in a colorless limbo.

The former Soviet Union, the United States and NATO struggle with the question of what to do about the many nuclear missile silos, sites and weapons stockpiles dotting the landscape inside both east and west Germany.

American military and NATO bases are easy to find in western Europe, especially in Germany. They are surrounded by fences posted with signs declaring the areas to be military reservations and therefore inaccessible to the average German citizen.

However, the average German citizen is aware that although the bases possess strategic and tactical missiles, the "big guns", the missiles with nuclear warheads, are hidden all over Germany in camouflaged sites.

One site, inside a fortified bunker covered with turf, in the middle of a cow pasture, is designated by the Department of Defense, SAC and NATO as Site 611. Less than half an hour outside of Berlin, near Potsdam, it contains six Pershing II missiles.

The Pershings possess warheads of 400 kilotons and are launched from massive twelve-wheeled tractor trailers. The Pershings have terminal guidance systems based on radar area correlation systems—the on-board computers compare images of the targets "seen" by the missile with images previously programmed into them. The range of the Pershings is limited, approximately 75 miles, but perfect for striking targets in east Germany.

The problem is that there are no longer any targets in east Germany, but the Pershings (and the Plutons and the Lances and the FROGS) are still scattered all over western Europe. Some have been dismantled and sold, some disarmed, but most are still waiting for either to happen.

At Site 611, the one dozen United States Army personnel stationed there were among those waiting. Technical duties consisted primarily of running checks on the fuel payloads of the missiles, detecting and correcting leaks, running system diagnostics on the ground and on-board targeting computers, making sure the satellite uplink frequencies to Cheyenne Mountain in Wyoming and NATO bases in the Mediterranean continued to signal "all clear", and in general acting as high-tech nursemaids and hall monitors.

The non-technical personnel serviced the trailers that held the missiles, checking the air in the tires, turning the engines over every twelve hours, and in general acting like janitorial staff.

No one was too concerned about maintaining the camouflage— every farmer, every cow and every woodland animal within twenty square miles knew they were there. Great squares of turf had fallen from the bunker, revealing the concrete beneath, but they were rarely patched up. Even the security guards patrolling the perimeter were relaxed.

It was light duty to pull, and though a Top Secret clearance was required just to get inside the foyer, no one was fixated on every security detail. The standard protocols were still observed, however.

At 0800 hours on Wednesday morning, when the officer of the day, Lieutenant Colonel Avery Simmons triggered the metal detector, not even Corporal Turnbull who held the sensor wand became unduly excited.

The helmeted M.P. waved the silver rod in front of Simmons's face and the squeal from the sensor came again. He looked at Simmons questioningly.

"Sir, I'm getting a—"

"I know what you're getting, Corporal," said Simmons impatiently. "I had some dental work done yesterday, remember? That's why I left early."

"Yes sir, I remember." Turnbull's questioning look didn't go away.

"Bridgework, boy. New bridgework."

Turnbull nodded. "Yes sir. But if I might ask you to open your mouth?"

Simmons groaned. "Oh, for Christ's sake."

He took off his uniform cap and tilted his head back, opening his mouth wide.

Turnbull bent down and peered up inside Simmons's mouth.

"Don't even think about sticking your fingers in there," Simmons snapped.

"Yes, sir. I mean, no sir."

Not having bridgework himself, or knowing anyone who did, the M.P. wasn't sure of what he was looking for. He saw gleaming steel affixed to back molars and a saliva damp pink arch adhering to the roof of the mouth.

"Can you pop it out, sir, and we'll try again?"

Simmons shut his mouth with a snap and pulled himself up to his full height. Glaring down directly into Turnbull's face, he said, "No, I cannot 'pop it out'. The standard procedure is to recalibrate the sensor. If you're unable to do that, I'll relieve you of duty and do it myself."

Turnbull backed away, speaking very quickly. "No sir, of course I can do that. But I'll have to log this in—see, every time the detector is triggered, a record is made, and I have to reconcile my log with the record and explain why I allowed entry into the facility."

"Corporal, I'm one of the men who drafted the security procedures at this site. You don't have to explain them to me."

Cap tucked beneath an arm, Simmons marched past the security station. Turnbull heaved a whistling sigh, then muttered, "Asshole."

Simmons walked down a short corridor, turned left, returned the salute of an M.P. standing there and entered the operations center.

The technical staff of the day shift—three men and two women— conducted the first of three diagnostics performed in a 24 hour period. They were seated before computer consoles, wearing headsets, tapping keyboards and gazing at the machine talk scrolling across their monitor screens.

Simmons stood and watched and listened. He didn't go to his desk in the corner or take off his jacket or hang up his cap. All he did was consult his wristwatch.

The tech staff had their attentions focused on the diagnostic. Lieutenant Taylor, the shift supervisor, asked questions in a monotone and received equally flat responses from the staff.

"Infra-red crosstie?"

"Enabled."

"Guidance system nexus?"

"Standby."

"Rear payload constriction flange?"

"Green."

"Tracking and control radars?"

"Enabled."

"Thermal imaging signature recognition systems?"

"Standby."

The droning conversation went on, then one of the women stiffened in her chair. "What the hell?"

Her monitor screen fluttered briefly. The words and images scrolling across her screen tore up in a jagged pattern of multi-colored pixels. All over the operations center, the staff swore and slapped keyboards.

"Kee-Rist!"

"I show a complete system failure-!"

"Goddammit-!"

Taylor shouted, "What's going on?"

He swiveled his chair and caught sight of Simmons for the first time. "Sir—"

Lieutenant Colonel Avery Simmons turned slightly toward him, then collapsed into a loose-limbed heap on the floor. His head struck the concrete with a sharp crack.

Taylor shouted for the M.P. who came in at a run. He kneeled beside Simmons and attended to him while Taylor tried to restore order to both the operations center and the system.

He went from station to station, tapping keys on each board. "Shit," he said. "I've never seen the effects of an electromagnetic pulse, but this sure seems like one."

"No way," said one of the women. "All the power would be out."

Another technician called out to Taylor. He was pressing the earpiece of his headset against the side of his head. "We're still linked to the NORAD mainframe in Cheyenne Mountain. This is a localized failure. Just in this site."

Taylor surveyed the blank, amber glowing screens then snarled, "Well, get on this, people! Boot up our back-up systems! Every goddamn techno-dweeb between Greece and Wyoming will be blaming us for pushing the wrong button or some such shit if we're not back on-line stat!"

Taylor took a small silver key from his pocket and went to a file cabinet at the rear wall. To do so, he had to step over Simmons's body. The M.P. was checking his pulse.

"How is he?" asked Taylor.

"He's nonresponsive. He's also very warm, like he's running a high fever."

The M.P. peeled back one of Simmons's eyelids, and both he and Taylor cursed.

Simmons's eye bore a milky glaze, like the membrane of an egg.

"Get him to the hospital," Taylor ordered.

While Taylor spun the dial of the cabinet's combination lock, then removed and unlocked the case of back-up diskettes with the key, Simmons was carried out of the operations center by the M.P. and a technician.

Simmons was rushed by ambulance to the General George S. Patton Military Hospital in what was once called the American sector of Berlin. He was declared dead enroute, thirty minutes before the wailing ambulance reached the emergency room, and less than ten after he collapsed.

While the chain of command was notified, Simmons's dog-tags were taken and preparations made to break the news to his next of kin, an autopsy was ordered by the chief of staff at the hospital.

A report to the German authorities was mandatory, in case Simmons had died from something contagious.

The doctor assigned to the autopsy was 41 year-old Captain William Bradfort. Post-mortems didn't disturb him—he had performed hundreds of them during his civilian employment by the Los Angeles County Medical Examiner's Office. He'd only had to perform eight in the 14 years he'd served in the armed forces, and usually the cause of death among military personnel was easy to determine—drug overdoses, car crashes, training accidents, and the occasional suicide.

The body of Lieutenant Colonel Avery Simmons posed a severe problem. Bradfort found that out when he took a temperature reading of the liver. It was at least five degrees warmer than it should have been. He duly noted the anomaly into his digital recorder.

When Bradfort opened up the abdominal cavity, his eyes bugged out and he said, "Jesusfuckingchrist!"

The fact that his outburst wasn't medical terminology and that a transcriptionist would render it into black and white for his superiors and God knew who else to read, didn't occur to him.

There was almost no moisture inside Simmons's body. The organs were all where they should have been, but they weren't glistening with blood or any other bodily fluid. The liver, which is the storage depot for the circulatory system, contained some blood—it was in the form of dark, gummy, congealed splotches.

Bradfort spoke rapidly into the recorder: "The subject's abdominal cavity shows very little moisture, indicating that the cause of death was extreme dehydration. I cannot explain this condition."

The captain picked up the circular bone saw, plugged it in and applied the whirling, razor-sharp edge of the blade to the top of Simmons's skull. Deftly, he cut away the top of the cranium, put it to one side and inspected the condition of the brain.

He didn't swear this time, but he grunted in disbelief. The brain should have been glistening with cerebrospinal fluid. It wasn't. The organ was dry, and rather than being a whitish-gray in color, it was pale beige, almost as if it had been seared briefly by an extraordinarily hot flame. Bradfort poked the brain with one rubber-sheathed finger. It was hard. Not rock-solid, but far harder than any human being's brain could possibly be outside of a mummy's.

Bradfort had never seen anything remotely like this in a human body, barely three hours dead. But he dredged up a memory from his past, over 20 years before during his second semester at Florida State University's medical school.

One of his fellow students had engaged in a sadistic impulse by covering it with the cloak of scientific experimentation. The guy had taken one of the lab rats and tossed it inside a microwave oven in the student lounge. Contrary to his expectations (and to his disappointment), the unfortunate rat hadn't exploded—it had simply stiffened and died.

Out of curiosity, Bradfort had taken the rat and dissected it. The major organs had burst, then hardened to a stone-like consistency—almost every trace of fluid in the rodent's body had boiled away. Though the condition of Simmons's organs wasn't as extreme, the similarities were frightening.

Bradfort examined Simmons's head. Both eyes were covered by a gelatinous film, as though the liquid within them had evaporated. He propped the man's head back and forced open his mouth so he could take a look at the tongue and the softer mouth tissues. What he saw brought another burst of profanity from Bradfort's lips.

Simmons's tongue looked like a shriveled, blacked piece of fruit. His teeth, the ones containing metal fillings, were shattered. Extreme heat would have caused the fillings to swell and fracture the enamel.

Adhering to the roof of Simmons's mouth he saw a mass of semi-melted plastic and metal.

Bradfort couldn't guess at its purpose, although it resembled dental bridgework. He studied it silently for nearly a minute, trying to make up his mind what to do. The standard procedure would be to remove it, tag it, and continue with the autopsy. He was baffled and a little angered by this unexpected problem that interfered with what should have been a perfectly routine post-mortem and a golf game he had scheduled for the afternoon.

Bradfort turned off the recorder went to the telephone, and called the chief of staff, who after listening to Bradfort's expletive-littered report, called the officer of the day, who in turn called an intelligence officer posted to the G2 department on base.

A Major Jacobs dropped by within the hour and stood by patiently as Bradfort, with a pair of forceps and a scalpel, removed the wad of metal and plastic from Simmons's mouth, taking a goodly portion of desiccated tissue with it.

The intelligence people played it safe and took the material to Ostara Development, a private solid-state physics lab and electronics firm near the Tegel airfield.

The researchers tried only a few tests before determining that the mass was made of plastic and metal. They also determined that it was bridgework subjected to a short burst of HPM, a high-power microwave, probably in the 1014 kilometer band. The burst was probably not over two seconds in duration, and was potent enough to interfere with sophisticated electronic equipment.

The people from G2 were aware of the incident at Site 611, but they said nothing to the researchers or their supervisor, a Doctor Iselda Abendroth. They did want to know where the HPM had originated.

"From this," Iselda Abendroth said, pointing to the smears of melted circuitry inside the plastic portion of the bridgework.

She told them that the bridgework was a highly advanced, almost unbelievable masterpiece of miniaturization. It was a microwave transmitter, set and timed to emit a HPM burst at a pre-determined time and place.

Of course, the burst had literally cooked Lieutenant Colonel Avery Simmons, but Abendroth doubted it was affixed to the roof of his mouth for the purpose of assassination. A gun, a knife or even a car bomb would have been simpler and far less expensive.

Abendroth theorized that such a powerful transmitter built on such a scale would cost upwards of three hundred thousand dollars.

The G2 officers knew that various scientists, both in and out of the employ of the U.S. government, had managed to produce some miniature HPM transmitter prototypes not much bigger than a bread-box, but nobody had ever made one as small or as powerful as this.

The G2 officers and Iselda Abendroth were in complete agreement on one point— not only was the thing extremely dangerous, the implications of how and where it had been found were terrifying.

Simmons's dentist was located and interrogated. He denied having any knowledge of the bridgework and he angrily swore he would take a polygraph to that effect.

The G2 officers took him up on his promise and administrated the test. He passed.

Simultaneously, another group of intelligence officers were investigating all of Simmons' civilian and military contacts in Germany. The day's duty log and personnel roster of Site 611 were requisitioned and studied. The systems at the site were back online, due to the quick rebooting of Lieutenant Taylor. He reported no further problems.

Within an hour of receiving this information, there was a great deal of covert activity among military officials. They moved to pass the word—and the buck—at once.

There were international calls over scrambler circuits from Germany to all military bases in Europe, then the intel went across the sea.

Twelve hours after Bradfort found the mass of metal and plastic in Simmons's mouth, a message was sent to the American Joint Chiefs of Staff via a backchannel. The backchannel under the control of the JCS is the Digital Information Relay Center in the Pentagon basement. Operated under 24 hour guard, and open only to those with the highest clearances, the center is linked to military commanders and installations worldwide.

It allows senior officers to communicate in single copy messages that are not filed or recorded. At banks of code machines, computer terminals and satellite up-link stations, technicians decipher incoming messages and route them through secured telephone lines to the proper people within the Pentagon.

The report from G2 regarding the system failure at Site 611, the manner of Simmons's death and what it could mean, was so chilling that the technician who received it sat stunned for a long moment. He pulled himself together long enough to email the data to a five-star general several floors above him.

The general looked it over, phoned the technician in the basement, and ordered him to transmit the same data to compatible equipment located in the West Wing basement of the White House. An NSA officer manning the equipment took the data up to the Oval Office. The

President looked it over and groaned. He said hoarsely, "This is scary as shit."

He dismissed the officer then picked up the telephone. He called a private number that rang a secured line within a secluded house in up-state New York. A man named Herne answered. Within moments, the jesses were loosed and he prepared The Falcon to take wing.

FOUR

June 1, The Eyrie, five miles north of Cooperstown, New York

WARING WHEELED his gunmetal blue P1800 Volvo along a road that curved up the side of the valley past fieldstone walls, tall hedges and drooping willow trees. The wrought-iron gate to The Eyrie Foundation was difficult to see from the back-country lane and the chiseled stone plaque bearing a bas-relief carving of a bird-of-prey with outspread wings was almost hidden by a tangle of ivy.

He drove up the steep gravel road among trees rich with green spring color and braked when he reached the grounds of the estate proper. He parked in a space near a flight of stone steps that led up to a portico supported by Greek columns. Terraced lawns rose up to an outcropping of dark granite, on top of which stood a multi-storied manor house made of red brick.

The building had two four-story wings and a baronial main hall. From the center of the roof stretched an octagonal tower with bay windows all around.

Although the mid-day sunlight was bright enough for sunglasses, Waring gloried in the cool, upstate New York air. He had returned from the oppressive heat and humidity of the tropical jungle barely 18 hours before. Several of those hours had been spent scrubbing dried mud and muck out of every pore. He had exchanged his T shirt and twill pants for a perfectly tailored, three piece black Brioni business suit with a tie of blue silk knotted at the collar of his white shirt.

With the strongbox he had carried from Brazil tucked under an arm, Waring took the steps two at a time. Reaching a flag-stone footpath, he strode along it and crossed through the portico. He glanced out at the courtyard, hearing the faint, musical tinkle of wind-chimes. A dozen men and women of varying ages, sizes and ethnicities sat cross-legged on woven reed mats. All of them wore thin cotton shifts of saffron. They focused their attention on a bearded, balding man who stood before them, holding a clump of broccoli in one hand and a turnip in the other. He wore only a linen loin-cloth, which to Waring resembled an oversize diaper.

Waring heard him intone, "To become a true vegan, you must become one with the vegetable—you must *be* the vegetable—"

Trying not to laugh, Waring pushed open two oaken double doors and entered the manor. Despite the sunshine, the foyer was gloomy and he tucked his sunglasses into a breast pocket. All of the dark, carved beams and wooden paneling always made him feel as if he were walking through the interior of a giant Bavarian cuckoo clock. He strode along the red Turkish runner that led toward another set of twin doors. These were closed and both bore plaques with the warning: Restricted! Foundation Faculty Only!

From his wallet, Waring removed a small plastic card imprinted with the logo of a nonexistent health club. He inserted it into the nearly invisible slot beneath the right hand door's handle. When heard a brief buzz, he opened the door, stepping into a small room that held only a water cooler, a wooden bench and another door – this one labeled Storage.

He used the card to open the door. On the other side was an old-fashioned cage lift. Only two buttons studded the interior wall of the lift. He pushed the red one and the lift descended smoothly to the underground brain of the Eyrie. Four elevators hidden on the grounds and the manor house dropped personnel down into a labyrinth of corridors, offices, laboratories and even temporary living quarters.

Mike Waring had been witness—and a participant—in a great deal of high strangeness in his life, but he even he had been impressed when Aladar Herne conducted him on his first guided tour of the subterranean complex.

The door slid aside onto a wide, cream-colored corridor lit by softly glowing neon tubes inset into the ceiling. He passed the sealed room known as the Cortex—it held the electronic ears and eyes patched into satellite transmissions. Inside the room, a team of controllers sat at computer stations, monitoring and collecting all of the SIGINT and HUMIT—Signals Intelligence and Human Intelligence—traffic.

Only Aladar Herne's inner circle knew the true purpose of the Eyrie Institute. Waring knew Herne employed a full-time faculty who maintained the cover story by holding seminars and classes in manor house and grounds above.

The real purpose of the Eyrie was to swoop in and ferret out the real facts about the current and future dangers to global stability and provide those facts to the intelligence agencies who wanted them—for a price. Waring still remembered what Herne had said to him upon his first visit, three years before: "We aren't academics—we get out in the field, and our hands get dirty, and sometimes bloody."

On paper, the Eyrie was set up as a sociological research program, sponsored by several government agencies, and most of the time it functioned as one. Congressional funding committees believed the CIA or the NSA, or even the Department of Education established the Eyrie. More than once, Congressmen put forth motions to pull the funding. Each time, the motions were withdrawn, upon "further consideration".

As he made his way toward the war room, he heard a female voice call out, "Mike!"

He turned toward Maggie Goodfaith as she beckoned to him from the open doorway of her office. She said, "I was told you'd be here today. That's good."

He arched an eyebrow. "Why is that?"

"Come inside and I'll tell you."

When Waring hesitated, she smiled broadly. "Do what the doctor asks and you'll get a lollipop."

Waring stepped toward her. "I'll take you up on that. My appointment with Aladar can wait if candy is involved."

Maggie Goodfaith was a petite, willowy woman in her early thirties. She was dressed simply in a knit sheath dress of a beige hue with the just the right type of jewelry—understated earrings, a gold necklace and only a couple of rings. Her ash-blond hair was skinned back from her well-sculpted face and gathered in a knot at the nape of her neck.

She went behind her desk and gestured to an armchair on the other side of it. "Sit, please."

Waring didn't move. "I recall talk of a lollipop."

Maggie blinked at him with her brown eyes. With a rueful smile, she opened a drawer and produced a red Tootsie Roll pop. Waring took it and sat down, placing the strongbox on the floor beside him. As he removed the paper wrapper, he asked, "What can I do for you, counselor?"

She nodded toward the strongbox. "May I ask what that is?"

"You may ask."

When she didn't so much as flicker an eyelash, he lifted a shoulder in a shrug. "It's a souvenir of my trip to the Amazon. Nothing to concern you."

Maggie nodded. "In other words...I don't have the clearance to know."

Reaching down, she produced a file folder from a drawer. She didn't open it but slid it across the desk top toward Waring. "But I do know something about your trip. Aladar shared your report on what happened in Brazil."

"And?"

"And…it's a little incomplete."

Waring inserted the Tootsie-Roll pop between his right cheek and his teeth. "I composed the report on my laptop on the flight back. I may have skipped over a few small details."

"They weren't small details, Mike."

Waring removed the candy from his mouth, twirling the stick between thumb and forefinger. "Maybe you should clarify."

"Your emotional reactions…anyone else would be suffering from a degree of trauma."

Waring stared at her with feigned innocence. "Anyone else? Like who? I'm the firm's only field rep."

Maggie Goodfaith sighed in exasperation. "And I'm the counselor here, Mike. Aside from being the only field operative, you're the only one of the Eyrie's personnel who has never had a session with me. I don't know why Aladar has given you an exemption but—"

"—I'm exempt because my services to the Eyrie are on a voluntary basis," Waring broke in. "I'm semiretired."

The woman's lips tightened. "So you're doing us the favor?"

"Rather more blunt than I would've put it, but yes…that's about the size of the situation." He returned the Toostie-Roll to his mouth. "If I have to take my retirement in increments, that's the way I'll take it."

Rather than respond to his comment, Maggie said, "Your personnel record might shed some light on your protected status. If you had a personnel record, that is."

Waring grinned around the lollipop stick. "There's nothing all that mysterious about me, counselor. I'm sure you've dealt with your share of agency spooks."

She nodded. "I have. But even agency spooks have birth certificates, medical records and fingerprints on file—all you seem to have are a collection of identities…Gay Lawrence, Stanhope Falcon, Malcolm Wingate, Michael Wadley—and finally Michael Waring."

"That's the least improbable sounding of all the identities, wouldn't you agree?"

"Apparently you worked as a licensed private investigator before being recruited by Army Intelligence. But there are a lot of gaps in your background. Years worth of them, for a man so young."

Waring sat up straight in the chair. "Are you asking for an origin story?"

"I'm more concerned with how you're dealing with what you went through."

"I don't need counseling at the moment, Maggie. I don't feel the least bit traumatized. When I do, perhaps we can discuss it over dinner and drinks."

She glared at him. "This freewheeling gentleman adventurer act of yours notwithstanding—you're too much of a wild bird to be allowed to fly free."

"And this bird you cannot change," Waring deadpanned. He picked up the strongbox from the floor beside his chair and rose. "If you like, I'll recite all the lyrics."

Maggie continued to glare at him. "I'm going to find out who you really are, Michael Waring…spook, ghost or Falcon. I don't trust what I don't know and neither should Aladar."

Waring took the Tootsie Roll out of his mouth and saluted her with it. "I'll apprise him of that, counselor. Thanks for the lollipop."

Maggie Goodfaith nodded, her eyes cold. "And thank you for your time—Falcon."

THE KNIFE incorporated three blades in one, spreading out from the stone hilt, like a "W", with the center blade being the longest. The metal was dull and tarnished, the edges notched. The haft carried a sunburst design in gold, and within the burst was inscribed a letter or Roman numeral—V. It looked very old.

Sarge Hardy turned the object over in his big brown hands and said, "It's called a Dag."

"What's that?" Waring asked. "Half a dagger?"

"You can see that it isn't," Sarge said with the quirk of his heavy lips meant to be a smile. "Besides, the German word for dagger is dolche." His British accent, still touched by his Brixton origins, lent his German pronunciation a peculiar lilt.

Waring sat at a table in the war room. A steaming cup of black coffee was nestled in his right hand, but he was more interested in the object held in Hardy's hands.

"The Dag," said Hardy, "is an emblem of the Geheimgericht, the Silent Tribunal, a sort of a medieval vigilante group that ran roughshod over Germany in the sixth century. The V symbolizes the number of Man and the number of knights who formed the first Tribunal under Charlemagne."

"Is it worth anything?"

Hardy heaved his broad shoulders in a shrug. "To antiquarians, maybe."

"The gunmen in Brazil weren't antique collectors," Waring replied. "They thought it was worth slaughtering a village full of Indians."

"Goetz never should have gone through Interpol," Hardy said. "If one of the neo-Nazi groups was hunting for him, it was like phoning in an appointment for your own hit with the Mob. The agency has been rotten with Nazis since the 1930s. One of its presidents ended up at the end of an executioner's rope in Nuremburg Prison."

Hardy returned the knife to the strongbox. As he shut the lid, he studied the symbol painted on it.

"Doesn't look like any Nazi insignia I'm familiar with," he said.

"It's the emblem of something Goetz called the Black Sun," replied Waring. "Mean anything?"

The horizontal crease in Sarge's forehead deepened. "There's Revelation 6: 12: 'When he opened the sixth seal, I looked, and behold, there was a great earthquake— and the sun became black as sackcloth, the full moon became like blood.' "

"I doubt that was what he was referring to, Sarge," Waring said wryly.

Hardy frowned. "Wait a second. There was a secret society in Germany, back before World War I, called the die Bruderschaft Schwarze Sonne…it was sort of an elite occult social club for industrialists and the very rich. Some historians believe it was the direct forerunner to the Nazi party. Alistair Crowley allegedly had something to do with it."

Hardy got up, walked to the nearest computer terminal and dropped into the chair. He began tapping the keyboard. "Let's see if we can find another reference to it somewhere…maybe in the NSA archives."

Steve "Sarge" Hardy was the undisputed master of data-dispensing and sifting at the Eyrie. His personally designed system was networked with hundreds of governmental agencies, universities and international think-tanks. A middle-aged former police detective, intelligence officer and data analyst, Hardy had worked with Waring since a set of unusual circumstances threw them together in London years before. Waring was living there under a different name and identity at the time.

Waring couldn't remember a time when Sarge hadn't been able to dredge up a bit of important data, no matter how obscure. When Waring agreed to work for the Eyrie, he brought Sarge along with him.

Hardy reviewed all the daily reports provided by the SIGINT and

HUMIT controllers looking for, as he termed them, "arcana." He applied this term to events both major and minor, events that appear superficially explainable, but on closer scrutiny, seem to fit the criteria of the Iceberg Principle. If he spotted an "arcana," Sarge red-flagged the report, marking it for further investigation. The origin point of an arcana was referred to as a dark site.

As Hardy tapped the keys and manipulated the mouse, he asked, "Have you talked to Aladar since you got back?"

"He knows I'm here."

As if obeying a stage cue, the far door swung aside and Aladar Herne rolled in, seated in his custom power chair. Not even the most shameless flatterer would have called Herne handsome, but he was definitely striking—more than a little on the unforgettable side. Despite being confined to a motorized chair, Herne gave the impression of great size due to the breadth of his shoulders and chest. Extremely well-dressed in a black suit, yellow shirt and black necktie, Herne's head was completely hairless—without even a trace of eyebrows. However a very black goatee framed his mouth and chin .A stack of file folders rested on his lap. He thumbed through one even as his chair silently eased up to the table.

Waring noticed several of the files were marked with the insignia of the U.S. Army, and several more with the symbol of the State Department. Looking at him over his silver-rimmed bifocals, Herne said without preamble, "We've got a bad one, Falcon."

Waring tensed at the mention of his code-name, employed only by Herne when a crisis was pending. With feigned civility, he said, "Good day to you too, Aladar."

If Maggie Goodfaith thought he was a ghost, Waring reflected, she had apparently never tried to check out Aladar Herne's background. Waring had heard whispers about Herne during his time as an Army Intelligence investigator but the man had never been characterized as anyone other than a mysterious Man In Black presence who was rumored to assume the unpublicized, extra-legal burdens from the shoulders of the bureaucracy—including the office of the President. He was known as a security consultant who commanded fees as high as fifty thousand dollars for one day.

Sarge glanced up from computer terminal "Am I a part of this?"

Herne nodded. "One of the reasons the Oval Office dropped this in our laps was the Eyrie's untraceable intel-gathering resources…and the fact that in the eyes of the global intelligence community, we're invisible."

Waring raised an eyebrow. "The President is involved?"

"I've just come from a video conference he arranged with the JCS. This is a top-priority, high-risk situation."

"What's its nature?"

"Little Boy."

Sarge said softly, "Shit."

Little Boy was the current code-word for a nuclear crisis in Europe.

"For a number of reasons," Herne stated, "it was decided the Eyrie would handle this —or rather you, Falcon, since this situation calls for your particular approach."

Thinking of the dead Indians in Brazil, Waring asked calmly, "What if I have something else to occupy my energies?"

He was tweaking Herne. It never hurt to remind the man that his alliance with the Eyrie was at his sole discretion.

Herne shrugged. "Suit yourself. But if you do, you may be dooming a good portion of Europe to a nuclear hell on earth. It will be very difficult to enjoy your next retirement increment during the aftermath."

Herne wasn't being melodramatic. Waring saw genuine fear in his eyes. Herne's high-handed manner irritated him, but he was honest enough with himself to know his reaction was superficial. It was simply that he disliked being considered anything other than a free agent. He nodded and said, "Go on."

The big man carefully recounted everything that had happened in Germany from the moment Lieutenant Colonel Simmons had entered Site 611. Opening an Army file, he fanned out four scanned photographs of the gadget found inside Simmons's mouth.

"I wish I could produce the actual device for our people here to study, but it's being held in Germany pending a final determination."

"So nobody knows how or why this thing got inside of Simmons?" Waring asked.

"Or how many other of these devices may be in other mouths right now," Herne said grimly.

Hardy listened to the briefing while his computer terminal scanned several files at once. "I may be able to offer a possible why. Microwaves operate on the fringe line between infrared and lower frequencies. A by-product is an electromagnetic pulse that fouls up communications and electronic systems. That's why people with pacemakers aren't allowed near microwave ovens."

"The G2 people already thought of that," Herne said. "The computer systems at the site came back on-line. They ran a diagnostic and everything checked out."

"What level diagnostic?"

Frowning, Herne consulted a sheet of paper from a folder. "A Lieutenant Taylor ordered a Level One and Two."

Hardy grunted. "Yeah, that's what I thought. I'm familiar with the systems used at those sites. Levels One and Two are routine automated procedures to verify system performance. He needs to run a Level Four, which is the most comprehensive type of diagnostic. That requires techs to physically verify operations of mechanisms and link-ups. With a Level Four, you can guard against possible malfunctions in self-testing software. Trouble is, it takes a while, and the system has to be taken off-line."

"That's probably why he didn't conduct it," Herne said, "After the failure, I'm sure he was worried about a reprimand. I'll memo the G2 officer in charge so arrangements can be made."

In one of the Army files, Waring came across a photograph of a woman. It was a head and shoulders shot of a dusky-skinned woman who looked to be in her late 20s or early 30s. Her dark, wavy hair framed a high-planed, full-lipped face. She wore a pair of wire-rimmed eyeglasses. She was obviously posing for an ID badge shot. She was pretty, in an impersonal sort of way.

"Who's this?" he asked.

"Our German expert on solid-state physics. Iselda Abendroth, Ph.D. She's head of the research department of Ostara Development, a private electronics firm that acts as a NATO consultant from time to time. According to G2, she's been exceptionally helpful to them. She'll be your contact in Berlin. We can't tell her who you really are, but she'll function as technical liaison with minimal access to the actual field operation."

"What's my cover?"

"A physicist from the U.S. Department of Energy. Since Abendroth has been around spooks before, she'll probably see right through you, but—"

"—Especially," interrupted Waring, "if I have to discuss solid-state physics with her. What am I expected to do over there?"

"Find out who is behind this and neutralize them. Find out if they've implanted any other military personnel and neutralize them, too."

"Kill them, you mean?" Waring inquired with exaggerated nonchalance.

"I said neutralize…you're free to employ your own definition."

"Mine doesn't include killing military personnel who could be victims, not conspirators. Any ideas who may be behind this?"

"Not many. Abendroth's firm, the Patton hospital and the U.S. embassy are under discreet surveillance by relays of men. They drive plumber's vans, utility trucks, that sort of thing. Two at a time and they're very good at it. They seem to know when they're being watched, and disappear. They haven't been identified as yet. Twenty years ago, I'd say they were working for the KGB or STASI."

"That's the problem with the end of the Cold War," Hardy commented with a smile. "It's not so easy to I.D. the players on the other side."

"True," said Herne, "but whoever they are, they're ruthless enough to snuff Simmons, and inventive enough to do it in a way that allowed them to tamper with a total of 24,000 kilotons of destructive force at the same time. That doesn't sound like much, since Cheyenne Mountain can deliver missiles of hundreds of megatons, but keep this in mind—the bomb that wiped out Hiroshima was only twenty kilotons."

Waring scanned the dossier on Simmons. He reviewed the hastily-compiled list of the officer's known associates in Germany when he came across a certain name.

"Julius Eicke," Waring read aloud. "Stockbroker. That's the second time in 48 hours I've come across the name of Eicke."

"What do you mean?" asked Herne.

In simple, unadorned language, Waring told Herne what had transpired in Brazil.

"Every piece of hardware was of German manufacture," Waring said, a cold note entering his voice. "The perps spoke German. And of course, the sainted Doctor Grimminger you sent me to rescue turned out to be Karl Gustav Goetz, formerly of the Reich Main Security Office."

If Waring expected Herne to react with dismay or shame, he was disappointed. Herne only nodded.

"I suspected as much. It's an axiom in the intelligence community that when Interpol makes a request of the State Department to diddle around in South America on behalf of a German-born, naturalized American citizen of a certain age, you can bet an ex-goosestepper is involved."

"Thanks for letting me in on your suspicion," Waring snapped.

Herne sighed, "Falcon, one way to keep the Eyrie operating with the freedom we have is to perform occasional favors for government agencies. That way, I can call in my own favors when I need to protect our people. I'm damn sorry about those Indians and what you went through down there, but I hope you understand that if I'd known the true nature of the request, I would've refused it."

Waring said, "You might not want to tell the State Department that I smell ex-goosesteppers in this mess. Or maybe not so ex."

Hardy looked away from his computer monitor and said, "Your sense of smell is as sharp as ever, Mike."

"How so?"

The man nodded toward the text scrolling across the screen. "I found a pretty comprehensive file in the NSA archives about German secret societies."

Herne scowled at him. "What does that have to do with anything?"

"We all know that the Nazi party was not just a military machine," Hardy answered. "The Nazis brought a completely new culture into prominence almost overnight and with the passive acceptance of most of the general populace of Germany. We shouldn't believe that the military defeat of the Nazis was the same as the cultural defeat of their ideas and philosophy."

"Like the Brotherhood of the Black Sun?" Waring ventured.

Sarge Hardy nodded. "Exactly."

Aladar Herne's eyes narrowed. "What are you talking about about?"

Hardy pointed to the symbol on the strongbox. "Historians claim that the abbreviation 'SS' stood for 'Schutzstaffel', but to Third Reich insiders, the abbreviation represented the words 'Schwarze Sonne'."

Herne stared at him expectantly, refusing to play straight man to Hardy's academic performance. Waring said helpfully, "Schwarze Sonne' means Black Sun in English."

The big bald man grunted. "That's what you think Goetz was referring to?"

"So you did read my report…yes, it's the only logical conclusion to reach."

Herne gestured dismissively. "Prewar Germany had more secret societies than braunschweiger and beer. The Thule Society, the Order of the Golden Dawn—"

Tapping his computer screen, Sarge said, "The Brotherhood of the

Black Sun was something special…only for the elite. It attracted more members than just disenfranchised Germans. To the members of the Brotherhood, the Black Sun represented a kind of energy source that radiated light which was invisible to the human eye. The very concept of it seems to have bordered upon the religious. The Brotherhood of the Black Sun was usually represented symbolically as a black sphere out of which eight arms extended."

Hardy nodded toward the image on the strongbox. "Just like this, I imagine."

Folding his arms over his chest, Waring said, "We know that the Nazis believed in a lot of hocus-pocus and superstitious rubbish. This doesn't seem much different from the rest of their master race delusions."

Hardy pressed a key on his console and the overhead lights dimmed. Simultaneously, light swelled from the four walls surrounding the table. The walls flickered and large text pixeled across them.

"I've accessed the World War II historical database from the National Archives," Hardy said. "This is compiled from a couple of O.S.S. reports, dated 1946. It was intended as a briefing document for the Nuremburg prosecutors."

In its present form, the Brotherhood of the Black Sun dates back to 1910 - 1912. It was a proto-Nazi occult group with connections to Aleister Crowley's Golden Dawn cult. But the roots of the society stretch back at least to the sixth century, and perhaps further.

According to tradition, a secret society known as the Silent Tribunal originated after the conquest of Saxony in 772 by Charlemagne. The powers of the Tribunal were wide. They exacted summary executions on any transgressor of Charlemagne's laws. The Tribunal's symbol was a three-bladed knife known as a Dag, and replicas of this instrument were stuck into trees as a warning to others that they were searching for a miscreant, and no interference would be tolerated.

This organization existed in various forms and names until it surfaced 50 years ago as the die Bruderschaft Schwarze Sonne. It is suspected that Hitler joined the Brotherhood shortly after 1918, when he was assigned to a highly secret counter-intelligence unit that engaged in acts of domestic terrorism, assassinating German leaders who had negotiated

Germany's surrender.

The Brotherhood was supported by the German High Command and it held secret courts and condemned people who they felt had betrayed the Aryan nation.

As time passed, the Brotherhood became a magnet for wealthy international businessmen. It is not an exaggeration to state that the Brotherhood of the Black Sun was the most important organization behind the rise of Nazism. Most, if not all, of the symbols used by the Nazis were ancient mystical symbols first used by the Silent Tribunal and then the Brotherhood The swastika, the death's head, the rune-inscribed daggers, and the S.S. lightning bolt were developed by the Brotherhood.

After Hitler reformed the German Worker's Party into the Nazi Party, he made it mandatory that high-ranking members of the party, and later the S.S., had to be inducted into the Brotherhood.

However, the ranks of this society did not pledge loyalty to Hitler-on the contrary, Hitler pledged his loyalty to the society. He claimed his true guidance came from supernatural sources.

The preoccupation with mystical lore may explain Hitler's obsession with collecting artifacts and icons from the ancient past. A primary belief of the Brotherhood was that in order to consolidate its position as the future masters of the world, it had to accumulate all the trappings of sacred kingship. There is no complete list of the artifacts supposedly in the Nazi's possession, but according to a report provided by a Lieutenant Goetz of the Reich Main Security Office, the relics are of immense spiritual importance to the inner circle of the society.

It is unfortunate that the Nazi defeat and reported death of Hitler has not ended the Brotherhood of the Black Sun's influence. It was clearly more than a political movement- it was a religion, a holy order, and religions can only be suppressed, not destroyed.

Herne nervously ran a thumb and forefinger over his goatee. "Why didn't any of this craziness come out at Nuremburg?"

Sarge Hardy was busy with his keyboard again. "Just a wild guess, but I imagine the prosecutors were worried that the Nazis on trial could make a fairly convincing insanity plea."

"It's no crazier than Mexican cartel drug-lords practicing black magic or Santeria," Waring said.

Hardy's computer was equipped to handle multiple functions. While Waring and Herne had been talking, he entered Julius Eicke's name, cross-referencing it with files on high-ranking Nazi officials.

The text blurred from the wall-screens and was replaced by a black and white photograph of a man in his mid-30s wearing the black uniform and peaked cap of an S.S. officer. The man was standing beside a small boy, his gloved hand resting on his shoulder. The boy wore the shorts and neckerchief ensemble of the Hitler Youth.

"Oberfuhrer Helmut Eicke, commander of the Brandenberg Division. The kid is his only child, Julius. The picture was taken in 1945."

Another black and white photo popped up beside the boy's head. This showed the smiling well-fed face of distinguished grey-haired man wearing formal evening clothes. "Julius Eicke as he appeared at a diplomatic function two years ago in Washington."

Hardy manipulated the mouse and superimposed the image of the man over that of the boy's. "A chip off the old block, looks like."

"If we suspected everybody in central Europe who had a family member in the S.S.," Herne growled, "then we'd have most of western Europe under surveillance. Not to mention South America."

"You wouldn't have to go to those lengths," Waring said.

"Are you making some kind of point?" Herne challenged

"Nazi garbage should have been flushed away a very long time ago Instead, some people, preserved aspects of it. And it's spread again, like a virus. Nazi groups, like the skinheads and some of these paramilitary militias, have been revived in America, Germany and other countries."

"We don't know if the Brotherhood of the Black Sun or Nazis or the Campfire Girls are behind this," Herne countered. "It's all supposition, no matter what Goetz told you."

"Until we have proof that satisfies you," Waring said, "let me assume the opposition is the Brotherhood. It makes sound tactical sense. So don't put the jesses on me."

"I won't, Falcon But if it is the Brotherhood they know how to make themselves invisible through protective coloration. Don't you think the Justice Department has tried to apprehend some of these resurrected Nazi groups with intelligence ties?" Herne squeezed the air with one fist. "It's like trying to prosecute smoke."

Sarge said softly, "Mike, these guys have a lot of protection. You're going to piss off a bunch of powerful folks if you lift the rock off this situation and find a bunch of Nazi bugs crawling out from under it. The alliance between American intelligence and the Nazis at the end of the war isn't something they want publicized."

"Exactly," said Herne. "If what you suspect is true, then the architects of the Nazi Party, the S.S. and the Third Reich are your targets. They've kept their secrets for a hell of a long. This is the old guard you're going up against."

"Hell's guard, more like it," Waring said. "But just to know where I'll stand with the intel-net in Germany, we should send a jacket to the G2 officer in charge about the Brotherhood of the Black Sun. He'll either accept the possibility or he won't."

"And if he doesn't?" asked Herne. "G2 may not want to accept the likelihood or the responsibility that bastards they absorbed into their own spheres are working against them."

"I know that, Aladar. I also know that over half a century ago, the Nazis missed being the first nuclear power by a hair. I think they're now rectifying that. You said you can't apprehend these people?"

"Yeah," Herne answered heavily.

Michael Waring's tone became low and cold. "These people—the Brotherhood, the Nazis, whatever they are—can't be prosecuted. But there's no reason they can't be run to ground."

FIVE
June 2, Berlin

JULIUS EICKE raised his crystal snifter of Asbach Uralt brandy to the four men around the table. "Gentlemen, I salute you."

The oak-paneled conference room in the Hauser and Hochbach office overlooking the Wilhelmstrasse gave an appropriately Old World setting to the function presided over by Eicke. The four men at the table responded to the toast with varying degrees of enthusiasm.

Eicke turned and raised his goblet to the oil portrait of Eric Eicke which dominated the wall behind him. "Prosit!" he said loudly.

Helmut Eicke had initiated his son Julius into the Brotherhood upon his 18th birthday. He had told him that the Brotherhood, unlike the Odessa group, was not an organization devoted to fulfilling Hitler's dream of a thousand year Reich. Rather, Hitler had failed to fulfill the Brotherhood's dream.

On that long-ago birthday, Helmut Eicke had said to his son, "Forget the Party, forget Hitler. He may have danced, but is The Brotherhood who called the tune."

Julius Eicke and every man in the elegant room knew the tune.

The portly and balding Professor Jorg Weisenburg was one of Europe's leading electronic specialists, or he had been until a heart condition had forced him to retire. His father had worked on Germany's secret electromagnetic research team, building on the discoveries of Marconi, Tesla and Hertz to construct offensive and defensive devices. Before the elder Weisenburg's work was completed, he died in the Allied bombing of Dresden.

Weisenburg had lost a father, but he gained his research papers and an undying hatred of western democracy.

That hatred was shared by the elderly, spectacled psychiatrist who sat next him. Doctor Hito Asoka had developed a number of psychological weapons to use against Allied prisoners of war, especially in the fields of behavior modification and mind-control. While still at university, Asoka had been enlisted into the Black Dragon Society, and after the surrender, he had asked to be inducted into the Brotherhood.

For the last forty years, Asoka had chaired the substance abuse program of Der Nachsinnen Anstalt, a medical clinic specializing in the treatment of wealthy Berliners for acute alcoholism and drug addiction. His program was copied all over the continent, and more than one staffer at the U.S. consulate with a drinking problem had been referred to his clinic.

The man seated beside Asoka was a rail-thin, crewcut, retired colonel of South Africa's Security Police. Born in Pretoria, he had moved to Frankfurt when his nation's apartheid policy had ended and was hired as a NATO security consultant. His name was Arlen deMilteer, and though he had fought against Rommel in Northern Africa as a very young man, he had always believed in his heart that the Allies were fighting on the wrong side.

Partly because of his German ancestry and the pride in his Aryan blood, he had been instrumental in helping hundreds of high-ranking German prisoners of war escape into South Africa. He had kept in contact with them, and they had put him in contact with the innermost circle of the Brotherhood. Through his numerous acquaintances in NATO , he kept the Brotherhood well-informed on military matters.

deMilteer didn't consider himself a true fascist— he was merely a well-bred racist of the old school who was horrified by the revolts staged in his country's black townships. He had no desire to live in a nation where the kafirs were treated as equals.

The man next to him wasn't sipping brandy, but a goblet full of orange juice. A thick-bodied, heavy-set man with black hair, his swarthy complexion showed a pale hue above his upper lip where he had recently shaved off a mustache. He wore a beautifully tailored Armani suit. He was more recognizable to newspaper readers and CNN watchers when he was mustached, bearded and with a colorful turban on his head.

His colleagues referred to him only as "Achmet", even though that was not his name. As the ruler of one of the most hated countries in the Mideast, Achmet was consumed with paranoia every time he set foot out of his own sandy, oil-rich nation. Because his face was so well-known, even to the average citizen, he was afraid his presence could compromise the security of the Brotherhood, so he always took pains to disguise himself. Although he knew the conference room of Hauser and Hochbach could not possibly be bugged, he insisted that he be called "Achmet" during his rare visits.

The Brotherhood tolerated this eccentricity, since Achmet's fears were not without grounds. Any number of intelligence and counter-terrorist agencies had kill-on-sight contracts on him. The Brotherhood made sure Achmet was always under their protection in Europe. Besides, the tyrant enjoyed a daily oil income of just under three million dollars, and he had already invested twenty million into the Brotherhood's coffers.

Achmet had joined the Brotherhood because he saw no reason to share his country's oil revenues with its dirt-poor citizenry, and he also saw the Brotherhood's project as the simplest, most practical way to end U.S. influence in his part of the world.

At the end of the table sat Ulrich Schreck, clasping his snifter with trembling hands. His bald head wobbled on his scarf-sheathed neck. He did not join the toast. Social fripperies only irritated him. He participated in the ancient rituals of the Brotherhood, but toasting the portrait of a dead man did not interest him.

Schreck had been involved with the Brotherhood since 1912, while Hitler was still hand-coloring postcards in Vienna. He had found and matriculated the man, transforming him into a shrewd orator and a frighteningly persuasive propagandist.

When the propagandist became fuhrer, then madman, Schreck had killed him, pulling the trigger himself. At Schreck's orders, his stunned aides had carried his body into the garden of the Reich Chancellery and burned it with gasoline. Schreck had chosen April 30, Walpurgis Night, to sacrifice Hitler. It was all part of an ancient ritual.

The Brotherhood of the Black Sun was not a large organization, nor did it need to be. It had a thousand year legacy that was preserved from generation to generation, although Schreck was concerned about passing on the torch to unworthy hands.

Even though the Brotherhood financed such noisy, crude groups as the Nationalist Front, the German Alternative, the Christian Identity Movement in England and the White Aryan Resistance in America, Schreck despised the drunken rabble. However, it was traditional to place several levels of attention-getting expendables between Brotherhood leadership and public relations efforts like the Nazi Party.

As well as the skinheads and neo-Nazis, the Brotherhood maintained a well-armed troop of soldiers, consisting primarily of ex-East and West German border patrolmen. Most of them had no place to go after the Wall collapsed, and were happy to find a new place for their talents. The majority of them spent their time in a special wing of the Nachsinnen clinic where Asoka had given them new identities and diagnosed them with a multitude of mental, emotional and substance abuse ailments. Any government official glancing through the patient records would find that these men were chronics, dangerous to the community and themselves, and their treatment was on-going.

Eicke drained off the brandy in his goblet and announced, "The news from Site 611 is excellent. The computers were re-booted with our program. No one is the wiser."

Asoka asked, "Did Simmons's illness raise inquiries of an unusual nature?"

Eicke nodded toward deMilteer. "Colonel?"

deMilteer shook his head. In his guttural Afrikaner accent he said, "The transmitter was found, I'm afraid, and at last report, it was taken to Ostara Development for study. They may not know what it is. I think we can assume everything is under control."

"Let us assume nothing," Eicke responded stiffly. "We have planned our campaign carefully and provided for all contingencies, but we must allow for an X factor."

Weisenburg said, "I'm familiar with the people at Ostara. One of the scientists there, a woman named Abendroth, may realize the transmitter's purpose—"

"—We have her under surveillance," interrupted Eicke. "My company has done with business with Ostara and I'm acquainted with Dr. Abendroth myself…she is very bright, but I doubt your excellent craftsmanship will be recognized. And if so, the end result is the same—we control the nuclear arsenal at Site 611. I also learned from my conduit in the U.S. embassy that an expert in solid-state physics is due to arrive tomorrow."

"Then we may have to reconsider the timetable," said Asoka. "Move it up."

" Good. When will we strike?" Achmet asked.

Eicke smiled at the dictator patronizingly. "His Excellency is premature. We do not intend to launch the missiles. The fear we will instill when the Americans and the government learn they do not have control over their toys will make them more than eager to deal with us."

"Fear," put in Asoka, "is the best motivator."

Achmet scowled. "What is the point of owning a weapon we will not use?"

Eicke kept his smile in place. "Our mission is what it has always been, Excellency. To seize control while Germany is in tumult. To force the NATO powers to recognize us as the true power behind the Republic. It is unimportant whether the United Nations shares that recognition, or even learns about us. We are not in this for publicity."

The last remark was a pointed comment about Achmet's apparent fondness for posturing and delivering threats on television.

Achmet glanced around the table. "That is all very well for you and for the rest of you. You promised that my nation would gain much from this undertaking. All I see coming out of this is a prolonged game of saber-rattling."

Schreck spoke up in a sharp, whip-crack voice. "The gain is that one of the conditions we set is the lifting of embargoes and sanctions against your country. You will supply Germany with oil, we will supply you with medicines, technologies and everything you need to rebuild your military."

Schreck turned from Achmet and lifted his blue eyes toward Eicke. "The news from Site 611 is excellent, you said. It is less so from Brazil, is it not?"

Eicke shifted uneasily. "Sir—"

"An entire village of Indians slaughtered," spat Schreck. "One of our aircraft and its crew destroyed. And the Dag was not recovered."

For all his devotion to the Brotherhood, Eicke did not share Schreck's obsession with relics, no matter how important they were to the lore and legend of the society.

"Sir," Eicke said patiently, "Goetz's body was finally found. The traitor is dead, the Brotherhood avenged. What else do you want?"

By way of an answer, Schreck hurled the contents of his snifter into Eicke's face. Eicke blinked as the liquor stung his eyes, but he did not otherwise move.

Placing his hands flat on the tabletop, Schreck levered his body erect. His arms trembled, but he forced himself to stand, his eyes blazing in his seamed face.

"After all these years," Schreck said in a low, deadly voice, "you still do not understand. We are conquerors. As in ancient times, we took the relics of national and religious power as symbols of our victories. The powers of rulership in these objects were transferred to us. It is more than an empty, symbolic gesture. It has an actual, functional reason."

Taking a deep breath, Schreck went on: "The Dag represents the roots of our Brotherhood. If it is in the possession of an enemy, those roots are cut. If we no longer control our past, then we will not command the present or the future. Do you understand me?"

deMilteer snorted. "I don't. You've kept me out of this black magic hocus-pocus horseshit so far, and I like it that way. Don't start dragging me into it now."

Schreck focused his gaze on the South African. For a moment, his face was convulsed by homicidal rage. Then, it relaxed. The furious flame in his eyes guttered out and he smiled. Then he laughed.

"Leave it to our Afrikaner friend," Schreck said, "to bring us back down to reality. Hocus-pocus horseshit, indeed."

The tension around the table broke and everyone shared a laugh, including Achmet. Eicke wiped the brandy from his face with a silk handkerchief.

Then, Schreck's hand darted inside his coat. It came back out gripping the Walther. The pistol spat a flat crack of sound. The bullet took deMilteer in the forehead, punching a neat, blue-edged hole barely quarter of an inch above his right eyebrow. deMilteer's head snapped back violently.

The high back and raised arms of his chair kept deMilteer from falling, though his body sagged down toward the floor. Cordite stung the eyes and nostrils.

Schreck met the stares of shocked faces with calm eyes. "Does anyone else care to speak of horseshit?"

There was no answer, and Schreck replaced the pistol beneath his coat. In a matter-of-fact voice he said, "I had already marked deMilteer for expulsion, so don't fear that his sudden vacancy creates either a problem or a vacuum. He served us well, but he showed signs of becoming an inconvenience."

Schreck turned toward Eicke. "Julius?"

"Sir!"

"You will use our contacts in Interpol, in the CIA, in the embassies or anyone else that is required to learn the identity of the man seen in Brazil. He will have the Dag if anyone does."

"I understand, sir."

Schreck carefully eased himself back into his wheelchair. He waved a diffident hand. "Get someone up here to clean this mess so we can continue with other business."

Eicke went to the telephone and picked up the old-fashioned French-style receiver. He dialed the mailroom and spoke to the supervisor. "Please send Xauz up to the conference room with six memo pads. At once."

In less than a minute came the pre-arranged double-knock signal at the heavy door. Eicke unbolted it and allowed Xauz to enter. He was a young man wearing the standard uniform of all Hauser and Hochbach male employees— a single-breasted navy blue blazer bearing the firm's monogrammed insignia on the pocket, white shirt and narrow black necktie. Only his footwear did not conform to the dress code— he wore pointy-toed American cowboy boots made of glistening rattlesnake skin.

Though Eicke was accustomed to Xauz's size, he nevertheless felt an instant's apprehension when the young man stalked past him into the room and insolently tossed the memo pads onto the table.

Xauz's arms and legs were like tree trunks, and great muscles rippled beneath the blazer with each motion. His closely-shaven head, bearing only a bristly covering of hair towered nearly seven feet above the floor. His forehead was high, and his grey eyes clear and alert.

Eicke gestured to deMilteer's body. "Get him out of here, Xauz. Then standby."

Xauz nodded and bent over deMilteer, sliding his huge hands under the corpse's armpits. He hummed softly as he swung the dead South African astride the wide yoke of his shoulders. Eicke recognized the tune. It was an Oi song—Nazi rock—recorded by Destructive Force. Though Eicke hated such music, it was instrumental in drawing street-level recruits from the dingy clubs and basement bars all over Berlin.

Xauz carried deMilteer through a door built into a carven oak panel. A passage led to the basement of the building next door, then to a fenced-off alley.

After Xauz shut the door-panel, the meeting resumed. Eicke would attend to cleaning up the blood and viscera personally, and he would also arrange for deMilteer to be found in his Frankfurt home, a recently fired Walther in his hand and a suicide note on the table. Numerous samples of deMilteer's handwriting were in his possession, and there was an excellent forger languishing at Asoka's clinic.

The next half-hour was devoted to fairly routine details regarding finances and the acquisition of new ordnance to replace that lost in Brazil. The Hit List of anti-fascist officials in the government who would oppose their terms was updated.

The meeting adjourned at six. Achmet left first, through the hidden wall panel that would bring him out to the alley, where his driver was waiting to take him to a private airfield. Asoka and Weisenburg left by the main door on the first floor. Inasmuch as they could prove they had legitimate business with Hauser and Hochbach , there was no reason for them to skulk through basements and alleys.

Eicke was left alone with Schreck. The old man's outburst appeared to have drained him. His hairless skull trembled.

"Are you feeling unwell, sir?" Eicke asked.

Without lifting his head, Schreck said hoarsely, "I should've killed that swine of an Arab as well as the Afrikaner. He will prove to be a problem."

Hesitantly, Eicke said, "Sir. We need no more dissension."

"True," Schreck replied bitterly. "We had enough of that in Brazil, didn't we?"

"We will find that man. We will find the Dag. You have my oath on it."

Schreck uttered a low, derisive laugh. "I trust you will obey that oath with more dedication than shown by Goetz."

With effort, Schreck raised his head. "Our Interpol contacts told us where to find Goetz. They also reported that someone leaked Goetz's radio message to the American State Department, and they in turn, contacted another agency. Find out what that agency might be. When you learn that, you will learn who that agency dispatched to Brazil. And you will find the Dag."

Schreck was not making a suggestion. There was no point in arguing with the old man, or of trying to point out that six Pershing II missiles were worth a hundred — no, a thousand—ancient ceremonial daggers. Eicke toyed momentarily with the notion of crafting a replica and offering it as the genuine article. But Schreck would see through the deception. And kill him.

"Julius," Schreck said quietly. "Did you speak the truth to Achmet when you told him the missiles would only be launched as a last resort?"

"Of course, sir."

"He is right. There is no point in owning a weapon you do not intend to use. We are not seeking a balance of power. "

Eicke's belly went cold. "Sir, is there a point in conquering a radioactive wasteland? The range of the missiles is limited. We would be destroying large pieces of the Fatherland we wish to repossess."

"Do you not think the Americans will figure that out and guess we are only bluffing?"

"I think they may suspect that, but they won't take the chance."

Schreck nodded. "Perhaps. Let me see the box."

Eicke hesitated.

Schreck raised his head and snarled. "The box!"

Reluctantly, Eicke went to the portrait of his father and grasped one of the mortised corners of the frame. It swung away from the wall on small, almost invisible hinges. Built into the wall was the military-grey metallic surface of a safe door. It bore no locks or handles. There was a glassy rectangle midway between the top and bottom hinges. Eicke placed four fingers of his right hand on the rectangle. The safe door buzzed and opened.

Eicke reached in and removed a black metal box about the size of a cigar box, but much heavier. He carried it carefully to the conference table and placed it before Schreck.

With one forefinger, Eicke slid a wafer of metal open on the top of the box. Within it were coiled fiber optical cables, coaxial input and output leads, and an entire layer of microprocessors. The box was the state of the art in miniaturization.

Schreck bent over it, one eyebrow lifted. "According to our friend Weisenburg, this little box can launch our missiles?"

"In conjunction with the rewritten programs," Eicke said. "The box is designed to be connected to a microwave transmitter that resembles a Citizen's Band radio antennae. Theoretically, we would drive the vehicle to within half a kilometer of the site, connect it with a keyboard and transmit the appropriate commands."

"Theoretically?"

"Obviously, sir, we have tested the device, but not on the actual missiles. To launch them would tend to invalidate our overall objective."

Schreck chuckled. "Would it? What if I suggested we alter that overall objective in order to bridge the gap between the theoretical and the practical?"

Eicke swallowed. He did not allow the fear, the hatred he felt toward the old man at that moment to show on his face.

"What is your answer, Julius?"

Eicke stiffened and thrust out his right arm. "Honor is Loyalty."

Schreck smiled and caressed the black box. "Yes. Isn't it just."

SIX
June 3, Berlin

THE LEAR jet knifed through the night sky, following the air corridor designated for Western aircraft. Looking out the window at the lights of Berlin below, Mike Waring reflected that only a few years ago, MiGs from the Eastern side would have buzzed them.

"We're on our final approach to Tempelhof airport," said the voice of Austin over the speaker.

Waring slipped on the headset connecting him to the cockpit. "Everything still green?"

"Yes, sir," replied the pilot. "Received a message from Herne twenty minutes ago. Green as the fields of Ireland. He said to tell you not to waste time soaking up the local Berlin culture."

"I've been to strip joints before," Waring said dryly.

Austin laughed. He was one of the civilian pilots for the Eyrie, generally employed only when a soft contact was to be made.

The jet descended in a steep glide toward the intersecting network of runways. Austin made a smooth landing and taxied the Lear toward an airside terminal.

Waring studied the airport. It was a huge, sprawling complex, sleek and ultra-modern in design. He tried to imagine what it had looked like seventy years ago, after the Soviet armored infantry divisions had finished shelling the hell out of it.

The jet rolled to a stop near the gates of an airside. As attendants chocked the tires and wheeled a ramp to the door, Austin emerged from the cockpit. He was a tall, rawboned man with a leonine mustache like the kind Wyatt Earp had favored.

"You can disembark now. Your luggage will be forwarded to the consulate, except your carry-on."

Waring shifted the position of the Ruger SR1911 in its shoulder holster beneath his black leather jacket.

"Customs have already been dealt with," Austin continued. "The chamber of commerce has sent a rep to meet you."

Austin employed the euphemism for the Verfassungschutz, the secret service. Waring was not looking forward to meeting them. He knew the officers consisted primarily of former Gehlen Organization men, and many of them were veterans of the S.S. Though most of the ex-Gestapo agents were probably retired or dead, Waring couldn't shake the echo of "Ehre Ist Treue" from his mind.

The main promenade of the terminal was crowded with camera-laden people. Waring caught at least a dozen different accents and dialects as soon as he entered. His eyes swept about, looking for his contact and simultaneously checking to see if anyone seemed unusually curious about him. He was not hard to spot—a tall dark-haired man with a hawkish cast to his features and a blue crew-neck sweater beneath his jacket.

Not too very long before, the Tempelhof had been the jumping off point for thousands of assorted spies, assassins, and miscellaneous intelligence agents serving at least forty different intelligence organizations of a dozen different nations. Most of the anonymous Cold Warriors had moved their base of operations to the Mideast and Africa, but Waring spotted several men and women carrying the spook aura.

He also spotted a pack of tattooed and shaven-headed young men, swaggering about the promenade, elbowing aside tourists and talking in loud, aggressive voices. As they approached him, an outside member of the pack swung directly into his path. Waring stopped and fixed a slit-eyed stare on the young man's face. His right hand made a casual show of stealing inside his jacket.

The man's eyes caught Waring's gaze. He blinked, and at the last second, veered to one side, avoiding him completely.

"Mr. Waring?" said a low, feminine voice behind him.

Waring turned, putting a smile on his face. The photograph of Iselda Abendroth had not done her justice. She was a beauty all the way, with leaf green eyes that contrasted nicely with her café'au lait complexion. She was full-lipped, and even the casual attire of slacks and flannel shirt did not conceal her athletic figure. She was surprisingly tall. With her mane of thick, russet hair, he guessed her to be five ten or so. Her gaze was direct and intelligent behind the lenses of her glasses.

She extended a hand and Waring shook it formally. "You're Dr. Abendroth."

"And you're a little late," she said. "Everyone is waiting, so we'll have to hustle."

Her English was perfect, touched only with a slight, yet charming accent.

They started moving through the terminal. "I'm to conduct you to the consulate. They asked me to meet you because embassy officials might be recognized here."

"The old watchers never sleep," Waring said.

"Something like that."

It was cool outside the terminal, a little above jacket weather. Waring glanced around casually at the crowds streaming in and out of the many glass and chrome doors. He saw nothing that made him suspect they were under observation, but the sixth sense that had helped him survive for so many years was on high alert. All he saw that seemed the slightest bit out of place was a VW mini-van parked at a service apron several hundred feet away.

The side panels were emblazoned with the words: *Der Volkkommen Stecker.* The Perfect Plug. Beneath the words was an illustration of a hand jamming a cork into the end of a leaky pipe.

Iselda Abendroth led the way to a grey Opel sedan parked at the curb. A sandy-haired young man was leaning against the rear door.

"This is Dave," said Abendroth. "Our driver."

Waring extended a hand. "Mike Waring."

"Good to meet you." Dave opened the door and Waring and Abendroth climbed in.

The Opel left the Tempelhof parking arena and took the cross-town extension. Even at close to 10 o' clock, the traffic was heavy.

"Why the consulate?" Waring asked.

"My office is under surveillance," replied Abendroth. "At least, that's what I'm told. The embassy has the least chance of being bugged."

"By whom?"

"That is what everyone is still trying to figure out." She looked at Waring quizzically. "Do you have any ideas?"

He shrugged and changed the subject. "I understand you've been a great help on the technical side of this."

It was Abendroth's turn to shrug. "Germany is the electronics capitol of Europe. I've acted as a consultant to your government and my own on a number of occasions."

"Your government?"

Abendroth faced him. "I realize I don't look like the standard German, Mr. Waring. My hair, my eyes and my skin may not meet the pure Aryan standard, but I am a native-born German nevertheless."

Waring smiled. "You misunderstand me. I'm curious about why the Republic needed your expertise, and if it was for a similar reason that sent me here."

Abendroth laughed sheepishly. "I apologize. I can be a little sensitive. My maternal grandfather was an American serviceman and though having a black American as a family member is hardly unique, it's not commonplace. I was on the receiving end of a lot of harassment growing up. Even now. Especially now."

"What do you mean?"

"I'm sure you're aware of the nationalistic fervor sweeping my country since reunification. The slogan is *Deutschland den Deutschen.*"

"Germany for the Germans," said Waring.

Abendroth nodded. "Anyone who doesn't have the prerequisite blond hair, blue eyes and pale skin is a target for harassment, even violence. Being born in this country doesn't make any difference, or make you safe."

"Sounds familiar," Waring said.

"Yes," Abendroth said bitterly. "I'm afraid it does."

The Opel exited from the cross-town onto Luisen Street. It was a fairly broad, smoothly paved avenue, wide enough to accommodate four lanes of traffic. Dave kept the car in the right hand lane.

As they were crossing a short bridge spanning the Spree River, Waring suddenly straightened. His eyes caught sight of a motion in the windshield mirror. He turned his head and looked behind them.

"We're being tailed."

"What?" Iselda Abendroth turned too, and for a handful of seconds she stared at the VW mini-bus several car lengths behind them. "You mean that plumber's van?"

"I saw it at the airport."

"So?"

"Intel reports one of the vehicles suspected of spying on the Patton hospital and your office was a plumber's van."

Abendroth's eyes widened. The van rushed up behind them rapidly. Waring could only see one figure in the cab, but in the cargo compartment, he glimpsed movement, and light glinted on something shiny and metallic.

The mini-bus hung on the Opel's back bumper for a handful of seconds, then it accelerated, swerved and came abreast of the driver's side door. The side panel of the mini-bus slid open about three feet, and Waring looked into a goggled and masked face.

The face was sheathed in a silvery, metallic-like hood that draped down over the shoulders. The thick goggles had tinted lenses. In hands covered by heavy, silver gauntlets, Waring saw a metal, parabolic dish a little over two feet in diameter. A gleaming rod, topped by a crystalline cone jutted out from the center. A thick, insulated cable stretched down from the backside of the dish and into the cargo compartment of the van. Even though the sedan's windows were rolled up, he heard the steady whine of an electric motor.

Waring didn't know what the dish was, but the crystal-topped rod looked like the muzzle of a weapon. Grabbing Abendroth's head, he shoved her down to the floorboard, at the same time drawing the Ruger with his free hand.

No noise, no light, no smoke came from the parabolic dish. But suddenly, Waring could feel intense heat, as if a giant acetylene torch had been turned on the car. The headlights of the mini-bus dimmed.

Dave, reacting to the sudden heat, looked back, glimpsed the dish and gave a cry of fear and anger. He accelerated, trying to outrun the van. The mini-bus kept pace, and its driver wrenched the wheel sharply.

Dave had no choice but to swerve onto the next side-street to avoid a collision. It was a narrow, cobblestoned lane, with old buildings on either side. The mini-bus turned with the Opel, hugging it close.

The glass on the window beside Dave's head suddenly darkened and cracked. Heat blasted inward. Dave shrieked in agony and clawed at his face. Then he wilted down over the steering wheel. With a jarring thump, the Opel jumped the curb and plunged down the sidewalk.

Like a coiled spring, Waring leaned forward and grabbed the steering wheel. He cursed and gritted his teeth. It was scalding hot. He gave it a twist to the left. The front tires left the sidewalk, slewed over the cobblestones and the rear end swung around in a semi-circle.

It bounced over the facing curb and hit the brick facade of building at an angle, its grillework almost inside a recessed doorway. Fortunately, Dave's foot had slipped from the gas pedal, but the sedan's momentum was still sufficient to nearly hurl Waring into the dashboard.

From the floorboard, Abendroth cried out, "What the hell's going on, Waring?"

As she heaved herself up, there was a squeal of brakes as the mini-bus sought to check its speed. It stopped, went into reverse and the metal dish swung around toward the Opel.

In one movement, Waring thrust open the rear door on the side facing the building and shoved Abendroth out onto the sidewalk. Only a space of four feet separated the body of the sedan from the front of the building. Both of them hunkered down at the rear of the Opel.

Instantly, the car beneath their hands became very hot. The back window nearest the van gave way in a spider-web pattern of cracks. Glass showered down onto the seat. The invisible torch was seeking

Waring and the woman out as they crouched down between metal and brick.

Waring felt his skin prickling, and the fine hairs in his nostrils seemed to vibrate. He felt, rather than heard, a feathery buzzing against his eardrums. His molars began to hurt, and his eyes stung, as if particles of sand were swimming in them. The gun in his hand heated up.

Though his vision was blurred, Waring fired the Ruger through the open back door, the bullet whipping out the broken window and punching a hole in the van's half-open side door.

The dish turned toward him, and Abendroth pulled him to one side. Waring closed the door, and he and the woman crawled along the car's length to the front fender. Waring could hear nothing but the motor of the van, the muted whine of the electric generator and the persistent buzz in his ears. The small space between the front of the car and the recessed doorway grew stiflingly hot.

A high-pitched shriek like a dozen boiling tea kettles split the night. The fuel tank of the sedan had ignited. The cap had been blown off by the pressure, and a foot-long jet of burning gasoline whistled through the vent.

Waring pulled Abendroth toward the doorway. He didn't waste time trying the knob. He put two slugs into the lock, flung himself at the door shoulder foremost, and he and Abendroth literally fell into the foyer of the building.

They rolled to one side, against the wall, just as the Opel's fuel tank let go. The entire rear end of the car ripped open, spewing burning gasoline in all directions.

The detonation was like a thunderclap. Waring felt the concussion against his back, despite the protection of the wall. A wave of fire crested and crashed through the open doorway.

Waring raised his head to eye-level with a window, pushing aside the heavy curtain. Through a part in the flames, he saw the dish withdrawn into the van. With a screech of rubber and a clashing of gears, the mini-bus leaped ahead and roared down the street.

"Are you all right?" Waring asked Abendroth, holstering the Ruger.

She nodded, hugging herself. She was scared, but still in control. She touched her face. "I lost my glasses somewhere. When the frames heated up and expanded, the lenses must've fallen out."

Waring ripped down a curtain and used it to extinguish the burning gasoline in the foyer. Abendroth helped him stamp out the flames, saying, "We've got to call the consulate and the fire brigade."

They heard windows on both sides of the street opening, frightened people shouting. The flames from the burning car were threatening to engulf the room they were in. Fortunately, the building seemed deserted.

"Let's find the back door," Waring said.

As they walked through the building, the first of the rising and falling wails of sirens echoed from the street. At the rear of the structure they came to a heavy door marked *Feur Ausgang,* the fire exit. The irony wasn't lost on Abendroth and she managed a shaky laugh.

They found themselves in a narrow alley. They strode quickly through it to a point up the block from the burning car. A crowd gathered around the fire truck as the firemen used foam spray to smother the blaze. Police cruisers sped toward the scene.

Abendroth stared at the dying inferno, the makeshift funeral pyre for Dave. "They almost got us, too," she murmured. "If not for you."

She glanced down at the nearly imperceptible bulge made by the Ruger beneath Waring's jacket. He knew the question she was going to ask, so he asked a pre-emptive one of his own. "What kind of weapon was that?"

Abendroth frowned. "It wasn't a weapon...not exactly. It looked like a miniature version of a Gunn Oscillator."

"A what?"

"A method of microwave generation, named for its discoverer, J.B. Gunn. Over 20 years ago, it was quite the advance in solid-state physics. The Gunn effect microwave devices replaced clumsy tubes used in radar and other applications. A lot of different types of solid-state devices were based on Gunn's findings."

"In other words," said Waring, "a Gunn gun?"

Abendroth laughed nervously. "A pretty obvious joke, Mr. Waring. During the attack, did you feel a prickling of the skin and pressure against your eardrums?"

"And my back teeth started to hurt."

"Microwave radiation interacting with your metal fillings. We were damned lucky we caught only a fractional spillover of the microwaves, or we would've ended up like Dave."

"Seems like pretty advanced gear."

"Not really. The principles have been used since the 1930s. Marconi may've invented the first so-called 'death-ray' using microwaves."

Still standing in the mouth of the alley, Abendroth removed a cell phone from her handbag. She glanced at it and swore in German. "I was afraid of this...it's fried."

They saw a pay telephone kiosk a hundred yards up the street and quickly walked to it. As she dialed the number to the consulate, Waring watched the arrival of fire engines and police cruisers. He smelled the sweetish odor of burned human flesh. Anger rose in him, but he tamped it down.

He knew the attack hadn't been made on impulse–there had been a leak and his arrival in Berlin was expected.

Abendroth hung up the phone. "They're sending a car to pick us up."

"Did you get a good look at the van?"

"You shoved my head down, so no. Did you?"

"A VW minibus, maybe ten years old. The front license plate was A398R. That doesn't mean much since it's probably phony."

"Does that mean it can't be traced?"

"Not that one." Waring nodded up the block behind her. "But that one may be a different story."

Abenroth stiffened but she didn't turn around. Instead, she dug into her handbag and produced a small compact. Popping it open, she made a nonchalant show of applying lipstick while she eyed the mirror. "Good thing I'm farsighted. Do you mean that florist's van?"

Waring nodded. The van was a much newer model and parked diagonally next to a storefront.

"What should we do?" asked Abendroth.

"Nothing. They've already made us. If we start acting twitchy they'll know we've made *them* and I want them to hang around."

Abendroth snapped the compact shut. "They could be what they appear to be."

"Could be...but professionals work in teams, like relays."

Iselda Abendroth glanced toward the collection of police cruisers down the street. "Should we tell the police?"

"Absolutely not. Let's see what happens when our ride gets here." Their ride arrived within five minutes. A young red-haired man pulled up next to the phone kiosk in a yellow Mercedes. Waring slid in the front seat beside him.

"The name is Darren," he said, flashing diplomatic credentials. Hooking a thumb over his shoulder at the police and fire department activity, he added, "Sounds like you two had a warm reception."

"Not very funny, Darren," Iselda snapped from the back seat. "One of your own people died."

"I wasn't trying to be funny, Dr. Abendroth," Darren replied contritely. "Poor choice of words on my part. But it's unsettling that the hit team was so goddamn bold."

"We may have a line on them," Waring said. "Interested?"

Darren's hands tightened on the wheel. "My orders from Major Jacobs are to bring you to the embassy as quickly and as directly as I can. If I don't, I'll be a candidate for a reprimand."

"We'll take the responsibility."

Darren sighed. "What have you got?"

"That florist's van. Cruise past it, see what it does."

Darren hesitated. "Are you armed?"

"I am. You?"

"No, but to hell with it. Dave was a friend of mine."

SEVEN

DARREN STEERED the car carefully around the van, giving it no more than a casual glance. He drove up the block to a cross-street, then hung a right. Expertly, he spun the wheel, did a 180 and parallel parked in a space between a Renault and a flat-bed truck. He turned off the lights, but kept the engine running.

As they sat in the car, waiting, the bells of a nearby church gonged eleven times. The florist's van appeared at the intersection, and turned left, away from them.

"They're not interested in following us," said Abendroth, relieved.

"Why should they?" Darren replied. "They saw us turn in the direction of the embassy."

Darren was an experienced tail. He waited until a full block of distance was between the Mercedes and van before he pulled out, turning on the lights again. The van took a circuitous route for the next twenty minutes. It rolled past the Kaiser Wilhelm Memorial Church, took a right, and then passed the Berlin Zoological Gardens.

The van turned off on Hardenburg Street, skirting the campus of Technische University. The traffic was still heavy, so Darren wasn't as concerned about maintaining as much distance between the Mercedes and the van as before. He wove in and out between cars, changing lanes every so often, hanging back, then accelerating.

The van's taillights suddenly shone bright as it braked for a left turn. Darren eased up on the gas and shifted to the far right lane. The van had stopped at a gated driveway. Beyond the driveway was a four-story stone building, set back at least a hundred yards from the street. The lawn was ringed by a very tall, wrought iron fence.

As the Mercedes cruised past, the gate swung open to admit the van, and it drove up to park in front of very wide entrance steps. Darren very quickly double-parked across the street.

Two men climbed out of the van. One opened the side door and removed a huge bouquet of flowers.

"A little late for a delivery," said Waring, leaning forward and staring past the bars of the gate. The two men were of approximately the same height and weight.

He got a better look at them when they reached the lighted porch. Both were blonde, the one carrying the bouquet a little taller and heavier than his companion. They both wore green coveralls with the name of the florist stenciled across the back. The tall man rang the bell, the door opened and they entered.

"What is this place?" Abendroth asked.

Darren reached for the car-phone. "I can find out."

"No," said Waring. "These people have access to sophisticated electronic gear. It's likely they have a monitoring set-up to listen in to all nearby radio and cell phone transmissions. They may even have the consulate bugged."

Darren frowned. "No way." But he didn't make the call.

"Move up the block a little," Waring suggested. "If this is a legitimate delivery, they'll be coming out soon."

Darren guided the Mercedes up the street, and then U-turned so the nose of the car was aligned with the driveway. By leaning forward, they could see the van.

Within three minutes, the pair of delivery men came out of the building and climbed back into their vehicle. As it rolled back onto the avenue, Waring said, "They've pulled a switch on us."

"What?" asked Darren, as he put the Mercedes into gear. "It's the same van."

"The same van, but different guys in the same clothes. They look enough like the first two to pass a quick inspection."

Darren seemed reluctant to accept Waring's assessment. "What do you want me to do?"

"We know where the first pair are. Let's see where these guys take us."

The Mercedes followed the van for 25 blocks at a discreet distance back into metropolitan Berlin. Night-clubs, cabarets, bars and strip-joints lined either side of the street. Neon lights glared in a variety of colors. People clogged the sidewalks. Music thumped from inside the clubs and raucous, drunken laughter seemed to come from every direction.

"Action city," Darren commented with a sour smile. "Think maybe they're looking to celebrate?"

The van finally stopped at a storefront. The name and illustration on the plate-glass window was identical to that painted on the van. A garage door beside the storefront rose, and the van moved beneath it before it was fully raised. The Mercedes rolled past, without slowing.

"Now what?" Abendroth asked.

"Let's get to the embassy," Waring said. "That building on Hardenburg needs to be checked out. I think we've found our dark-site."

"You know," said Abendroth, "you don't talk like any representative of the Department of Energy I've ever met."

"How many have you met, Dr. Abendroth?"

"You'd be surprised, Mr. Waring."

Darren chuckled, and drove them through winding and twisting streets until they reached an alley off Clayalee leading to a chain-link gate. He braked in front of it, spoke briefly into the car phone and the gate swung open for them. He parked the Mercedes in an underground garage full of different makes of cars.

"Our secret fleet," Darren said. "The ones without diplomatic plates."

Darren led Waring and Abendroth to a back entrance of a white-stone building, into a dimly-lit hallway and then into a small, window-less room.

There were three men sitting at a round table. Darren left the room. Abendroth knew them, and made quick introductions. Major Art Jacobs was the representative of both G2 and NATO intelligence, Lieutenant Roman Taylor was the shift supervisor at Site 611, and a middle-aged man introduced only as Solezer was a section chief of the Verfassungsschutz.

Solezer looked Waring over with bleak eyes. Waring knew the long-nosed German had been in the business long enough to realize that he was a specialist, and that his name and credentials were fake. Then again, Solezer probably wasn't his real name, either. Waring guessed him to be ex-Gehlen Org.

The discussion began slowly. Waring briefed the three men on the attack, and Abendroth offered her opinion on the technology used against them. Jacobs and Solezer only grunted. They were cagey with each other, regardless of their common cause. It took Solezer five minutes of monosyllabic answers before he admitted that the Russians had been informed of the current situation.

"Just what," Waring asked, "is the current situation?"

Jacobs nodded to Taylor, who without preamble, declared, "The Pershings at the site are no longer under our control."

By the lack of a reaction, Waring realized this was old news to both Jacobs and Solezer. "Bring me up to date, Lieutenant."

"After the system crash, we re-booted as quickly as we could. The database was downloaded from our mainframes, so the only software we actually needed to install were secondary analogues—access codes, targeting and trajectory programs , recognition signals and launch commands. Everything seemed to work fine, so I just relegated the cause of the crash to a glitch. When Simmons collapsed, there was too much excitement to run a Level Four diagnostic. Besides, we needed to re-link with Cheyenne Mountain ASAP."

Taylor took a very deep breath. "When the Major informed me of the probable cause of Simmons's death, I immediately suspected an electromagnetic pulse. I was ordered to conduct a Level Four diagnostic. I did. Superficially, the system is fully operable. But evidently, the software we used to re-boot it had been tampered with."

"Tampered with?" asked Waring. "Explain."

"One of the diskettes had been replaced with one containing a program that infiltrated the primary and rewrote it—like a virus. On the surface, everything is green. But the launch code has been rewritten and our attempts to delete it resulted in an immediate lock-out. I'm afraid that if we try to physically disarm or remove the war-heads, the launch code will be transmitted."

"There's no way to interrupt the link between the computers and the missiles?" Waring asked.

"We don't know, yet," Jacobs said. "This new program could have insinuated itself so completely in our systems that anything we do could trigger a launch. That includes moving them."

Waring nodded. "Any idea who made the software switch, Lieutenant?"

Taylor cleared his throat. "Aside from me and the other shift supervisors, you mean? There are only two keys to the program disk locker. Each supervisor is handed one at the beginning of the watch. The second is kept in a combination lock cabinet. Neither I nor the other three supervisors had the combination."

"But Lieutenant Colonel Simmons did," said Jacobs. "Hard to believe he would turn traitor, but all evidence points to it."

"Maybe not," Iselda Abendroth said.

Solezer looked at her levelly. "You think he may be innocent?"

"He may have done the software switch, but he may not have had full knowledge of what he was doing."

"We considered the possibility of brain-washing and hypnotic suggestion and drugs," said Jacobs. "But his whereabouts and movements over the last three months are fully accounted for. That kind of conditioning, of thought-pattern reversal, requires a long time and a specialized environment, no matter what you see in the movies."

"I've been brought on board as a consultant because of my expertise in solid-state physics," Abendroth said, an edge to her voice. "The effects of microwave radiation on the human body go far beyond simply cooking it from within. Exposure in the 0.5 kilohertz to 30 megahertz range increases the gamma globulin and leukocyte count in the blood, enlarges the thyroid and causes deviations in brain patterns. Even at low intensity, microwaves can seriously alter the rhythm of brain-waves, causing drastic perceptual distortions. Since our adversaries possess a variety of microwave devices, I believe Simmons had his mind tampered with."

Solezer allowed himself a small smile. "It was revealed years ago that the Soviet Union was bombarding the northwestern United States with low frequency microwaves. As I recall, they were trying to influence behavior by electronic means. It wasn't very effective, since America began a massive military build-up."

"You're not suggesting Russians are behind this?" Jacobs demanded.

"Did you read the jacket?" Waring asked.

Solezer's jaw muscles tightened. "I read it. Ridiculous. If the Brotherhood of the Black Sun ever existed, it died when Hitler did."

"I don't buy the Nazi theory, either," said Jacobs. "There's no intel indicating any major movement either by the neo-Nazi groups or what's left of the Odessa network."

Waring said grimly, "Let's stop side-stepping, gentlemen. Both of you know all about the Brotherhood. Hundreds, even thousands of S.S. men became part of Interpol and CIA operations after the war, not to mention the Gehlen Org. It may be bad taste to mention it, but the vipers we thought had been driven away seventy years ago have reared up and sunk their fangs in our collective asses again."

Solezer's eyes narrowed. "I was a Gehlen man. I was never a Nazi."

"I'm not implying that you were or are," Waring responded. "But what about this acquaintance of Simmons'…Julius Eicke? You read the report on his father—"

"We know about Eicke's father," broke in Solezer coldly. "It's hardly a revelation. Would you hold a son responsible for the sins of the father, Herr Waring?"

"We checked out Eicke and his firm," said Jacobs. "Impeccable credentials. Simmons was only one of a dozen American officers who are clients of Hauser and Hochbach. Eicke deals in stocks, bonds, hedge funds, mutual funds, that sort of thing. He and his company have always been very pro-American."

Iselda Abendroth shifted uncomfortably. "Eicke has recently done business with Ostara…buying microwave data transmitters and power amplifiers."

"What did he need those for?" asked Waring.

She shrugged. "He's under no obligation to tell us what use he has for them, but since he runs a brokerage, that kind of equipment would most likely be applied to computer networks."

She paused and added hesitantly, "There's something else—I've been invited to a soiree at his home tomorrow evening."

"You have?" Jacobs demanded.

"Not just me," she replied defensively. "Several executives of Ostara."

Waring smiled. "I hope your invitation is a plus one."

She frowned at him. "I don't understand—"

"Can you bring a date?"

She continued to frown, and then said uncertainly, "I think it's a fairly informal get-together, so I don't see why not. You'd be my date?"

"Unless you've already got one, then yes—that's the idea. I'd like to get a read on who we're dealing with. If Eicke is a member of the Brotherhood, seeing us together in his own home might make him nervous enough to become careless."

Jacobs said stiffly, "I've met Eicke at functions here at the embassy. He's been subjected to background checks and thoroughly vetted. If he has any Nazi connections beyond his old man, we couldn't find them."

"That doesn't mean that he finds the philosophy uncongenial," said Waring. "The fact is—this embassy, Major, and your agency, Solezer, probably has a few people lurking around who do appreciate that philosophy. The trap laid for me points to it."

"It's extremely likely," said Abendroth. "Remember, Nazi scientists made the first breakthroughs in microwave researches. Not all of them are dead."

"Assuming your suspicions are true," said Jacobs, "what's their objective with the Pershings?"

Waring shrugged. "Blackmail, maybe. To force NATO and the German government to deal with them, to accede to whatever demands they make. Or maybe they simply intend to blow up a large piece of real estate just to show they can. The missiles are only a means to an end."

"If that it so," said Solezer, "then they will make a demand of both our governments very soon."

"They may want to keep their success a secret as long as they can," Waring said. "They may not make a demand until they're certain we're on to them."

Jacobs sighed and dry-washed his face with his hands. "We're up against a tight timetable, but we don't know by whose schedule. Those missiles are virtually time-bombs, and we have no idea in hell how long or how short the fuses are."

There was a knock at the door. At a curt, "Come!" from Jacobs, Darren entered, holding a sheet of computer printout.

"We have the vitals on that building on Hardenburg. It's a privately owned substance abuse clinic, run by a Doctor Hito Asoka. He's a very reputable psychiatrist, sometimes makes the rounds on talk-shows. He has no ties with any Fascist or Marxist doctrines. The place is as clean and upstanding as it can be without having a halo around it. However, here's an interesting item—the place has a special wing in the rear for the more-or-less permanent care of chronic cases. You know, heavy-duty juicers and dopers. This wing is patrolled by armed guards and attack dogs."

Solezer fluttered a dismissive hand. "Many institutions have that kind of security."

"State-run mental asylums, maybe," said Waring. "This one has two of the blackhats holed up inside."

He locked gazes with Solezer. "We need the full treatment. Do you agree?"

Solezer returned that unblinking stare for a few silent seconds, then shifted his eyes toward Jacobs. "Very well. I authorize a wire-tap and round-the-clock surveillance. My people will interact with yours, Major."

"These people are pros," said Waring. "So don't send in agents dressed as vacuum cleaner salesmen or put paving crews outside on the street."

Both Jacobs and Solezer glared at him. "We're not amateurs," snapped the G2 officer.

"Neither are they," said Waring. "They've already scored three times against us."

Darren said, "Your luggage arrived a little while ago, Mr. Waring. Do you want it brought in here?"

"Yes, thanks."

Solezer stood up, military trim and ramrod erect. "I will see to the surveillance, Major, and contact you when my people are ready."

He nodded to Abendroth and pointedly ignored Waring as he left. Jacobs looked at Abendroth and Taylor. "You two are dismissed. Thank you for your time, doctor, and I apologize for the incident this evening. Quarters have been arranged for you here. Under the circumstances, I think it's best you remain here tonight."

Abendroth opened her mouth to say something, and then closed it. As she walked to the door, she murmured, "Guten nacht, Herr Waring."

Darren returned with two large vinyl-covered cases on a hand-truck. He dumped them, took a quick look at Jacobs' face, then left, shutting the door carefully behind him.

Waring heaved the larger case onto the table and unlatched it. He removed a Remington Autoloader USAS-12 shotgun and a pair of rotary drum twenty-round magazines. He checked out the mechanisms of the weapon, sighting down its length. Waring laid it aside and lifted out a combat harness.

Jacobs watched Waring's inspection of the ordnance with a sour expression. He made a noisy show of unwrapping the cellophane from a cigar, setting it afire with a big Ronson lighter and snapping it shut with a loud click.

"Something on your mind, Major?" Waring asked as he looked over his Ruger.

"I don't know who the fuck you really are, or who the fuck you think you are," growled Jacobs around the cigar, "but you're some kind of spook. But you're not from the Company. Otherwise you wouldn't have such a hard-on about Nazis and this Black Sun shit. At least not in Germany."

"Why not?"

"We don't give much of a damn about who played on whose team seventy years ago. Double-U Double-U Two is a very long time ago. They're on our side now."

"Alliances of convenience under extenuating circumstances are one thing, Major. But those circumstances are pretty goddamn inconvenient now, wouldn't you say?"

Jacobs blew a wreath a smoke. "I read the jacket about this Brotherhood of yours. There's not one shred of proof or supporting evidence beyond that old O.S.S. report."

"You sound pretty positive, Major."

"You know something I don't?"

By way of a reply, Waring opened the second, smaller case. He removed the protective bubble wrap and tossed the Dag onto the table.

Jacobs looked at it with a bored eye. "That supposed to mean something?"

"It's the supporting evidence. An ancient relic from the early days of the Brotherhood. It was in the possession of a former Gestapo intelligence officer who held onto it for nearly seventy years as way to balance out some of the evil he'd done during the war. The Brotherhood wants it back. They killed a village full of Brazilian Indians to get it just three days ago."

"Why do you have it?"

"Bait. Or flypaper. Take your pick."

Jacobs sighed. "Listen, Waring—if that's your real name, which I doubt—the surviving Nazi guard are scattered all over the world, living new lives under new identities. They want nothing more than to spend the rest of their days in peace, not spend them resurrecting the Third fucking Reich."

"You think the rise of neo-Nazism in Germany coinciding with the fall of Communism is just happenstance?" Waring asked.

"What else?"

"Tactics. If the Brotherhood kept the driving spirit of Nazism alive, then it was to their benefit to help the western democracies destroy Communism in Europe. It's easier to fight one enemy than two."

Jacobs snorted. "Bullshit. You're talking about some kind of long-range objective, planned over seventy years ago. If that were so, they'd have to take into account that a lot of their people would be dead by now."

"They recruited new people. While Allied intelligence was busy assimilating them into post-war intelligence networks, the Brotherhood was busy assimilating new people into their network."

"You're paranoid."

"Experienced. These guys couldn't operate without elements in the government giving them Get-Out-Of-Jail-Free cards. Same way the Mafia or the Medellin cartel gets a grip on a country or a city. They don't have to conquer with guns and bombs. Not when somebody on the inside hands them the keys on a silver platter, simply by looking the other way."

"We're talking terrorism here, Waring. Plain and simple, not a scheme to build a Fourth Reich."

THE FALCON

"When's the last time you were briefed on international terrorism, Major?"

"I keep up with the latest intel."

"Then you've heard of the Third Position. The slogan is 'Hitler and Mao united in struggle.' Two extremes of the political spectrum coming together in dead center. An alliance of convenience, to spread death and terror around the world."

"We used the ex-S.S. guys to help us fight the Communists. They were beaten, the Reds weren't. It was expedient."

"That fight is over," said Waring quietly. "The circumstances of the alliance no longer exist. Past time to treat these people as what they really are."

Waring slammed an ammo clip into the butt of the Ruger and jacked a round into the chamber. "I'm taking them out," he said very calmly. "With or without your help."

SCHRECK WHEELED himself through the doorway, rubber wheels squealing on the bare cement floor. The small room was packed with chassis after chassis, module upon module of electronic gear. A bank of monitor screens flickered with grey and white images. Pilot lights of a powerful radio glowed red and green. Two complex recording units with vertically mounted spools and an eighteen channel console ran the length of one wall. A locked file cabinet stood in a corner.

Dolf stood before one of the monitor screens and he turned as he heard the squeak of rubber. "I've cued the tape for you, sir."

Schreck didn't reply. He wheeled his chair to the screen and watched the video of the mini-bus assault on the Opel. The incident had been recorded by the team of observers in the florist's van. It had been delivered late last night to the clinic hidden inside a bouquet of flowers. Schreck, who had quarters in the Nachsinnen, had been called by Dolf to look at the recording. Dolf was wearing the neat white coat of a hospital attendant. Beneath it, in a hip holster, was a compact FIE Titan .380 automatic.

Schreck watched the explosion of the Opel, replayed the file and watched it again. "Nicely done."

Dolf cleared his throat. "Fast forward it, sir."

"Why? The nigger and the American went up in smoke, that's what is important."

"Not exactly, sir." Dolf steeled himself for Schreck's outraged reaction. His hand stole beneath his coat and his fingers touched the butt of the Titan. He kept his eyes on Schreck's right hand, making sure it didn't dart inside his coat to grab the Walther holstered there. Dolf had heard of deMilteer's expulsion, and he had no intention of having his employment terminated in the same manner.

Schreck did not show any anger, but Dolf didn't feel relieved. Schreck's long fingers pressed a button on the console and the images on the monitor screen sped up. Flames licked crazily and people raced to and fro as official vehicles careened around corners and disgorged passengers, all to an inhuman tempo, like an old Benny Hill comedy skit.

Dolf leaned forward and pointed. "There, sir."

The pace of the images returned to normal. The quality was poor, dim and backlit by flames dancing from the burning automobile. A man and a woman emerged from the mouth of an alley, paused and approached a telephone kiosk. They faced the hidden camera.

"How did they escape?" asked Schreck.

"I'm not certain, sir. According to Otto, the oscillator operator, the American was armed. We hadn't counted on that."

"Why would a representative of the Department of Energy be armed?"

"I don't think that is who he really works for, sir."

The man's face swelled in the screen as the lens of the camera moved in for a closer view.

"Freeze it," Dolf instructed.

Schreck complied, tapping the mouse.

The man appeared to be gazing directly into the room. His pale eyes shone with a predatory glitter, his mouth a thin, grim line. Backlit by the fire behind him, he looked like a warrior prince from Teutonic legend.

"That man is not a scientist," said Schreck flatly.

"No, sir. He is not. I believe he is the same man we saw on the riverbank in Brazil."

"The same man who destroyed our aircraft and shot down two of your comrades?"

"Yes, sir. Though I only caught a glimpse of him when I put the searchlight on him, I'm sure he is the one. The swine was carrying a strongbox."

"That man is no swine," muttered Schreck.

"We retraced his path on the riverbank and found Goetz dead in an underground passage. Obviously, this man found Goetz alive."

"And," said Schreck, "Goetz gave him the Dag."

"Our latest intel indicates this man's name is Michael Waring. We checked and though there is a personnel record of a Michael Waring employed by the Department of Energy, his credentials seem incomplete."

"A cover," Schreck snapped. "The U.S. has dispatched a specialist, and I doubt, even with our contacts, we will learn his real identity. But that is meaningless. I know who he is."

Dolf was startled. "You recognize him?"

Schreck did not answer. He said, "Contact Julius. We must neutralize this man, and Julius can take care of it in a less spectacular fashion than the last attempt."

Dolf did not move. "With all due respect, sir, I request the contract. The men he killed in South America were friends of mine and—"

"—Contact Julius!" Schreck barked. "Immediately!"

Dolf quickly scuttered away, making sure Schreck didn't turn around with the Walther in his hand. Schreck ignored him. He pushed his wheelchair back and studied the hard, unforgiving face on the screen.

His lips drew back in a smile. For the first time in decades, Schreck was filled with fear, and he took a secret delight in the emotion.

It was somehow fitting, even inevitable, that this dark-haired, pale-eyed warrior would have the Dag. Although there was a faint scar on the man's face, Schreck could see the much deeper scars on his soul. This was a warrior of many battlefields, a man who had always emerged victorious, stained with the blood of his enemies. The man had been wounded, true enough, but each wound was a badge of honor, each scar representing a triumph.

This man was no mere soldier, performing his duty for God and country.

Schreck had told Dolf that he knew who the man was, and he did, without knowing anything about him at all.

Schreck knew, with a terrible certainty, that the dark man was a predator—with the glint of the hunting hawk in his eyes. He was Vengeance and Justice and Death.

EIGHT

ISELDA ABENDROTH'S office at Ostara Development held few clues to her interests. Works of art covered the walls—black and white Japanese block prints, swirling abstracts and colorful Expressionistic scenes from turn of the century Europe. A framed diploma from M.I.T. hung on the wall behind her desk.

The desk was very large and very old, with many pigeon holes. A framed, hand-tinted photograph of a black man wearing the uniform of the U.S. Army was the only personal item on it.

Waring assumed the man in the photo was Abendroth's grandfather, but he didn't question her. He was more interested in the device she was fiddling with on the desktop.

It was a metal, oblong gadget studded with dials and buttons, about two and half feet long by two wide. A glass covered digital read-out dominated the face, and a telescoping antenna extended from the top.

"This can detect and register microwave radiation at up to 500 yards," she said.

"What if it picks up emissions from microwave ovens?" Waring asked.

Abendroth carefully pointed out dials and controls. "It can be adjusted to register wavelengths of certain frequencies. Ovens usually operate on the 10.13 band. The Gunn oscillator emits radiation in the 10.14 kilometer band."

The sun set over the Berlin skyline. On their way to Eicke's home, Waring had accompanied Abendroth to her office to pick up the device so it could be turned over to the surveillance team posted around the Nachsissen clinic. At last report, approximately eight hours of constant observation had turned up nothing unusual or suspicious. The wire-taps hadn't been hooked in, and Abendroth had cautioned against using long-range listening devices since their energy transmissions could be detected.

Iselda Abendroth wore a strapless cocktail dress of coral which showed off her firm figure to good advantage. She had applied cosmetics with restraint. In her stilt-heeled shoes, she was almost as tall as Waring. He wore a tailored white dinner jacket and black slacks.

Abendroth stowed the device inside of a large, leather carrying case and Waring helped her close it. Major Jacobs hadn't been happy about them driving across Berlin without an armed escort, but Waring pointed out that it was extremely unlikely another hit had been scheduled so soon, and even if it were, the radiation detector would let them know if the "Gunn gun" was being deployed again.

Besides, Waring wanted to be seen, particularly at Eicke's home. Although he hadn't mentioned it to Abendroth, he knew they were under surveillance and more than likely being followed. He counted on it. He had done this sort of thing before, exposing himself to the enemy. It was the equivalent of a matador shaking a red cape and shouting, "Hey, Toro!"

They went out into the parking lot and Abendroth put the device in the back seat the Volvo the embassy had provided. She turned it on and raised the antenna and then climbed behind the wheel. She drove so Waring could have his hands free—the Ruger was snug in its shoulder rig under his jacket.

As they passed the company's sign, with its graphic of a nude woman standing amidst a sea of floating stars, Waring asked, "Ostara. Does that mean anything special?"

Abendroth smiled. "Ostara is the Teutonic moon goddess. Her festival is celebrated each spring, like Easter."

She glanced over at him. "Do you have a deity, Mr. Waring, besides the god of the gun?"

Waring didn't look at her. He scanned the area ahead of them and checked their backtrack in the side mirror. "I don't worship guns, doctor, any more than a stonecutter worships a chisel."

"So they're just the tools of your trade, is that it?"

"That's how I think of it."

"And what is your trade, besides masquerading unsuccessfully as a physicist?"

"On-call sanitation expert." He didn't smile when he said it.

Abendroth glanced again at the sharp profile. She'd worked with intelligence agents before, but this man was different.

"Don't you ever find it tiring?" she asked. "Going to wherever you're ordered to go to clean up somebody else's mess?"

"I'm not ordered," Waring replied. "I pick and choose. I can only do so much, so I go where the need is the greatest."

"The need for what?"

"Scale balancing, loose end tying. Running my prey to ground."

"Prey?" she echoed. "What are you—a raptor?"

"More often than I care to admit…and yes, I do find it tiring. This very well may be my last hunt. I think I've lost the taste for it."

Waring turned his head toward her, and for a moment their eyes met. A horn blaring from behind them commanded Abendroth's attention—Waring's hand made an instinctive streak to the butt of the Ruger. Both of them eyed the mirrors. A young man in denim astride a motor scooter signaled for a left turn behind them. He was wearing a bright, shiny white helmet.

Abendroth let out an uneasy laugh. "Just a kid."

Waring kept his eyes on the mirror until he was positive the woman's assessment was correct. The rider turned off left and disappeared into the mouth of an alley. Waring released the butt of the automatic, but he didn't relax.

Iselda Abendroth drove through a suburban neighborhood and pulled up before the baroque façade of town house that Waring guessed dated back at least a century and a half, probably to before the days of Bismarck. Somehow, its dark stone walls had withstood the ravages of two wars.

They climbed out of the car, Iselda wrapping a pashmina around her bare shoulders. Waring preceded her up the flight of stone steps to the front door. A tall, crewcut man in butler's livery looked them over with a sour expression. Iselda spoke to him in German, gesturing toward Waring and the man stepped aside.

"I didn't know anyone had butlers anymore," Waring commented lowly.

"Herr Eicke is very old world," she replied.

The interior of the house belonged to another era too. The drawing room was filled with dark leather furniture, massive oak tables and dominated by a huge hearth that could have easily accommodated the Volvo. Fortunately, it was not lit. Waring's first quick impression was of an expanse of hanging tapestries, stands of old armor, swords and pikes and other relics from the Teutonic Middle Ages.

When introduced by Iselda, Julius Eicke greeted Waring with a formal, old-world courtesy, clasping his hand tightly and bending from the waist. The man wore light gray trousers, and a dark gray blazer with an old-fashioned coat of arms sewn over the breast pocket. With his silver hair, he presented the image of a monochromatic ghost. He spoke only in German. Waring had the feeling that by doing so he was sending the message that since Waring was in his home, in his country, he should use his language.

"Are you a doctor of physics like Iselda here?" Eicke asked, his gaze traveling up and down Waring's body, from the toes of his shoes to the top of his head. His tone sounded doubtful.

"No, I'm a consultant from the United States," Waring replied. "I just arrived. I'm indebted to Dr. Abendroth for bringing me."

Eicke's gaze flicked to Iselda. A thin smile stretched his lips. "Dear Iselda. So many people may have so much to thank her for in the days to come."

That, Waring reflected, was as ambiguously menacing a remark as he had ever heard.

Eicke directed him toward the bar and excused himself, greeting another couple who had just arrived. Iselda drew him away. She whispered, "Julius can be rather reserved—don't be offended."

Waring replied, "I'm not—not yet, anyway."

With Iselda's arm linked through his, Waring acknowledged introductions, carefully maintaining the air of a polite, but not too observant visitor.

He noted the guests were of a curious assortment, even for cosmopolitan Berlin. While he spoke routine formalities, Waring's mind catalogued and evaluated. A number of the guests fell into an expected pattern—minor bureaucrats, middle-aged industrialists accompanied by their second or third trophy wives, affable lobbyists and even a couple of German military officers. Several Japanese men were present, although they gave the impression they were only there as favors to Eicke. They stood apart in their black suits, eyes masked by sunglasses. Waring tagged them as Yakuza and he wondered if they were connected to Hito Asoka.

Iselda became engaged in a conversation with a colleague from Ostara—a blond haired woman named Kaja with a discreetly plunging neckline who seemed more interested in watching Waring than listening to Iselda.

Waring's casual roving attention was caught by three men who definitely seemed out of place in the baroque setting of the drawing room. Although wearing expensive suits and holding drinks, they looked tense, unable to relax. They were all of type—tall, broad-shouldered and almost stereotypically Nordic. Whenever they caught Waring's gaze, they glanced away. He guessed them to be ex-military.

As Waring strolled through the room, he heard fragments of conversation concerning immigrants, the socialists, and the economy. No one sounded particularly optimistic. In fact, he heard anger in the voices of more than one man.

"More and more of them allowed to come in every day—"

"We have been betrayed—"

"It is the liberals who need to be taken care of—Hitler knew how to do it in the old days."

Waring drifted across the room to a glass-fronted case. Sipping from the wine glass he snagged from a passing waiter's tray, he idly regarded a taxidermist's mounted recreation of a brown-feathered hawk pouncing on a snarling hedgehog. He was trying to identify the species of hawk when a rough male voice asked, "Are you interested in taxidermy, Herr Waring?"

Turning, he looked into the face of a man in his late thirties or early forties. His blond hair was cropped in a short buzz-cut. Waring recognized him as one of the tense men who had made a poor show of not watching him. He held a half-full beer stein in his right hand.

"My interest is more in birds," Waring said. "You know my name, but I don't think we've been introduced."

"My name is Veit." He took a noisy slurp from the stein and wiped at the line of foam on his upper lip.

"Just Veit?"

The man didn't respond to the query. Waring received the impression he was inebriated—or trying to appear so. Veit said bluntly, "I was told you were a physicist...not an ornithologist."

Waring felt slightly surprised the man pronounced the word so clearly. "I am a physicist...and my interest in birds is restricted to the raptors...eagles, hawks and falcons."

Veit indicted the mounted hawk with his mug. "That's a Western Marsh Harrier...a male. You can tell by the reddish-brown feathers."

Veit took another sip of beer and stared directly into Waring's eyes. "What color are *your* feathers, Herr Waring?"

Waring felt an inner chill. His masquerade hadn't fooled a professional soldier, half-drunk or not. Without waiting for an answer, Veit turned sharply on his heel and strode away.

Waring became aware of Iselda Abendroth's hand on his elbow. "We can leave anytime," she said.

"So soon?"

She smiled wanly. "I'm only thinking of you. You must find this deadly dull."

Waring looked toward Veit, who had rejoined his companions across the room. "I wouldn't say that, exactly. But, if you're ready to go—"

He allowed himself to be guided in the direction of the doorway, where Julius Eicke stood welcoming late arrivals. The gray man favored Waring with a narrow eyed stare. "Leaving so early, Herr Waring?"

Waring smiled politely. "I'm rather busy…what with all my consulting. Thank you for allowing me into your home."

Eicke matched his smile. "You are welcome. I looked forward to talking a bit more with you."

"About solid-state physics?"

The man's smile widened. "Yes…and a few other subjects as well. Perhaps in the future, if your schedule pemits."

Iselda Abendroth and Waring left the house and returned to the Volvo parked at the curb. As he opened the door for her, he asked, "Shall we check your detector?"

Iselda turned to the device on the back seat, looked at the gauges and announced, "Nothing."

Waring settled into the passenger seat "Do you think you could find that florist's shop we went by last night?"

After a second of surprised silence, Abendroth said, "Sure. I guess so. Why?"

Waring nodded toward Eicke's home. "If he's involved in this situation, he's too smart to have anything in the house that will implicate him. We already have the clinic covered. I want to double-check we haven't overlooked a secondary site."

As she started the engine, she inquired, "What about that plumber's van?"

"Jacobs said there was no company called the Perfect Plug. It's likely that van is inside the florist's garage. It's certainly not here."

Iselda put the car into gear. "Is that why you wanted to come with me to this get-together?"

"Partly. But it's more an old practice of mine—Know thine enemy."

By the time the Volvo reached the area of the florist's shop, the time was close to 11PM. They drove past the storefront. The window was dark, the garage door down. There was no signal from the detector in the back seat. Abendroth had to drive slowly and tap the brakes several times to avoid running over drunken bar patrons who kept stumbling into the cobblestoned street.

Loud music blasted from the neon-lit nightclubs and strip-joints. Packs of young people, arms entwined in drunken affection, clogged the sidewalks.

Abendroth managed to find a parking space a hundred yards or so down the street. Checking the detector, she announced, "Still nothing."

Waring opened the door and got out. "Stay here."

Abendroth didn't say anything, but she climbed out of the Volvo and joined him on the sidewalk. She stared at him with amused, defiant eyes. Waring sighed once, and they walked up the sidewalk to the florist's. They were forced to step aside once to make way for a weaving collection of drunken, laughing girls. They glanced at Waring and Iselda and made comments about how overdressed they were.

Standing in front of the shop, Waring peered through the window and saw only what he expected to see—flowers, flowers and more flowers, and a large rack holding an assortment of cards. The door was locked, and the garage door was secured from the inside.

"Think there's a back entrance?" Waring asked.

The sound of glass shattering against stone cut off Abendroth's response. Waring spun around. Three men reeled across the street toward them. One had dropped a beer bottle on the cobblestones. All of them appeared drunk, but they walked faster than drunks would have been expected to.

They were young, shaven headed, wearing metal-studded denim jackets, fingerless leather gloves and provocative smiles. One was of medium height and build, another rather small and acne-spotted.

The third was one of the biggest men Waring had ever seen and he had seen quite a few. Rather than the heavy laced boots his companions wore, his feet were shod in pointy-toed cowboy boots.

"Hey, Auslander," said the big man in reasonably good English. "They're closed. Find another place to buy your nigger bitch flowers."

Waring sized him up quickly. He was huge, nearly seven feet tall and probably tipped the scales at over 300 pounds, none of it fat. He was also doing a very poor job of pretending to be drunk.

His two companions laughed at the giant's wit. Waring recognized the smaller man's jawline—he'd seen him only a short time before astride a motor scooter.

Waring stepped in front of Abendroth. She breathed, "Don't. It's a trap."

Waring knew it was a trap. If it was sprung successfully, he and Abendroth would be written off as just two more victims of random neo-Nazi violence. He also knew the trap was prepared on impulse, a surveillance team forced to act as assassins. The three weren't professionals, and that made the situation a little less formidable.

Staring into the hulking giant's face, Waring asked mildly, "What's your name, son?"

The young man blinked. After a second's hesitation, he said with a smirk, "They call me Xauz. What's it to you, foreigner?"

"I always want to know the name of every asshole I kill. Makes record-keeping easier."

Xauz gaped at him in outraged surprise. "You fuckin' Amerikanisch—I'll tear your head off and shit down your neck!"

As Xauz crossed the intervening few feet of sidewalk, Waring saw that the smallest skinhead had pulled a sawed-off ball bat from beneath his jacket. Waring stepped back, hand closing around the butt of the Ruger.

Metal glinted from the knuckles of Xauz's right fist. Waring sprang to the left, away from the brass-reinforced punch. As Xauz's fist brushed the shoulder of his jacket, Waring slashed the barrel of the Ruger across the bridge of the giant's nose.

Blood sprang out, splashing into Xauz's eyes. He stumbled forward, pawing at his face. He slammed into the garage door with a loud bang! and uttered a scream of rage and pain.

Waring whirled on his companions. The little man with the ball bat stared too long at Xauz. Waring smashed the frame of the automatic against the side of his head, splitting the scalp. Blood pouring down his face, he staggered against his companion.

The skinhead pushed his senseless partner out of the way and rushed forward, head down, hands balled into fists. Waring didn't use the Ruger on him. He pivoted on one foot and drove a roundhouse kick into the man's lower belly. The skinhead folded over Waring's leg, then flopped down on the sidewalk, making gagging sounds.

Xauz turned, breathing heavily through his mouth. He glared first at Waring and then the Ruger in his hand. He didn't move.

Deliberately, Waring handed the automatic to the wide-eyed Abendroth. He faced Xauz and smiled. Xauz charged at him, hands outstretched.

Waring quickly stepped inside the man's outflung arms and kicked his right kneecap. The pop of the patella being forcefully removed from the femur was clearly audible, even over the throbbing beat of music.

Xauz went down on the sidewalk, plucking at his maimed leg and howling in agony. He gaped up at Waring with astonished horror. His right hand was splayed out on the sidewalk, and Waring put the heel of his right shoe on it, twisted sharply and heard the bones crack. Xauz screamed as Waring maintained the pressure. He bent and pulled the brass knuckles from his hand.

Waring slipped the knucks over the fingers of his right hand and waited until the belly-kicked skinhead shambled erect. He breathed in great, bubbling gasps, hands over his stomach.

Without putting much of his weight behind it, Waring snapped a jab to the skinhead's jaw. Metal met flesh and bone with an ugly crack. The man staggered a few feet, then fell in a loose-limbed heap to the sidewalk.

Waring turned back to Xauz. He was still smiling that small, cold smile. At the sight of it, Xauz managed to control his pain and tried to force himself to his feet. Through clenched teeth he hissed, "Schutzig auslandisch schwein."

Waring waited until Xauz had achieved a half-crouching posture, then he delivered the toe of his right foot full against Xauz's chin. He went over on his back, his head striking the sidewalk.

Waring strode over to him and Xauz cringed away, scooting on the seat of his pants until his back was pressed against the garage door.

"The master race," Waring said, his voice heavy with contempt. He gestured to Abendroth, who slipped the Ruger into his hand. He went to one knee beside Xauz and planted the bore of the automatic against his forehead.

"I'm going to ask you a few questions," Waring said softly. "If you don't answer them, if I think you're lying or if I simply don't like your attitude, I'll blow your head off and shit down your neck. Do we understand each other?"

Squeezing his eyes shut, Xauz nodded several times. "Ja, ja."

"Who do you work for?"

" Hauser and Hochbach."

"What do you do?"

"Mail room clerk."

"Who ordered you to kill us?"

Xauz hesitated, and Waring dug the bore into his forehead.

Xauz choked out, his voice nasal and snuffling, "No one. My orders were to watch the store. See who showed up. That's all."

"So you did this on your own initiative. A skinhead with ambition. Who gave you the orders?"

"Herr Eicke."

Waring stood up and holstered the Ruger. "Do you know what a Dag is?"

"Nein."

"Doesn't matter. Tell him I have it."

Waring took Abendroth by the arm and led her back to the Volvo. She was trembling. "Want me to drive, doctor?"

Abendroth gave him an angry look and quickly slid behind the wheel. When they were mobile again, she snapped, "Why did you brutalize that kid?"

"He intended to do more than brutalize you," Waring replied.

"You may very well have crippled him."

"I may very well have educated him. Size, strength and arrogance counts for only so much. He'll have time to think about that over the next few months while he's walking around on crutches."

Abendroth gripped the steering wheel tightly. "I'd be more prone to agree with you if I didn't suspect you took pleasure in doing that to him."

"You think I enjoyed it?"

She glanced at him. "Didn't you?"

Waring took a breath and pursed his lips and then decided to say nothing.

NINE

WHEN WARING and Abendroth entered the office in the consulate, Major Jacobs was waiting for them. He ignored the radiation detector Abendroth placed on the table and snarled, "Just what the hell did you hope to accomplish with that stunt at the florist's shop, Waring?"

"To draw the blackhats out in the open."

"And to draw a lot of unwanted attention!"

Abendroth looked from Jacobs to Waring and demanded, "What're you talking about?"

"The major had us tailed," Waring said.

"What?" Abendroth said raggedly. "Then why didn't they help us with those skinheads?"

Jacobs didn't answer. He kept glaring at Waring. "We had the florist's shop covered, Waring. There was no need for you to go there."

"Good of you to share that with me."

"Now, because of that little street theater performance of yours, the 'blackhats' won't go near it."

"They don't have to," Waring replied. "We have a name and a place. Julius Eicke and Hauser and Hochbach."

Jacobs sighed in exasperation. "Didn't we go over that already? Eicke is clean—"

"—And one of the skinheads, maybe all three, works at his firm," Waring interrupted. "Solezer can arrange formal charges against them. They're low-level thugs, not pros. One of them will spill and we can go after Eicke all nice and neat and legal."

Jacobs thought that over for a handful of seconds. He opened his mouth to speak, but the telephone on the table rang. Jacobs picked up the receiver and spoke into it. Then he fell silent, just listening. After a minute, he hung up. His face had paled by several shades. He sank into a chair and rubbed his forehead.

"What is it?" Waring asked.

Jacobs cleared his throat and began speaking in a monotone.

An ambulance had picked up the three young men Waring had left on the sidewalk. They had been ferried to the nearest hospital. Less than ten minutes after they had been admitted to the emergency room, two men —one with a raincoat slung over his right arm— entered the emergency room and announced they were relatives of the three young men.

The admissions nurse informed them that the men were being treated and their injuries were such that it was unlikely they would be released that night. Whereupon one of the men shot the nurse through the head with a .380 caliber automatic.

Then the two men walked quickly into the examination room where the trio of skinheads was being attended to by a pair of physicians. The man with the raincoat flung it aside to reveal the muzzle of an Uzi. He shot down the two doctors.

The largest of the three skinheads screamed something before several bullets perforated his shaven cranium. The other two were dispatched by a prolonged burst of autofire.

The pair of raiders calmly left the emergency room. On their way out, the man armed with the .380 shot a security guard who tried to block their way. The nurse was dead, so were the three skinheads and one of the doctors. The other was on the critical list with multiple gunshot wounds. The security guard was expected to die before dawn.

The entire sequence of events had happened in the past 45 minutes.

"Oh my God," Iselda Abendroth gasped when Jacobs finished his account.

She looked at Waring with horror-stricken eyes. Then, with one hand covering her mouth she ran out of the room. Waring didn't go after her. There was nothing he could say.

A frustrated and angry Jacobs stared at him. "So much for nice, neat and legal, Waring. Your leads just evaporated."

"No," said Waring. "I forced their hand. They killed three of their own to keep their secrets, but they know they'll have to make a move very soon. We have to get busy to checkmate it."

"How do you figure to do that?"

"By hitting their dark-site when they least expect it."

"When?"

"Tonight."

"Goddammit, we don't have any evidence that the clinic is anything than what it appears to be."

"That's why we need to hit it. Get Solezer over here with maps of the sewer lines in the Hardenburg district."

Jacobs chewed his lower lip for a moment. The friction between two military veterans accustomed to playing out a mission their own way heated up the small room.

Waring said calmly, "Major, let's knock off the game of 'push-me-shove-you'. We don't have the time for it."

Jacobs snorted and picked up the phone. He muttered into it for a few seconds then dropped the receiver back into its cradle. "Solezer's on his way."

"Good. I'll order us some coffee from the dining room."

The pot of black coffee arrived before the Verfassungsschutz officer. Waring had just finished his first cup when Solezer walked in. He was carrying a briefcase.

To Jacobs he said, "Here is what you requested."

Solezer spread out a large chart on the table and Waring went over his plan, point by point. Solezer mentioned certain problems and even made a few useful suggestions.

"You've used these sewers before?" Waring asked.

Solezer nodded. "Before The Wall came down, we occasionally infiltrated agents into East Berlin through them."

"A pretty clandestine border crossing," Waring replied. "And smelly, too."

Solezer ignored the comment. "I have little doubt that you can penetrate the clinic. Whether you can get out is a different matter altogether. After last night and tonight's event, those inside will be on full alert."

"I've taken that into account. The risk factor is high, but acceptable."

"I suggest a reserve standby force, waiting to execute a diversionary tactic if you need assistance."

Waring considered the proposal. "Agreed, as long as it's a strike force of no more than twenty men. And keep the unit incommunicado from all outside contact from the moment you brief them."

Solezer angled an eyebrow. "What are you implying, Herr Waring?"

"Nothing. I'm making a straight-from-the-hip statement. There's a leak somewhere between the consulate, G2 and your secret service. I don't know who, and at the moment, I don't care. I just want to make sure I won't waltz into another trap."

Solezer didn't become angry or huffy. "I understand. My department will provide you with the newest and best equipment."

"Thank you," said Waring.

A rendezvous and timetable was set. Waring shook Solezer's outstretched hand and the secret service officer left the room.

Jacobs drawled, "You must be slipping. You didn't offend him this time."

Waring didn't reply. He poured himself another cup of coffee.

Jacobs watched him sourly and asked, "What if you get in there and find absolutely nothing of value? It'll be a pretty embarrassing diplomatic incident."

He seemed pleased by the possibility.

"I don't embarrass easily, Major. If that's the case, you can watch me eat crow with a side order of humble pie."

"What if you get in there and find a hell of a lot more than you expect? You're just one man."

Waring shrugged, sipped at his coffee. "I'm one man who makes a point of paying my bills. If the second scenario is the case, then I'll pay off what I owe and add in a lot of interest."

THE REPORT of the massacre at the hospital reached Eicke at a little after midnight. His butler summoned him from the party when the secured line between his private office and the Nachisessen clinic rang.

Asoka provided the details. Eicke was shaken, appalled and greatly disturbed by the vision of the next day's headlines. He demanded to know who had ordered the murders.

"Ulrich, who else?" Asoka said. "When the report of the accident came in from one of our informants on the police department, Ulrich dispatched Otto and Dolf to the hospital."

"I thought as much," Eicke said bitterly. "What Ulrich has done is intolerable. Our men have acted like cheap thugs."

"There's more," Asoka said. He hesitated, then said, "According to Otto, Xauz said he had a message for you, something the American told him."

A chill crept up the buttons of Eicke's spine. "A message for me?"

"Evidently. Xauz probably told him that he worked for Hauser and Hochbach."

"What was the message?"

"The American told Xauz to tell you that he has the Dag."

Eicke swore into the mouthpiece, and swore again when he noticed that his hands were shaking. "Did Otto tell Ulrich about this?"

"Of course," answered Asoka. "And Ulrich flew into a rage. He demands that the American be apprehended at any cost, and forced to reveal the Dag's whereabouts. He even said something about storming the U.S. embassy, or kidnapping the Abendroth woman and holding her for ransom."

"Jesus Christ," Eicke muttered.

"It is my opinion that Ulrich is suffering from a severe dissociative disorder," said the Japanese psychiatrist. "Partly due to age and partly due to a long-term psychosis. We can no longer trust his judgment."

"Of course not," Eicke snapped. "This sort of violence will only anger the very people in the government we wish to influence. If they come to believe we are common terrorists, or a left-over scrap of stormtroopers, they will not even consider our proposal. Your friends from the Black Dragons will withdraw their support, too."

"I agree," said Asoka. "Ulrich must be isolated from the circle."

"Easier said than done," Eicke replied. "Many of the soldiers in the special wing are undisciplined hoodlums, loyal to Ulrich, not to our objective."

"They are expert survivors, Julius. They may not be loyal to our cause, but they will not wish to leave the sanctuary I've provided for them."

"We'll have to move up our timetable," Eicke said. "I'll draft the communiqué tonight. In the interim, remove Ulrich from the general population. If anyone in the wing asks, just say that he needs special medical treatment."

Asoka agreed and hung up. Eicke sat at his desk, swiftly calculating the odds of how soon he could expect the Berlin police or the Verfassungschutz to ask him questions about Xauz. He knew the young giant should have been eliminated, since the Brotherhood's security could not be compromised, but the public manner in which it was done raised far more problems than it solved.

Ulrich, unfortunately, was becoming a security risk as well. If the old man continued to be intractable, he would notify Asoka to kill him, preferably by injection, introducing an embolism into his bloodstream. Because of his advanced age, the few soldiers loyal to him would not become unduly suspicious.

It would be a very difficult decision to make. He admired Ulrich Schreck as he admired no other man, with exception of his father. But it was Ulrich who had told him to plan for all foreseeable contingencies, as a good strategist should. In contemplating Ulrich's death, he was simply following his advice.

Certainly he would regret killing the man—Ulrich had almost single-handedly kept the Brotherhood of the Black Sun from being consumed in the same inferno that consumed the Third Reich.

Through the S.S., Ulrich had seen that the Brotherhood maintained its own research centers and factories, many of which even Hitler and Himmler didn't know about.

Eicke couldn't help but chuckle at the memory of how the Allies had raced hither and thither all over Germany to recover the Reich's legendary "secret weapons."

When the Allies did discover a few research centers, all they found were frustratingly incomplete documents, isolated parts of obviously complex components and a treasure trove of electronic odds and ends that could have belonged to just about anything.

Ulrich, Eric Eicke and Jorg Weisenburg had overseen the completion of many of the so-called "secret weapons", including the miniaturized microwave transmitters. The Brotherhood had access to technology as much as five years or more ahead of the most advanced industries.

But Ulrich looked on the technologies developed by Nazi scientists as mere toys. As much as he disparaged Hitler as a madman, Ulrich himself was just as obsessive and perhaps just as insane. He believed in reincarnation, Atlantis, and a world of Aryan gods lying just beneath his feet.

Though Eicke believed in the basic philosophy of the Brotherhood, he was a pragmatic man. He didn't entertain for one second that any of the myths and legends about an actual black sun were anything other than parables.

Ulrich had told him that the concentration camps were never designed to simply imprison the racially inferior—he claimed they provided the raw material for mass human sacrificial rites.

Julius Eicke and Ulrich Schreck were in complete agreement in one area, at least —human freedom led only to unchecked lunacy. Freedom and democracy never worked. They led only to self-indulgence, conflict and waste, and perpetuated the stagnancy of the human mind.

The nuclear missiles were, like humanity in general, only tools to be used to build a better, cleaner world. Eicke had no intention of launching them, because he knew that many people in the German, Russian, British and American governments believed in the tenets of the Brotherhood.

The world was out of control, freedom and democracy led to revolution and chaos, and the Brotherhood would transform Germany into the prototypical nation of the future, a standard by which other countries would measure themselves.

The Brotherhood of the Black Sun would not accomplish this through armies or death-camps or brutal repression. Eicke knew that nuclear blackmail would accomplish only so much. The Pershings were only fulcrums to move the government and NATO to the proper position to agree to their terms. After all, the agreement would be covert, and every European nation would benefit.

In the final analysis, the world of politics was only a chess game, the pieces were property and the game was only played by the elite who hid behind closed doors.

With nuclear missiles as keys, those doors would be unlocked and the Brotherhood of the Black Sun would be invited to join in the game.

TEN
June 5

IT WAS nearly 2:30 AM when Waring entered the pump house some eight blocks from the Nachisessen clinic. He felt keyed up and anxious to get moving. The need for sleep was something he had learned to turn on and off. He could accumulate it, to have a reserve for times when he might have to go for a long period without it. This was one of those times.

Solezer and a pair of Verfassungsschutz men waited for him inside the little cement block building. Waring pulled on the rubberized black wet suit while Solezer explained the operation of the ear-transceiver and throat mike to him. It was a very simple device— the flesh-colored transceiver fitted snugly into Waring's right ear, and a thin but tough filament stretched down to a small microphone that adhered to a spot near his larynx.

Iselda Abendroth and Jacobs were stationed in a truck a block away from the clinic with the radiation detector. If it picked up microwave emissions, Abendroth would let him know over the comm.

Solezer handed him the diving mask. The unit was self-contained, equipped with a very small oxygen tank that provided enough air for at least fifteen minutes. There was no need for bulky back-tanks that would interfere with his movements or speed.

One of the men handed Waring a waterproof knapsack. Inside it was his Ruger, his combat harness, the broken-down Remington Autoloader with one ammo drum, and night-vision goggles. There were also a few odds and ends that Waring thought might come in handy.

Solezer eyed the weaponry uneasily. "I thought this was primarily a recon mission, Herr Waring, not a commando raid."

"A recon mission can turn into a raid at a moment's notice," Waring replied, shrugging into the knapsack. "If that happens, I want to be prepared for it. I hope to get in and out without any contact with the people inside."

Solezer glanced at his watch, and gestured to his two men. They lifted away the heavy manhole cover, revealing the entrance to Municipal Sewer 501.

"My people are all in position," Solezer said. "On rooftops, in parked automobiles and we have a Hotspur Hussar Land Rover standing by as well."

"Let's hope I don't need it."

Waring adjusted the oxygen flow into his face mask, gave the thumbs up signal, and clambered down metal rungs into the dark, concrete cylinder. He clung to the last rung then dropped down into the sewer. It was about ten feet in diameter and filled almost to the top with a steady rushing stream that carried Berlin's sewage. The current wasn't overpowering, but Waring allowed himself to be carried along with it.

Waring detached the waterproof flashlight at his waist and shone it ahead of him, looking for the intersection where he would have to turn off to the right. It came up very quickly, and Waring kicked his flipper-shod feet against the current until he made the turn. He rolled and flowed down the sewer, aiming the flashlight up at the concrete tunnel's roof.

He saw the iron circle marked 83, and Waring seized the bottom rung of the short, rust-eaten ladder that stretched down from it. He pulled himself up from the main current and hung there for a moment, steadying his breathing. Lifting the face mask up to forehead, he touched the throat-mike.

"I'm here," he whispered.

Abendroth's crisp tones sounded in his ear. "No signals from the detector."

"Acknowledged."

Waring pushed up against the manhole cover, trying not to shove too hard, because he couldn't guess what lay on the other side. He was forced to wrap his legs around the ladder and use both hands to push. Rust showered down from the rim. Finally, the heavy metal disc shifted and he managed to shoulder it up and to one side without making too much noise beyond a grinding sound.

Waring struggled up, panting from the exertion. He stood in complete darkness and rather than turn on the flashlight, he opened the pouch and removed his combat harness. Slipping night-vision the goggles over his eyes, he saw a low-ceilinged chamber, a maintenance tunnel of some sort with walls made of blocks of rough-hewn stone. The blocks looked very old.

He guessed led to the basement or sub-cellar of Doctor Asoka's clinic. Waring activated the microphone and whispered. "I'm in."

"Acknowledged," said Abendroth. "All clear."

Waring kicked out of his flippers, strapped on the Ruger, and snapped together the Remington. Cradling the shotgun in the crook of his left arm, he walked slowly down the dark shaft. Despite the goggles, the room was still too dimly lit to be seen clearly. He walked carefully some 50 feet before the passage curved to the left. Just around the curve was a heavy metal door. It was locked.

From a pouch on the harness, Waring took a small squeeze tube of thermite paste. He spread it around the edges of the hinges, and he stepped back quickly. As the paste was exposed to oxygen, it flared into a clinging white fire which burned through the hinges until the door was held upright only by half-liquid threads of metal.

The flames died and Waring gingerly tugged at the door. It grated, hung for a moment, and then fell toward him. Waring caught the heavy panel and carefully eased it down to the floor,

He peered into a wide, high-ceilinged room. Stacks of wooden crates were arranged neatly across the floor in a rectangular pattern. An old coal-burning furnace squatted against the far wall.

Waring inspected one of the boxes. Using his combat knife, he pried up the wooden lid. The crate contained a dozen handguns, Glock 17's. He checked another crate, this one longer and narrower. It held six Heckler & Koch HK-94 auto carbines, the same ones the men on the Madeira River had carried.

Waring opened several other crates, more or less at random. He found incendiary grenades, blocks of C-4 plastic explosive, clips of ammunition and Kevlar vests. There was enough hardware to supply a small army. He found no electronic paraphernalia, nothing that seemed to relate to microwave emitters inside people's mouths.

Tapping the throat mike, he said softly, "I've found something. This place is definitely dirty. There's enough ordnance in here to take a city."

Jacobs's voice filtered into his ear. "Then get the hell out, Waring. Solezer can arrange for a warrant and have the place busted by noon."

"Negative," Waring whispered. "The rest of the stuff, the microwave gear, must be upstairs in the clinic. That's the real evidence."

Abendroth's voice, touched with concern, said, "Waring. Mike. You've done enough. Let the authorities handle it from here on out."

"It's easier to go up than the way I came in," Waring replied. "That is, if I can find a way out of here. Standby. Don't call me, I'll call you."

Waring looked around the room. By the eerie, wavering infra-red light he saw no way out of the chamber. No door or stairway.

Waring paced around the supply depot, looking for a concealed panel or a trap-door or even a dumbwaiter shaft. He didn't look long before overhead lights blazed into life with such suddenness he was momentarily dazzled.

Waring pushed the goggles up on his forehead and squatted down near a crate. He heard the sounds of footfalls and then metallic clinkings, as if a key were being inserted into a lock. He risked a quick glance around the corner of the crate.

A man was stepping out from inside the furnace. He swung the door to one side and bent low to enter the arsenal. He had long blond hair, tied back in a flowing ponytail. He was wearing the white coat of a medic. Whistling tunelessly, he walked over to a crate less than ten feet from Waring's position and lifted the lid.

Drawing an F.I.E. Titan automatic from beneath the coat, he ejected the clip, took a fresh one from the crate, and slid it into the butt. As he was holstering it, he turned and saw the metal door lying flat just outside the room.

He bellowed in surprised rage and pulled the pistol, looking wildly around the room, the gun in his hand questing for a target. Waring wasn't certain if the room was soundproofed, so he didn't use either of his guns. The man stepped toward the open doorway.

Sidling up behind him, Waring butt-stroked the back of his head with the stock of the shotgun. The man went down on his left side, eyes glassy. He pointed the little automatic at Waring's mid-section. Waring kicked the pistol aside and struck twice more with the stock of the shotgun. The man slumped down unconscious.

Moving quickly, he bound the man with his own belt and improvised a gag with strips torn from the white coat. He dragged the man to a far corner and arranged a number of crates around him.

Waring entered the furnace and saw a light switch on the wall. He also saw a flight of narrow stairs that stretched up at least twenty-five feet. He turned the light out, fitted the night-vision goggles over his eyes again and climbed the stairs very quietly. They creaked beneath his weight.

When he reached a door at the top of the steps. Waring carefully edged it open and found himself in another room. He smelled it before he could see it. Garbage cans were arrayed in rows along the wall. He moved to a door at the far end of the room and pushed it open slightly and saw a kitchen—very large and well appointed with modern appliances.

Stepping to the nearest window, he peered out beyond the wire mesh. At first he could see only neatly trimmed shrubbery, then a man wearing a white coat appeared around a corner. A lean Doberman pinscher strained against the leash the man had wrapped around his left hand. In his right he casually carried one of the auto carbines.

Waring's underground route had brought him directly into the special wing of the institution, where the arsenal and the men who used it were sequestered. The wing was probably connected to the main building by a single corridor.

Waring glided silently through the kitchen, the rubberized fabric of the boot-sox on his feet making almost no noise. He went through a huge dining hall and found himself in a corridor dimly lit by low-wattage overhead bulbs encased in wire cages. Numbered doors lined with corridor walls.

A small circle of glass was set in each door. Waring peered through one. All he saw was a tiny room, almost a cubicle, with a snoring man sprawled on a narrow cot.

Waring moved on, senses alert, finger on the trigger of the shotgun. He heard the murmur of voices somewhere ahead of him, so he slowed his pace. The voices came from inside one of the rooms, so Waring very carefully peered through the glass in the door.

He saw a heavy-set Japanese man engaged in a heated discussion with a very old, bald man in wheelchair. The room looked far more spacious than the other he had seen. Both men were speaking in rapid-fire German, so Waring had difficulty in understanding the entire exchange, but at one point the old man addressed the Japanese as "Asoka."

It seemed odd that the director of the institute would make personal visits with his patients, especially at after three in the morning.

Asoka said patronizingly, "As much as I enjoy our frequent word and wit battles, I must insist you restrict yourself to your quarters until further notice."

The old man trembled with rage. He rattled off a guttural stream of German words which Waring guessed were insults.

Asoka sighed heavily. "I wish you could just try to be reasonable, Ulrich. You have no idea how happy it would make me."

Asoka turned toward the door, and Waring slid away from it, his back pressing against the wall. He recalled what Goetz had said: "Ulrich is nearly 100."

He didn't know who Ulrich was, or had been, but something in Asoka's voice made it certain he feared the old man.

The corridor opened up into a room filled with armchairs, bookladen shelves and tables scattered with newspapers and magazines. A flat screen TV dominated one wall. Waring kept going on through it. He entered another corridor then, came to a sudden stop.

Two men stood in the corridor. They were clad in the white coats of clinic attendants, but the way they held their Titan automatics showed plainly they were combat veterans.

One of the men spoke into a compact walkie-talkie. The other snarled something in German and gestured with his gun. Waring understood enough of what he said to get the gist: it had something to do with putting down his weapons and raising his hands or having his brains blown out.

"No habla," Waring said.

In excellent English, the heavier of the two snarled, "You habla as well as I do, fuck-face. Drop the shotgun, or I'll put my initials in your forehead."

Waring eased the gun down, barrel first, to the floor. Then, with a flick of the wrist that came of long sleight-of-hand practice, the barrel came up. Waring squeezed the trigger. The sound of 20 gauge buckshot exploding from the bore of the Remington was deafening. The heavy man took the shot in his lower belly. As though he had been slapped off his feet by a giant invisible hand, he catapulted backward down the corridor.

Diving headfirst, Waring went into a somersault and the bullet fired at him from the second man seared the air well above him. Coming out of the roll, Waring triggered the shotgun again. The shot pounded the man's chest, picking him up and knocking him down like a disjointed puppet.

Waring regained his feet and ran, leaping over the shattered bodies of the two Germans. He kept his finger on the Remington's trigger. Waring had chosen it as his Close Assault Weapon because it was fairly lightweight, could be manipulated with one hand, and the recoil was manageable because of the gun's gas system operation.

Into the throat mike, he said, "Situation critical. I've been discovered."

An alarm klaxon began warbling the second after he said it.

There was no response from the transceiver, only a crash of static.

Doors began opening, voices shouted questions and curses. A man in boxer shorts popped out of a room just as Waring passed. He made a grab for him. Waring laid the barrel of the Remington alongside his head, and he staggered back into his room.

Waring hated to be chased. Even in his early days he always played the role of predator. Only rarely was he the hunted, and even in those situations, he always turned the tables on his pursuers. Waring decided to turn them now.

He veered toward a pair of double doors and shouldered them open. He was standing in a tiled shower room. At least a dozen shower heads projected from the wall. Each shower stall was separated from the other by a waist-high tiled wall.

Waring started turning on water faucets, adjusting the temperature to scalding hot. He went from handle to handle, letting jet streams of water spray down and produce billowing clouds of steam. The steam would mask his movements, and the noise of the spray would cover any sounds he might make. Using the barrel of the shotgun, he smashed the neon bulbs of the overhead light fixtures and then squatted down in a corner, between a bench and a row of lockers. He had a clear view of the doors.

The steamy air became stifling. The night-vision goggles gave all surfaces a strange, unshadowed appearance. The heat radiating from the shower stalls was like a glowing, molten bath.

The doors burst open, and three men armed with auto carbines rushed in. One tried the light switch and cursed when it didn't work. They coughed when they inhaled the hot steam. The infrared light of the goggles made the men stand out as dark blobs, the only cool things in the room.

Standing shoulder to shoulder, they opened up with the carbines, raking the dark shower room with hammering autofire. The racket was ungodly as streams of slugs shattered tiles, ricocheted from the chrome shower heads and stitched holes in the walls.

None of the bullets came near Waring's position. Resting the shotgun across his left forearm, he squeezed the trigger.

The man closest to the Remington was blasted off his feet and hurled against his companion who, in turn, staggered against the man next to him. Bullets went wild, chewing up the ceiling panels. Plaster dust and chunks of dry wall rained down.

The Remington boomed three times.

Two of the men were swept back through the double doors, carbines falling from nerveless hands. The third was smashed violently against the wall, blood exploding from a plate-sized cavity in his torso.

From the other side of the doors, a frenzied voice shrieked commands in strident German. Waring recognized the voice of Asoka. The pudgy psychiatrist was screaming about the noise, fearing it would be

heard out on the street.

Waring doubted that, but at least he wouldn't be subjected to grenades being lobbed at him.

Standing up, he made a quick circuit of the muggy room, making sure there was not another way in or out. There wasn't. Tilting his head back, he studied the ceiling panels, wondering if there might be decent-sized crawlspaces.

Waring tried the throat-microphone again. The static still hissed in his ear, but this time he heard Abendroth's voice, faint and faraway. She sounded frantic, calling his name over and over again.

"I'm reading you, doctor," Waring said.

"Thank God. Some sort of jamming umbrella went into effect a few minutes ago. It took us awhile to boost the signal."

"When the alarm went off, the jamming frequency was probably activated automatically."

"Where are you?" she asked. "We've had reports of gunfire."

"I'm inside the clinic proper, probably on the first floor. I'm bottled up in a shower room."

There was a sudden crash of static, drowning out most of Abendroth's response. "——out of there?"

"Repeat," said Waring.

Beyond the double doors, Waring heard noises of activity—hurried footfalls, whispering voices and the steady squeak-creak of wheels.

Abendroth's voice came again, overriding the static. It was urgent, holding a note of terror. "—read me? Goddammit, Mike, do you read? Respond!"

"I'm here."

"You've got to get out of there fast! Now! The radiation detector has just registered a strong signal! They've powered up one of their microwave emitters, probably the Gunn oscillator!"

Waring glanced toward the doors.

"Mike! Acknowledge! Mike!"

"Acknowledged. Tell Solezer to prep his unit."

The squeaking outside the doors stopped.

A low hum sounded and Abendroth's response, if she had one, dissolved in a blur of static.

ELEVEN

WARING INSTANTLY grasped the strategy. The blackhats would maneuver the Gunn gun up to the closed doors and flood the shower room with microwave radiation. Then, at their leisure, they would recover his corpse, fried from the oscillator and parboiled from the steam.

The whole room was beginning to heat up. Not the muggy heat from the steam, but a dry, baking heat that made his skin prickle. He felt a maddening pressure against his ear-drums.

Fiery pain suddenly seared the calf of his right leg. The blade of his sheathed combat knife was melting the rubberized wet-suit beneath. Waring snatched it out and flung it away, scorching his fingers in the process.

Going to the wall furthermost from the doors, Waring tapped the tiles with the stock of the shotgun. After several tries, he was rewarded with a hollow echo. Bracing his legs wide, and shielding his lower face with his left hand, Waring began firing the Remington at the wall. Round after round after round blew the tile and plaster and wood to bits.

He kept pumping the trigger, hoping the heat from the Gunn gun wouldn't ignite the cartridges in the Ruger or the shells inside the Remington's ammo drum. Dust floated in the air, mixing with the steam and drifting planes of cordite smoke to make an impenetrable and eye-irritating fog.

Waring stopped firing, and using the stock of the shotgun as a bludgeon, he battered his way out of the shower room.

Men were waiting for him in the weight room beyond. They drove him back with a steady fusillade of small arms fire. Waring didn't return it—to find a target meant exposing himself to the hail of bullets.

The gunfire tapered off and ceased. A laughing voice called, "Hey, Amerikanner—hot enough for you?"

In fact, it was. The heat in the shower room became unbearable. The steam drew sweat out of him and the microwave emissions dried it out instantly. Fortunately, he was not in the center of the room, or he would have succumbed by now. Still, the invisible fan of radiation was reaching him.

He risked a quick peek through the hole into the room beyond. It was filled with exercise equipment, lead weights and benches. He didn't get a good look because the gunfire resumed.

Waring hugged the wall, hearing slugs snapping through the hole to smash more tiles.

A new voice cut through the gunfire, as sharp as a whip crack. *"Halten, halten, idiotischs!"*

The firing stopped again. The voice called out, in English, "American. Can you hear me?"

Waring didn't respond. He gulped air in great gasps.

"You will not be harmed if you come out. I want only one thing from you."

Throat dirt-dry, tongue like a piece of shoe leather, Waring managed to husk out, "The Dag?"

"Where is it? Is it safe?" The sharp voice hummed with tension, with want. "Name your price."

He heard Asoka's voice, speaking in low, beseeching German.

"Ruhe!" the sharp voice said. Then, in English: "What do you say, American?"

Waring knew he couldn't stay much longer in the super-heated shower room. Pretending to go along would at least buy him time.

"I'm coming out," he called.

He rose slowly and peered around the edges of the hole. He still saw no one. He started to step through.

Then the lights went out.

Nobody in the weight room moved or spoke for a second or two. They were stunned and uncertain in the sudden darkness. Waring did not hesitate. He charged forward, his night-vision goggles dimly illuminating six figures near the doorway.

The Remington roared and the figures went in all directions, two to the left , two out the door and two down to the floor. Waring dropped into a crouch just in time to avoid a bullet that whistled over his head. He fired again, and saw one of the shadow-shapes fall heavily against the wall. Three more explosive shots cleared the room entirely. When he squeezed the trigger again there was nothing but a dry click.

Dropping the Remington, Waring drew the Ruger and rushed for the door. A man standing just outside it reacted to the rustle of his wet-suit and slashed out with the barrel of his carbine.

The night-vision goggles caught most of the impact, and the blow cracked the lenses. Waring was immediately in the dark, but he rolled away and fired the automatic in the direction of the blow.

The .45 caliber round took the man in the right shoulder. The sound of steel-jacketed destruction maiming the man's shoulder was ugly, but the awful animal howl he uttered was worse. The wounded man lurched down the corridor, wild with pain, dazed from the shock of impact.

"Schiessen! Schiessen!" he screamed.

The answering burst of carbine fire from his comrades was quick and deadly. A dozen .30 caliber slugs at close range chopped his head to pieces and nearly cut him in two.

Pulling off the ruined goggles, Waring ran down the corridor in the opposite direction, unhooking the flashlight from his belt. A carbine cracked from behind him and he turned a corner. He pressed the throat-mike.

"Iselda, are you there?"

Her voice, static free, said, "Yes. We managed to short out the power to the clinic. Hope it was in time."

"It was, thanks. The jamming umbrella is down, as well as the Gunn gun."

"Good. Solezer's people are moving in. Try to stay alive until they reach you."

"No promises," said Waring.

He stopped beside a small window and knocked the glass out of the pane with the Ruger. The window was barred on the outside, but Waring had an unobstructed view of the front of the clinic.

From across the street, two members of Solezer's unit fired a missile from a Grail Blowpipe launcher. The missile impacted on the wrought-iron gate and blew it askew on its hinges.

The Hotspur Hussar Armored Land Rover roared to the gate, the barricade remover smashing into the gate and knocking it aside. A machine gun began chattering from a window above Waring, the bullets striking sparks from the vehicle's body.

A small port opened on the roof of the Land Rover, and a two-foot long projectile sprang from it. Waring heard it smash a window on the floor above and then the slamming concussion of a flash bomb. The machine gun fire ceased.

A dozen helmeted men in body armor, armed with the stubby West German G11 rifles, came running through the open gate and across the lawn. More autofire sounded from inside the clinic, and two of the men went down.

The rear door of the Land Rover opened, disgorging six men, also wearing body armor and carrying the G11 rifles. They rushed the front door, and vanished from Waring's field of vision. He heard steady gunfire, some from handguns, much more from automatic weapons. People were shouting and swearing and running.

Then he heard a new noise. Screams of women, hoarse shouts of terror from men. The legitimate patients of the clinic were awake and terrified as the noise of battle mounted.

The mercenaries fought back stubbornly and skillfully, for they had nothing to lose, and therefore everything to fight for. It was crucial that they be kept too busy to dip into the collection of weaponry in the sub-cellar.

Waring left the window, intending to be as great a threat —or great-er—to the mercenaries inside as the specialists were outside.

ASOKA WHEELED Schreck into the monitor room in the base-ment. Picking up the phone, he tried calling Eicke, but the phone was dead. Dolf was nearby, holding a flashlight in one hand and a Gewehr 3-A3 assault rifle in the other.

The chubby psychiatrist perspired freely, his shirt already soaked through. Schreck sat in the wheelchair, watching his frantic activities with a derisive smirk.

Sliding open the drawers of the file cabinet, Asoka tossed matches into each one. The hardcopy documents were all of flash paper, and they ignited instantly. Though the documents were encrypted, there was al-ways a chance that a clever cryptographer could decipher them.

"You seem worried, Hito," Schreck said with a smile.

Asoka ignored him, though he was far more than worried. He was terrified. He had no idea how many men were besieging the clinic, and the possibility they outnumbered the mercenaries was bone-chilling. Not counting the soldiers the American had killed, there were only forty-five defenders. He had to concentrate on the problem of escape.

Dolf said worriedly, "We cannot stay here."

Schreck wheeled himself to a switch-studded metal panel on the wall. "True. So let us even the odds a bit."

He flicked the switch that started the emergency generator, suddenly il-luminating the entire interior of the building. The monitor screens flashed to life. They showed nothing but snow. Dolf got busy resetting them.

Schreck said cheerfully, "Now that power is restored, our men can contend on equal terms with the visiting team."

His gnarled fingers touched another switch on the panel. "And we can also compound our visitors' handicap."

Asoka rushed toward him. "Don't! Ulrich, for the love of God-!"

Schreck yanked the Walther from inside his coat and waved off the Japanese psychiatrist with it. "Back off."

"Ulrich," Asoka pleaded. "That is monstrous. Please, don't do it."

"Shut up, you fat piece of shit!" Schreck snarled. "It's seventy years too late to retreat into your Hippocratic oath!"

Schreck threw the switch, closing the circuit that controlled all the doors of the legitimate patients' rooms.

From the monitor console, Dolf announced, "I've got cameras two, four and eight reset."

On the screens, panicky patients stumbled out of their rooms in wild confusion. Some wandered dazedly in the corridors, and others headed toward the front door.

Asoka, Schreck and Dolf watched as a quartet of armored and helmeted raiders smashed down the front door with a battering ram. A group of mercenaries waited for them in the foyer. They had built a barricade from heaped furniture. The Verfassungschutz specialists exchanged fire with the mercenaries. Stray patients wandered into the crossfire. They seemed indifferent to the bullets.

The raiders stopped firing, but the mercenaries shot through the patients. The invaders were forced to retreat back out the door.

Schreck laughed and looked up at Asoka's sweat-filmed face. He smiled sweetly. "I wish to leave now."

Asoka turned away from Schreck, covering his face with shaking hands. Schreck raised the Walther and squeezed the trigger. The bullet hit the psychiatrist near the base of the skull, shoving him forward face-first against the wall. He slid down it lifelessly.

To Dolf, Schreck said, "Let's go, my boy. Our work here is done."

WHEN THE power came back on, Waring's first thought was of the Gunn oscillator trained on the shower room. Reversing direction, he sprinted back down the corridor. When he reached the double doors, he saw two of his kills still lying on the floor outside them, but the microwave emitter was gone.

He heard gunfire down the hallway, and distant, masculine screams. He loped in that direction.

Rounding a corner, he saw a row of barred windows with the glass knocked out of them. Three white-coated mercenaries fired handguns out the window. One of them wore the silver protective garb. He was positioned behind the parabolic dish of the oscillator. It was much larger than the one Waring had seen the night before. It was mounted on a wheeled, tripod type of contrivance. A heavy cord ran from the electric motor on the base of the dish to a wall outlet.

The oscillator operator was swinging the dish back and forth out the center window. The wave of invisible radiation fanned out and washed over Solezer's men on the lawn. Five of them were writhing in horrible agony on the ground, screaming, convulsed with the awful pain of their bodies cooking from within.

Even as Waring ran forward, he glimpsed the rifle in one Verfassungsschutz specialist's hands explode with enough force to shred his face and hands and send pieces of the weapon flying like shrapnel.

Waring increased his pace. Because of the heavy fire and the boot-sox on his feet, the mercenaries didn't hear his rushing approach. But they certainly felt it.

The first shot from the .45 took a man in the head, lifting the top of a dark blonde scalp and flinging it up toward the ceiling.

The second round punched a mercenary in the side of the neck, sending him cartwheeling down the corridor, leaving a red spray in his wake.

The hooded oscillator operator frantically tried to swivel the dish toward him. Waring launched himself over it. He collided with the soldier and both of them went down, but Waring's knee jammed deep in the man's gut.

The oscillator fell over, the funnel of radiation splashing against the ceiling.

The man beneath Waring was strong, perhaps stronger than he was, but his movements were hampered by the heavy gloves. He closed one hand around the barrel of the Ruger and struggled to yank it away.

Waring couldn't get to the man's eyes because of the goggles, and the soldier couldn't claw Waring's because of his padded hands, so they wrestled and wrenched at the pistol.

For a very long moment, they were motionless, locked in straining combat, sweat breaking out on Waring's forehead, breath coming in harsh gasps from beneath the mercenary's hood.

The mercenary jacked up a knee into Waring's left kidney. He ignored the pain and grabbed a fistful of silver hood. He pulled on it at the same time the man arched his back and bucked Waring off.

Waring threw himself backward, using the man's strength against him. The hood came away, but the mercenary didn't release his grip on the gun barrel. Planting a foot against the man's sternum, Waring levered him up and over.

The man's bare head landed in the parabolic dish of the oscillator. He had time for one, high-pitched cry and a convulsive shudder before there came a sound like a paper bag bursting.

A nauseating stench filled the corridor. Bile rose in Waring's throat as he carefully walked around the silver dish. The mercenary's head was out of shape. His brain had cooked and exploded within the skull. Only the scalp kept his cranium intact. Viscera oozed from the eyes, ears and nostrils.

Waring yanked the cord from the wall outlet and the electric hum ceased. It seemed strange that such a ghastly, deadly weapon worked off house current, like any other appliance.

He fired a round into the electric motor of the oscillator, just to make sure the bastards couldn't use it again.

TWELVE

WARING CONTINUED down the corridor, following the sound of heavy, continuous gunfire. He went through a door and realized he was in the main building of the institution. Sidling up to a corner, he hazarded a quick look around it.

In the front foyer, three mercenaries directed carbine and pistol fire out the battered-down front door from behind an overturned table.

The bullet-riddled bodies of at least four patients, three men and a woman, lay in their own blood on the floor. They had been caught in the crossfire between the table and the open front door.

Waring announced his participation in the firefight with a triple burst from the Ruger.

The first bullet hit a mercenary broadside, punching a deep, ugly cavity in his right rib-cage. Bullets two and three spun the second mercenary around like a top, blood spurting from mortal wounds in his head and upper back.

The third mercenary swung his body and pistol toward Waring, rising from behind the overturned table. He snarled in silent rage.

A rifle burst from one of the specialists outside the door opened his skull in a spray of crimson.

In a crouch, Waring crept across the floor to where a carbine rested in the outflung hand of a dead mercenary. Grabbing it by the barrel, he backpedaled, knowing that he was just as likely to be cut down by friendly fire as he was the enemy's.

He went through a side door and up a short flight of carpeted stairs leading to a long hallway. The windows faced the front lawn.

At least ten men were blazing away with carbines out of a bay window. A crate of ammo clips was pushed against the wall.

The mercenaries had arranged themselves in two rows, so while one line reloaded, the other line could keep the invaders at bay. The fire from Solezer's unit had accounted for three of them already.

Waring had no intention of making a kamikaze charge down the corridor. He had little doubt he could decimate the mercenaries, but there was also little doubt he would stop at least a dozen .30 caliber slugs in the process.

Waring inspected the ceiling. This stretch of corridor had interlocking acoustical panels in the ceiling. He holstered the Ruger and slid the Heckler & Koch through his combat harness.

Springing into the air, Waring grasped the top edge of the doorframe, a ledge about two inches wide, and he chinned himself up until he was able to push one panel aside.

He clambered up into a crawlspace. He crawled along cross-pieces of two-by- fours joined with heavy rafters, putting his weight on the wood. When the sound of gunfire was very loud, he stretched out on a rafter and carefully tugged a corner of a panel aside.

The mercenaries were almost directly below his position, their backs to him. Waring unslung the auto carbine and inserted the barrel into the small space between the tiles. Gripping it in his left hand, he made sure his body was shielded by the rafter before he squeezed the trigger. He didn't have to aim. Every man below was a target.

Over the rattling roar and the clink of ejected cartridges, Waring heard cries of shock, pain and anger. Return fire raked the ceiling, showering him with panel chips and splinters.

He withdrew the carbine and shifted position. He felt the rafter beneath him shudder as a couple of rounds nicked it. He dropped the empty weapon and slid back, weathering the storm of bullets that chewed up the panels only a foot below him.

The autofire ceased, to be replaced by the rapid scuff and scutter of running feet. Clinging to the rafter with one arm, Waring drew the Ruger and swung down, kicking out several bullet-blasted panels. He dropped lightly to the floor.

Six of the mercenaries ran down the corridor, one supporting another. They left four of their number leaking crimson on the floorboards.

Waring went after them, pausing only long enough to pick up a carbine and slam a loaded magazine into it. He duck-walked beneath the bay window. A fusillade of shots still zipped between the bars, pockmarking the opposite wall.

He ran full out down the corridor. One of the mercenaries turned and sent a strafing burst of .30 caliber slugs toward him. Waring managed to slap himself against the wall, avoiding the swarm of lead. He brought his carbine into target acquisition, finger tensed on the trigger.

Then he saw the naked woman.

She pirouetted from a room, dancing, twirling on her toes like a ballerina. She was young, blonde and very graceful, and she crooned a song in a lovely, melodic voice. She blocked Waring's line of fire, but he knew the mercenaries could have cared less if she put herself in front of theirs.

Waring bounded forward, catching her and falling with her to the floor just as a stream of autofire burned the air where she had been posing. Lifting his head, he saw the men turn left through an arch.

The woman beneath him stared unfocusedly at Waring. She smiled and caressed his face. *"Liebchen,"* she murmured.

Waring pushed himself up and away from her. She seemed content to remain on the floor, singing softly to herself, so he started running again.

The entire building suddenly shuddered, shaken by a tremendous concussion. The floor heaved beneath Waring's feet, sending him stumbling sideways against the wall. Plaster fell from the ceiling, and he heard windowpanes shattering all over the building.

From the sound and feel of the explosion, Waring guessed that a grenade had detonated—whether it was due to the actions of the mercenaries or the specialists, he wasn't certain.

Waring turned left, beneath the arch, into a long, carpeted corridor. Almost at once, a door opened at the far end of the hall, and a man was framed there, with a Gewehr rifle at his shoulder.

Waring dropped to the floor and fired once. The rifle was already stuttering. It sent a stream of lead pouring into the hall. The slugs swept high, and by the time the gunner got his aim adjusted, blood was squirting from his chest where Waring's shot had hit him. The man hurtled backward, his arms flailing, the rifle clattering to the floor.

Waring stayed low and ejected the spent clip from the Ruger, slamming in a fresh one detached from his combat harness. He chambered a round and got carefully to his feet, moving to a window. The glass was broken out of it. He peered out past the bars.

Running, falling and leaping figures filled the grounds of the clinic. Smoke was pouring from a corner of the building, and flames lanced out of a ground floor window.

He saw a specialist, apparently blinded by the smoke, take half a dozen shots in his Kevlar vest and fall down. Immediately, a pack of mercenaries surrounded him, the little Titan automatics snapping viciously. The bullets ripped the secret service man's face to pieces.

Waring put his carbine out of the window and fired three times in quick succession. At each shot, a mercenary fell.

Some of the mercenaries looked up at the window and raised their weapons. Waring ducked back as a storm of shots ripped through the window and peeled long splinters from the opposite wall.

In the distance, came the howling and woo-wooping of fire engines and police cars. Waring smiled grimly, wondering what cover story

Solezer would be forced to concoct on the spot.

Turning from the window, he crept to the room at the end of the hall, out of which the mercenary had popped.

Waring didn't waste time checking out the room. He simply threw himself at the door with a flying kick, knocking it off its hinges. He had both the Ruger and the carbine spitting flame and lead.

No one was in the room. It was a janitor's closet, loaded with mops, buckets, a hot water heater and a deep, rusted laundry sink. Waring searched the walls and floor with his eyes. Near the sink, he felt the floor give just a bit. He put a round from the .45 into the floor beneath the sink. The bullet punched a hole, and a gout of powder mushroomed up. Not linoleum or cement, but mortar.

It was a false floor, mortar over wood.

He began a methodical search for the concealed switch and found it in the sink. The hot water handle lifted up and out. Hidden pivots creaked. The wall the sink was attached to swiveled open, revealing the dark throat of a small elevator shaft.

Snatching up a handful of rags, Waring wrapped them around the greasy cable and slid down. He leathered the Ruger and managed to navigate the cable still holding the Heckler & Koch HK-94.

The shaft wasn't very deep, perhaps only twenty feet. He alighted noiselessly atop the lift car and used the barrel of the carbine to flip open the square emergency roof hatch. He leaned back against the wall of the shaft, anticipating a storm of gunfire blasting up from below.

When the gunfire wasn't forthcoming, he dropped down into the car. The cage door was open and beyond it was a short corridor forming a T, with hallways branching to the left and the right.

There was also a gutshot mercenary, lying face down in a thickening pool of the blood. He was the one Waring had wounded upstairs. When he died, his comrades had simply dropped him and gone on their way.

Waring wasn't sure which way was their way, so he paused at the crossbar of the T and tested air-currents with a moistened forefinger. He felt air moving from both directions, so on impulse he turned down the left-hand path.

The corridor led to a room filled with video monitors, electronic gear and file cabinets with open, smoking drawers. A pudgy man sat on the floor with his face jammed against the wall. Blood and brain matter were clotted on his collar.

Waring toed him away from the wall and onto his back. The con-

torted face and glazed eyes of Asoka looked up at him. Judging by his expression, his last sensation had not been pain, but sorrow.

Waring glanced at the images on the monitor screens. There were scenes of white-coated mercenaries surrendering to the Verfassungsschutz specialists, and a few who still were trying to dig in and shoot it out. A handful of walking wounded frantically stumbled toward cover.

On one screen was the image of a blond mercenary pushing a man in a wheelchair down a concrete-walled passageway toward a metal paneled door. Several armed men were clustered at the door, and Waring recognized them as the same Germans he'd been pursuing.

Waring whirled and dashed from the room, down the corridor, past the intersection, and through the right-hand hallway. The door at the end of the passage was closing, pushed from the outside. It shut with a heavy thud before he reached it, but he still slammed into it. The impact hurt his shoulder, and sent jarring pain through his entire side.

He bounced back from it, the wind all but driven from his lungs. Stepping back, he examined the door. It had a combination lock, but no handle or knob.

He backed up half way down the corridor and unlimbered the carbine. Holding down the trigger, he emptied the clip at the lock. He stood fast as ricochets whined and screamed around him, striking sparks from the sheet-metal and digging long gouges in the walls and ceiling.

When the firing pin clicked against the empty chamber, he dropped the carbine and drew the Ruger. Holding it in a two-handed grip, he blasted the same small area of the door with .45 caliber wrecking balls.

The circular lock was smashed, shattered and finally fell out to clatter on the floor.

Waring ejected the clip, took a spare from the harness and slid it into the pistol's butt. He ran forward, launching a kick at the door. It crashed open.

He found himself in a long, low tunnel, evidently part of the of the old sewer system he had used to enter the clinic. Stagnant water lay ankle-deep, and rats scuttled on the curving stones.

He heard an engine start down the passageway. Chambering a round into the pistol, Waring sloshed through the water, following the sound. The stone floor slanted upward at a gradual angle, out of the standing water. He saw damp footprints and the tracks of wheelchair tires on the dry stones.

He reached the top of the ramp just as a mini-bus bearing the Perfect Plug logo rounded a bend in the tunnel and was lost from view.

Waring pressed the throat-mike. Static crackled and hissed in his ear. When the power had been restored to the clinic, the jamming umbrella opened up again. He could only hope that one of the Verfassungsschutz agents would spot the vehicle, but he was pretty sure that the mini-bus would emerge blocks away from the hellzone.

Waring walked back down the passageway. He returned to the elevator and took it back up to the janitor's closet. The sound of battle had nearly faded, except for distant and sporadic gunfire. He walked down the hallway toward the front door of the clinic.

Solezer was there, speaking into a walkie-talkie. Blood streaked his face from a minor laceration on his forehead.

"How did your recon mission go, Herr Waring?" he inquired politely.

THIRTEEN

The mop-up went slowly.

Little pockets of resistance still had to be dealt with, patients had to be rounded up, the dead tagged and bagged. The place was honeycombed with hidden rooms and secret passages.

When a specialist brought up the mercenary Waring had tied up in the subterranean arsenal, Jacobs suggested it might be fruitful if Waring had a long, quiet talk with him. The G2 officer said it was likely that the mercenary could cast some light on where all the concealed rooms and cubbyholes might be located.

The mercenary was more than willing to co-operate, on the condition he be given a pain-killer. One of Solezer's specialists found some medical supplies and gave him an injection of morphine. The man was so grateful, he even drew a crude map indicating all the secret boltholes he knew about.

By the time all that was accomplished, it was nearly 8AM.

Waring went through every room, accompanied by Abendroth and Jacobs. They found bodies and wreckage and spent cartridges, but no sign of any advanced microwave gear.

The fire and police departments were angry with Solezer— the fire department because the fire in the clinic had been caused by an incendiary grenade shot out of a mercenary's hands by one of his specialists, and the police department because they had not been informed of the raid.

Solezer was angry with Waring because a recon mission had turned into a major incident, with many Verfassungsschutz casualties. A small army of media was clustered at the gate of the clinic, and the police were hard-pressed to keep them all back.

In an antechamber off the kitchen, Abendroth found a metal-paneled, padlocked door marked DANGER! HIGH VOLTAGE! The door was locked. To be on the safe side, Solezer ordered one of his men in the underground room to turn off the emergency generator. Waring shot out the lock, and opened the door.

By the glow of flashlights, they found strange machines, some with parabolic dishes five feet in diameter, and tiny little devices small enough to fit inside someone's mouth.

Abendroth examined the gadgets with complete concentration, occasionally murmuring to herself.

Solezer ordered the power to be restored, and when the lights came up, he took Waring aside. Early morning sunlight streamed in through the windows.

Four medics came by, struggling with a body bag. It was unzipped over the head, and Asoka's face stared up at them.

"That was the man who kept the secrets," Solezer said. "Until someone put a bullet in his brain."

"That someone used a .38," Waring replied. He touched the butt of his holstered Ruger. "I use a .45."

"So I've noticed by the number of corpses."

"If you have something to say, say it."

"Very well." Solezer's face was inscrutable. "What right did you have to continue marauding through this institution after Major Jacobs ordered you out?"

"If I had done what he said, by the time a warrant was processed, every bit of evidence would have disappeared. You know there's a leak."

"I also know that we don't know a verdammt thing more about who controls the missiles than we did two days ago."

"At least we've blown the cover off one of their safe houses."

"And staged a minor war," Solezer said. "Eleven of my people are dead, six are seriously injured. I don't find that much of a trade-off."

"To be honest," said Waring, turning away, "neither do I."

Solezer grabbed his arm and spun him around. "I'm not done with you, Waring."

Waring glanced down at Solezer's hand, then fixed his eyes on Solezer's face. "I'm damn sorry about your people, but if you had tried to play this out legally, your people would have walked into an ambush and the casualties would have been far greater. Your problem is that you haven't been taking the Brotherhood seriously. I hope that's changed."

Solezer's cell phone suddenly trilled. He released Waring and took the phone from an inside pocket of his coat.

Waring stalked away from him. He didn't blame Solezer for being angry, but deaths were the luck of the draw. It was part and parcel of walking the hellfire trail, and Waring knew the odds were he would fall on that trail as well, sooner rather than later.

He found Abendroth sitting on the floor with the gadgets spread out around her. She reminded Waring of a kid on Christmas morning, busy opening all her gifts. Jacobs squatted down near her. She looked up at his approach.

"Mike—this isn't like any sort of solid-state hardware I've ever seen."

"You don't know what it is?"

"I can venture a fairly good guess."

"Don't keep me in suspense."

Abendroth gestured to the parabolic dishes. "These emitters, the oscillators are the clue. They transmit a very strong, very focused beam of radiation. They're all set for an exceptionally high frequency, not like the Gunn guns."

"And?"

"And, any one of these oscillators could transmit a signal to penetrate a missile silo and trigger a launch."

"From here?" Waring asked.

Abendroth shook her head. "No, but the range doesn't have to be close, either. Theoretically, you could mount one of these oscillators on a vehicle and drive to within a klick or two of the silo and send out the appropriate frequency. It would have to be linked with a portable computer terminal or telemetry box to get the transmission code pulses just right."

"Who could do this?," demanded Jacobs.

Abendroth shrugged. "You. Me. Anyone with even the most superficial knowledge of microwaves...and an electrical generator inside the vehicle."

"Any names occur to you that might fit the designs of these gadgets?" Waring asked.

"Too many," replied Abendroth. "Keep in mind that as early as 1935 there was talk coming out of Germany about death-ray projects, among other things. The Nazi military establishment had encouraged every kind of research in the field of lasers, radar and microwaves. Any number of scientists could have worked on these kinds of emitters."

"Name one," Waring suggested.

"Jorg Weisenburg," Abendroth responded. "He used to be on the consulting staff of Ostara. He retired a couple of years ago. I remember him talking about some remarkable solid-state research and experiments his father was involved with for the S.S. during the war. It's possible that this gear is the product of those experiments."

"Would the personnel files of Ostara have his last known address?"

"Maybe. I'll check it out."

Solezer was suddenly there, folding up his cell phone. "I've just finished talking to my director," he said. "The 'blackhats' as Herr Waring so quaintly refers to them, have made contact. Terms and conditions. I'm instructed to go to your embassy where we'll receive the full update."

"Christ," Jacobs said tonelessly. "This is like something out of a bad movie ... or a nightmare."

"Yes," said Waring. "And the bad movie and the nightmare are just now starting the second acts."

EICKE HAD gone to bed rather late, waiting until the last of his guests had gone home. Though he felt comforted by Asoka's assurances that he would deal with Ulrich, his nerves continued to be on edge.

He had devoted several hours to making a videotaped communiqué to the Federal Republic, making sure it ended up in the hands of the director of the secret service.

Once completed, it had been dispatched to the offices by a courier. Then, Eicke was chauffeured to his palatial home in the Prenzlauer Berg district.

Eicke took two sleeping pills and set the alarm clock for eight. He finally dozed off shortly before three o'clock.

He was awakened at quarter to six. It wasn't the clock, the telephone or one of his five person serving staff, but a cold, round thing pressing against his forehead.

Eicke's eyes snapped open, blinked and focused on the black barrel of the pistol. His body jerked, but a terrifyingly familiar voice spoke from only two feet away.

"Don't move," the voice said. "Not one fucking millimeter or I'll spread that turd you call a brain all over the pillowcase."

Eicke lay rigid, frozen, barely breathing. He husked out, "Ulrich."

"Very good, Julius. You can obey simple commands. Not bad for an incompetent imbecile."

Eicke's eyes adjusted to the gloom. The faint light of dawn peeking in between the curtains showed him two men. One was Schreck, gripping his beloved Walther P-38. The other was a tall blonde man standing behind the wheelchair, holding a Glock 17. A long Sionics noise suppressor was screwed into the muzzle.

Eicke tried to speak, but Schreck pressed the bore of the pistol harder into his forehead.

"Shut up. Shut up. I am very angry with you, understand? This morning's disaster was the final straw. You leave me no choice."

"Disaster?" Eicke murmured, his voice pitched low to disguise the tremble. "What are you talking about?"

"The clinic was overrun. I was forced to flee. They are on to us, Julius."

"Overrun? By who?"

"By the secret service and the American."

"How could this have happened? We had no warning!"

"I tried to explain it to you, Julius. I tried to warn you. The American warrior has the Dag. As long as it serves his energy, his vision, he will be brought into conflict with The Brotherhood. We cannot destroy the Dag, so we must destroy the warrior."

Eicke had regained some his composure. "It wasn't the Dag that brought him into conflict," he said as scornfully as he dared. "It was our conduit within the consulate. The idiot followed the man's orders to follow our observation team to the clinic."

"He had no choice, did he, without raising the American's suspicions? No, Julius, you cannot transfer the blame for this morning's catastrophe. You will take full responsibility."

"What about Hito?"

"Dead. I killed him myself."

Sheer terror flooded Eicke. He felt his bowels loosen, and he tried to jackknife up out of the bed, but Dolf leaned over and slammed him back down, a hand jammed cruelly over his mouth. Eicke breathed in panicky whistles through his nostrils.

"Forget about your servants, Julius. We have eliminated them from the game."

Dolf removed his hand, and Eicke began to babble. He claimed his rights as a high-ranking member of The Brotherhood, he told Schreck that he did not have the authority to do this.

"This entire operation was organized and planned under my direction," he said. "Simmons was my contact, as is our conduit inside the American consulate. I've already sent a communiqué to the director of internal security. Only I have access to the black box. So you don't dare kill me."

Schreck leaned back in his wheelchair and moved the gun muzzle back from Eicke's forehead.

"Much of what you say is true," he said meditatively. "The Brotherhood owes you much. Despite the fact that Helmut, your own father, once told me to kill you if you put personal interests ahead of The Brotherhood's."

Eicke's eyes bulged. He was too shocked to speak.

Schreck chuckled maliciously. "Oh, yes. He told me shortly before he died that egotism was your fatal flaw, and I must make sure you were expendable."

Eicke became angry. "I am not expendable, you crazy old fuck! The Brotherhood needs me—you need me!"

"Actually," said Schreck calmly, "I need only the black box. And to get that, I need only a small part of you."

Schreck glanced up at Dolf and nodded. Eicke began a screaming rush up from the bed, but the Glock in Dolf's hand made a sound like a rubber mallet hitting concrete.

Blood bloomed in the center of Eicke's forehead and the back of his skull broke open. He fell back limply onto the bed, his eyes gazing sightlessly at the ceiling.

Schreck looked at the red and grey mess spattered on the pillow under Eicke's head and made a noise of disgust.

"I prefer the .38," he said. "A cleaner kill."

Schreck lifted Eicke's slack right hand by the wrist. With a forefinger he traced a line just below the wrist bone. "About here, I should say."

Dolf nodded and stuck the Glock into his waistband. From a coat pocket he withdrew a heavy clasp knife. He opened the five-inch blade and thumbed the cutting edge.

It was exceptionally sharp.

THERE WAS a portable television and DVD player on the table of the small room when Waring, Jacobs and Solezer entered.

Darren made adjustments on the player and greeted everyone with a nervous smile. A large padded envelope was on the table. Nodding to it, he said, "That arrived from your office a few minutes ago, Mr. Solezer."

Jacobs dismissed Darren and he and Waring sat down. Solezer removed a DVD from the envelope and inserted it into the player.

An image flashed onto the screen. It was not a particularly melodramatic or even sinister image. It showed the shadowy head and shoulders of a man sitting in some shadowy place. The videographer had taken great pains to show nothing but a dark human outline.

The image spoke in a harsh, electronically distorted voice.

"Inasmuch as you will play this communication for the Americans, I will speak in English and save you the time and trouble of interpreting.

"My name, the organization I represent, are not important. What is important is that we control six thermonuclear missiles at an American missile site. That control cannot be wrested from us without incurring the most terrifying consequences. I should not have to add that what we accomplished at one site, we can accomplish at another."

Jacobs muttered, "You sonofabitch."

The image said, "We have no intention of launching the missiles—at least, not yet. That is entirely up to you. We want Germany returned to the Germans. We have had enough of wasted time and opportunities, self-indulgence and corruption and decadence. We must reclaim our land, our superiority in the global community. We cannot do that while a weak and pallid democracy persists in allowing freedom to destroy us."

Solezer snorted.

"Germany is finally one nation again," the image droned on, "but the freedom prevents us from sharing a united purpose. We must be disciplined and driven. Our people cry out for such a discipline. Our young people are desperate for a sane and safe Germany. We can save ourselves. Such a goal can be accomplished in a relatively short time, without bloodshed, without incident."

The man on the screen paused, as if for effect, and continued, "All we require is a covert cooperation between the Bunestrat, the Bundesprasident, the Bundeskanzler and the organization I represent. We will ask for certain legislation to be passed, certain laws to be created or repealed, certain trade agreements to be made. We realize the wheels of government turn slowly, and we can afford to be patient.

"However, you cannot afford to ignore us. Within a fortnight, a motion to amend the constitution regarding the immigration laws will be presented to the Bunestrat. The motion will be carried as a show of good faith. If it is not, then we will be forced to take extreme measures. If the motion is carried, then we will communicate with you again. If it is not, further communication is unnecessary. You know our position. Let us know yours."

The image faded and was replaced by hissing snow.

Solezer reached over and turned off the television. "On the basis of this tape, my superiors in Bonn are convinced of a substantial plot against the security of the Republic."

"No shit," said Jacobs. "Has a course of action been discussed?"

"A show of thinking it over, at least for the moment," replied Solezer.

"Two weeks is a long time to pretend to go along with these people," Waring said. "The longer they have the missiles in their hands, the greater the temptation to play their trump card."

Solezer rubbed the back of his neck. "Herr Waring, not every member of my government may be pretending. There are a number of officials who were elected to their positions by subscribing to the tenets of Deutschland den Deutschen—Germany for the Germans. Their sympathies lie with what the man in the tape described as his own."

"Even so, I can't believe they'd allow a shadow government to pull their strings," Waring said.

"And why not?" demanded Solezer, some heat entering his voice. "Wasn't my country the puppet of the U.S., NATO, the United Nations and the Soviet Union for over 50 years?"

"We're talking a large and well-financed Fascist conspiracy here," Waring said. "Do you want your country's strings pulled by a conspiracy?"

"Don't be so naive," Solezer replied, voice rising. "The entire world is part of a conspiracy! You think your country is any different? A select few decide all the issues."

"A neat, self-serving philosophy," said Waring. "Justifies allowing totalitarianism to take over. The problem is, you'd have too many secrets to keep."

"So?" Solezer's tone was challenging. "We Germans have always lived by the credo of the good of the Fatherland outweighed the good of the people."

"Seventy years ago those slogans worked. But they won't wash in today's political climate. If your own citizens won't censure you for knuckling under to blackmail, the rest of the world will."

Solezer's eyes slitted. "And how would you deal with it, Herr Waring?"

"There are only two ways to deal with blackmailers. Expose them or kill them."

Jacobs cleared his throat noisily. "Waring, Solezer—we're being a little premature. Let's find out which way the parliament jumps, then make plans."

Solezer did not take his eyes off Waring. "Whatever plans are made will not include American intelligence. This is now a matter of internal security. We will proceed from this moment on with utter stealth and complete secrecy. Do you understand me?"

"I understand how stealth and secrecy are effective against an enemy," said Waring. "But when a democratic government practices them against its own citizens, you divorce everyone in that democracy from any understanding of the circumstances affecting their own lives. If that's your standard, then you don't have a government. All you have is a conspiracy."

Solezer and Jacobs exchanged glances. Solezer said "Ja, as an American you would of course be the expert on the topic of stealth and secrecy practiced against one's own people—"

"—The first order of business," Waring interrupted, "should be to grab Julius Eicke and this man Weisenburg. Lean on them. Find out who the old man in the wheelchair is, why he was willing to trade my life for the Dag—"

Solezer stood up so quickly his chair fell over backward. "Enough!" he shouted, eyes wide and wild. "I am the authority on this matter. It is not open for debate, for suggestions, for plans or counter-plans! If I were not in your country's embassy, I would have you arrested, Waring, as an enemy of the state! I still might, if you set foot on German soil again!"

Motions sharp and violent, Solezer ejected the DVD, shoved it back in its envelope and stalked from the room.

After he had slammed the door behind him, Jacobs said dryly, "I think you struck a nerve."

FOURTEEN

WARING'S FIRST move after he went to his quarters was to get out of the wet-suit. Not only was it uncomfortable, Solezer would probably have him arrested for stealing government property if it wasn't returned to the secret service.

He rang Abendroth at her office. She sounded damnably clear-headed and alert. He was beginning to feel the effects of too little sleep and too much exertion.

"I found Professor Weisenburg's address in the personnel records," she told him. "It's over a year old, but since he's lived in the same place for nearly forty years, I doubt he's moved. Would you like me to call him?"

"No," Waring replied. "If he's involved at all, once he learns what happened at the clinic, he'll probably make himself scarce. No point in forewarning him."

"He lives at 88 Lindenalle. It's a residential section not too far from the Berliner Ring."

"Thanks. What are your plans for the day?"

"After I turn these gadgets we found over to Research, I'm going home, taking a bath, then a long nap. Care to join me?"

"That may not be wise, doctor."

"If you want me to call you Mike, I insist you call me Iselda."

"That may not be wise, Iselda."

"I'm too tired to care, Mike."

She hung up.

Holstering the Ruger in the shoulder rig, Waring slipped on his jacket, stowed two extra clips in the pockets and went down to the garage in the embassy basement, making sure to avoid Jacobs. No one was there.

Waring glanced over at the board from which keys hung from numbered hooks and started to take a set belonging to an Opel, when he heard the sound of metal on metal.

Following the sound through the parked cars, he saw a pair of coveralled legs sticking out from beneath a canary yellow Mercedes.

"Hello," he said quietly.

The legs twitched in startlement. Darren slid out from beneath the car's engine block, tools in hand, eyes wide with surprise.

"Mr. Waring. Shit, you scared me."

"Not only do you drive them, you work on them, too?"

"Sometimes. If it's minor stuff like changing the oil filter. What can I do for you?"

"I need wheels and directions to Lindenalle."

Darren stood up and thumped the hood of the Mercedes. "I've just serviced this one and she carries some light armor in the body work. As for directions, I'll drive you."

"Not necessary."

Darren smiled sheepishly. "I'm afraid it is, sir. I'm supposed to escort you and chauffeur you whenever you leave the embassy grounds. If the secret service wants to lean on you, they'll be less apt to do it with a consulate staff member as a witness."

Waring considered it for a second, then nodded. "Let's do it, then."

Darren hurried to a booth at the far end of the garage, unzipping the coverall. "Give me a minute to wash up and ring upstairs."

"I'd just as soon you didn't do that."

Darren looked at him earnestly. "It's my job, sir. If I don't let my relief know I'm off the grounds, I'm in deep shit. The garage has to be manned by someone."

Waring's eyes narrowed. "As long as he's the only person you talk to."

"It will be, sir. You have my word."

JORG WEISENBURG had been an early riser for most of his life. But after the death of his wife two years previously and the diagnosis of his heart condition, he tended to sleep until ten or so every morning.

When Inga, his wife of 47 years had died, Weisenburg had found fewer reasons to get out of bed at all, much less at the crack of dawn. Though The Brotherhood had given him something of a new purpose, he still felt hollow.

Julius's scheme had been an interesting diversion, a tactical problem to solve. He had involved himself with it primarily to interrupt the tedium of his daily life. He consciously did not dwell on the repercussions if it was successful or unsuccessful.

When he awoke at a little before ten, he heaved himself out of bed and turned on his favorite mid-morning news program while his breakfast tea was steeping. He was unprepared for what he saw and heard, and his own reaction to it.

The usual banal banter between the program's hosts was absent—instead, on the screen of the small flatscreen TV on the kitchen wall were scenes of carnage—tongues of fire licking from the ground floor window of a building that was horrifyingly familiar, the sound of gunfire, running figures outlined by flames and the flashing lights of official vehicles, and an on-the-spot correspondent speaking excitedly about the unbelievable events occurring at Der Nachisessen Anstalt. A news ticker across the bottom of the screen told him that the video had been shot several hours before, in the pre-dawn hours.

Weisenburg's weak heart gave several painful spasms. He gasped and sank into a kitchen chair, his face suddenly filmed by cold sweat. Blood pounded so loudly in his ears that he almost missed a second report of a massacre at a local hospital late the previous night.

With trembling hands, he reached for his medicine box and gulped the pills that would restore his heartbeat to its normal rhythm.

His thoughts raced wildly, out of control. He thought about all the microwave emitters he had constructed and stored at the clinic—he thought about Hito, who he was very fond of, and he thought about poor deranged Ulrich, who he admired but feared, who lived there.

Then he wondered why he had not been apprised of the raid on the clinic. He didn't dare call Hito, so he phoned Julius on his secured office line. There was no answer, which was disturbing since Julius was punctual to the point of anal retentiveness about being at his office at nine sharp, every morning.

He called the general switchboard of Hauser and Hochbach and was connected to Julius's secretary, who told him that Herr Eicke had not yet arrived. She seemed a little puzzled, but not concerned.

Weisenburg was more than concerned, he felt frantic. He dialed Julius's home,—the man old man did not carry a cell phone—there was no answer, even though any one of five servants should have picked up.

Weisenburg stared at the TV. On the screen, a young man, face covered with blood, was being rushed past the cameras toward a waiting ambulance. He looked very young. Memories of Dresden, of the Russian assault on Berlin, filled his mind.

He suddenly felt so repulsed by the images and memories of violence that he nearly vomited. It was no longer a game or an intellectual or engineering puzzle. It was terrifying, sickeningly real.

He could think of only one reason why he couldn't reach Julius—the man was either in custody or in flight, leaving him, Hito and Ulrich to fend off the authorities who would shortly be baying at their doors.

Moving faster than he had in years, Weisenburg rushed into his bedroom and began tossing clothes into an overnight bag. He made sure he had his passport and sufficient cash. He didn't want to use credit cards, since that would leave a paper trail. He dressed quickly and carelessly and trotted to the front door. Fragments of a plan began to take shape in his mind— he would take a taxi to the airport and book passage on a flight to Brazil—no, Canada—no, Switzerland—no, he wouldn't take a flight at all, he would pay the cabman to drive him to Poland. All this careened through Weisenburg's brain as he locked the front door and turned to leave the stoop.

"Professor Jorg Weisenburg?" a cold voice asked behind him.

His heart gave a great lurch. The world seemed to tilt to one side then the other. When it steadied, he felt strangely calm and he turned around slowly, attempting an air of dignity.

"I am he." Since the voice addressed him in English, he would respond in kind.

A tall man stood at the bottom of the stoop. He was dark-haired, with eyes like chunks of blue ice. The hawk like face, though dispassionate and cold with resolve, was not cruel or brutal. This man was a professional, and Weisenburg decided to extend him professional courtesy.

"Who are you, sir?" he asked.

"My name is Waring," the man said. "I need to ask you a few questions about solid-state hardware. Microwave emitters, specifically."

"I am not under arrest?"

"I don't have that authority, sir, though I'm sure it can be arranged."

"I understand." Weisenburg saw a yellow Mercedes parked behind the man at the curb. "Shall I accompany you?"

"Yes, to the American consulate."

"Sehr gut."

Weisenburg stepped down to the sidewalk. The man glanced down at the bag in his hand.

"Going someplace, Professor?"

Weisenburg laughed. His relief was such that he felt almost giddy. "Ja, ja, I am. With you, remember?"

Waring was a little surprised by the man's attitude and behavior. He had half-expected not to find him home, and if he did, to encounter stiff-lipped German resistance. Weisenburg had the air of a man who had been harboring a secret for a very long time, and now welcomed the opportunity to share it with someone, anyone.

A closed delivery truck, painted a drab olive green, suddenly rolled forward. Waring had noticed it parked a hundred yards down the block when he arrived, and had pointed it out to Darren.

Taking Weisenburg's arm, Waring quickly pulled him to the side of the stoop behind a four-foot high brick wall that doubled as a planter. Weisenburg allowed himself to be led without question or protest.

The truck accelerated and roared past them. As it came abreast, two ports in the cargo compartment suddenly slid open. Waring pushed Weisenburg down behind the wall just as machine gun barrels were thrust out of each port. Darren threw the Mercedes into reverse and backed up, shouting something at Waring which he couldn't catch.

The whole street filled with the staccato hammering of autofire. Lead swept across the front of the ornamental wall, punching craters into it, shredding flowers and smashing the front windows of Weisenburg's home.

Even before the machine guns began to chatter, Waring had thrown himself over Weisenburg, behind the shelter of the wall. The Ruger was in his hand. The truck raced past and jolted to a stop fifty feet up the street with a whine of brakes. The guns stopped stuttering. Its driver maneuvered the truck around in a U-turn, intending to come back for another broadside.

Waring came to his knees and fired a round at the truck. The bullet glanced off the side. It was armored. The truck had halfway completed the turn.

Waring took a breath and held it. He steadied his gun hand on the top of the wall. The sound of the truck faded into nothing. He closed his ears to it. He brought one of the gun ports on the truck's opposite side into target acquisition. The small, rivet-rimmed oval was clear and sharp. In the center was the slender black barrel of the machine gun.

He shifted the blades of the front and rear sights a fraction to the right. The tension in his mouth relaxed. His eyes took a dreamy quality. Waring squeezed the trigger. He fired three shots, all in the space of three quarters-of-a-second.

Three bullets tore through the right-hand gun port, entering an area that could have been covered by the palm of child's hand. The distance was a hundred feet.

The gun barrel withdrew in a jerky, convulsive fashion. The second barrel was pulled back smoothly.

The truck completed its turn, seemed to hesitate, then roared on past. Waring stood up, pulling the white-faced Weisenburg to his feet. Darren leapt from the Mercedes, a Browning .45 caliber automatic held in both hands. Assuming the Webber combat stance, he fired several rounds at the retreating truck. He only stopped shooting when Waring shouted at him.

"Forget it, it's like a tank," he said. "And we've attracted enough attention for the morning."

People were streaming from their homes, opening windows, shouting questions and yelling for someone to call the police.

Waring manhandled Weisenburg into the rear of the Mercedes and got in beside him. "Put your hands where I can see them, Professor."

Weisenburg obediently placed his shaking hands on his knees. Darren climbed back behind the wheel. He was enraged.

"Let's get after these motherfuckers!"

"Just what I had in mind," Waring said.

As Darren threw the Mercedes into pursuit down Lindenalle, Weisenburg kept his eyes glued to the floorboards.

"They were after you," said Waring.

"Ja. I suspected as much. But who are 'they'?"

"You don't know?"

Softly, Weisenburg said, "Not Hito."

"No, not Hito Asoka. He's dead."

The Mercedes took a curve with a squealing of rubber. Weisenburg grabbed blindly at an arm rest. His eyes filled with tears.

"Dead...how?"

"Shot through the back of the head with a .38."

Weisenburg took a deep gulp of air. "Who did it?"

"I don't know. In his last moments, he was in the company of an old man in a wheelchair."

Weisenburg sat frozen for a moment, then whispered, "Ulrich."

"Ulrich?"

"Ulrich Schreck. The spiritual leader of der Schwarze Sonne. A brilliant strategist."

"How does Julius Eicke fit into this?"

Before Weisenburg could answer, Darren wrenched the wheel and the Mercedes swung west at a corner. They gained rapidly on the truck. The area the vehicles raced through was an industrial district, containing large, ugly red brick chemical works, and vacant lots. Overgrown walls, many bearing seventy year old bullet scars, reared from the weed-choked ground.

The truck turned to the left around the corner of a soot-stained factory wall. Beyond it, Waring saw docks and the waters of the Landwehrkanal.

Darren eased off on the gas and the Mercedes slowed to a crawl. It slowly nosed around the corner of the building. There, facing the Mercedes, not more than 200 feet away, stood the armored truck.

Waring was so intent on it, he didn't notice Darren reaching down and fiddling with a knob on the dash. A sheet of partition glass lunged up between the seats. With a pneumatic hiss and a thump, its top edge slid into the narrow metal channel running the width of the roof.

It was a standard feature of government vehicles that might have to transport prisoners.

Face taut, Waring tried the door. It wouldn't open. He reached across Weisenburg and grasped the left-hand door latch. It was locked from the dash controls.

Bringing out the Ruger, he reversed it and struck the partition with the butt. Not surprisingly, the glass did not even crack, much less break. He knew every window in the Mercedes was bulletproof.

Darren looked over his shoulder. His face was expressionless. He brought the car to a full stop and climbed out. He left the engine running.

"What is going on?" Weisenburg asked. "I don't understand."

"I'm afraid I do," said Waring.

Without looking back, Darren casually approached the truck. He paused to light a cigarette, shielding the lighter from the breeze with a hand, then continued on toward it. He waved at the cab.

One of the gun-ports in the cargo compartment opened, a burst of autofire chewed up the asphalt, tracked Darren, caught him and sent him reeling backward, arms windmilling, clothes flapping as though he faced stiff wind. He fell onto his back, arms outflung, the cigarette still burning between the fingers of his right hand.

"Leiber Gott," Weisenburg croaked.

The telephone hooked on the back of the front seat suddenly rang. Weisenburg jumped at the sound of it. Waring picked it up. Without preamble, a voice spoke. It was the same sharp tones he had heard outside of the shower room.

"We've never been formally introduced, but I had to speak with you nonetheless."

"Didn't we exchange a few words earlier this morning?"

"Wunderbar, you recognize me. I wasn't sure if you would, with all the other distractions."

"Is this Schreck?"

There was a moment of silence, then: "You deduced my identity with Jorg's help, I imagine."

"Do you want to talk to him?"

"No need. I had him marked for expulsion. It is my good fortune that I snared both of you in the same net."

"I take it you're in the truck?"

"Yes. I was forced to fire the gun that killed your driver, since you seriously wounded Otto. You are a magnificent marksman."

"Darren was a member of your Brotherhood?"

There was a burst of genuinely amused laughter from the receiver. "By no means. He was simply one of a network of contacts we maintain in embassies of many countries all over the world. Normally, they are not asked to compromise their positions so blatantly, but he was such a greedy young man, I knew tempting him with the promise of a fortune and a new identity would be sufficient for him to completely betray his country."

"Honor Is Loyalty," Waring intoned.

"For very few, I'm afraid. Today, most men are loyal only to themselves."

"What you're loyal to is obvious, Schreck. Like the Dag."

There was pain in Schreck's reply. "Yes. I realize that by killing you, I may forfeit an opportunity to have it again in the Brotherhood's power, but I cannot risk leaving it in your possession. If I cannot have it, I must have your life. You are a warrior, and its energy cleaves to you, it inspires you, it alters probabilities. You should have died in Brazil, you should have died many times in the clinic, but the power of the Dag was with you. I cannot have that power turned against me. The energy circuit you share with the Dag must be broken, and regretfully, that means you must die."

"You're afraid of me, is that it?"

"Do not seek to draw me into a —what is the word?— macho debate. Yes, I am afraid of you, nor am I ashamed to admit it. Without the Dag, you are a nuisance. With it, you are a true threat to my plans, to the very existence of the Brotherhood."

"What *are* your plans, Schreck?"

"Don't be a fool!" Schreck's voice was angry, insulted. "You think I'm the villain of the type of cheap cinematic melodramas you Americans love so much? You think I'll reveal anything to you before you die?"

"How are you going to arrange our deaths? Another Gunn oscillator?"

"No, none of Jorg's toys today. This is a simple explosive device, nothing too fancy. Half a kilo of Titadyne attached to the oil pan of your car. The device is hooked to the battery which, obviously, you cannot reach. When I hang up, the timing apparatus of the bomb, which is connected to the fan of the motor, will be set in motion. Thirty seconds after I break the connection, the Titadyne will explode."

"You're a good one to talk about melodrama, Schreck. Why go to all this trouble?"

There was a sigh. "It is not every man whose mind, whose heart is pure and fierce enough to tap into the energies of the Dag. Such a man is owed explanations. Auf wiedershen, warrior. I salute you."

The voice ceased speaking. A dial tone buzzed out of the receiver. Waring replaced it on the hook and glanced at his wristwatch.

"Are we just going to sit here?" Weisenburg asked.

"Only for another twenty-eight seconds, Professor."

FIFTEEN

TWENTY-EIGHT seconds wasn't much time to formulate a plan. It wasn't even worth using the phone to call anyone, since all Waring had time for was to give a very brief overview of how and why he and Weisenburg came to be blown to bits.

But because The Falcon was one of those men who by nature must keep on fighting while there remained any chance at all, he swung swiftly into action. The bomb might detonate while he was making the attempt, but he had to take the chance.

He raised the Ruger and smashed out the plastic covering of the dome light in the roof of the Mercedes. With steady fingers, he unscrewed the small bulb and dropped it to the floor.

He jacked a round out of the Ruger. He spit on it, making sure it was wet all the way around. Then he thrust the bullet up into the empty bulb socket, jamming it against the two terminals.

There was a tiny flash of blue sparks as the current passed through the wet copper and short-circuited the electrical system. Schreck's words about breaking power circuits had given him the idea.

The motor jerked, and ceased to throb.

Waring sat and waited. Less than fifteen seconds remained. If the fan-belt continued a full revolution after the engine stopped, it would still actuate the timing mechanism, and detonate the bomb. Another three seconds passed.

And nothing happened..

The voltage from the battery to the timing mechanism had been cut off, so the bomb would not explode.

"Why did you do that?" Weisenburg asked, frowning.

Waring didn't answer. He looked over at the truck. When Schreck realized the car's engine was no longer running, more than likely he would command a more direct assault. He wasn't sure if a bullet striking the Titadyne beneath the Mercedes chassis would detonate it but he didn't want to find out.

Telling Weisenburg to crouch down and protect his face, he raised the Ruger and emptied it at the partition. The gun thundered in the close confines of the Mercedes in a deafening rhythm.

The bulletproof glass resisted the bullets, catching them in its polymer coating. Cracks spread in a network of interconnecting lines, but it did not break.

But Waring had blasted a crude "X" pattern across the face of the partition, putting several rounds into the center, where the lines intersected.

Leaning back, bracing himself against the seat, he launched a straight leg kick at the center of the "X". From the corner of his eye, he saw the truck lurch into motion.

Waring kicked again, ignoring the needles of pain shooting up from his ankle to the knee. The partition gave a bit. He kicked again, and the pane of glass folded inward, the top edge popping out of the slot on the ceiling.

Leaning forward, he grasped the top and threw all his adrenaline-charged strength into wrenching and yanking the partition down and from side-to-side. He managed to open a space large enough for him to fight and elbow his way through from the back to the front seat.

To Waring's surprise and relief, the truck gave the Mercedes a wide berth, rolling past it and toward the street between the factory buildings. In retrospect, it wasn't so surprising—the Mercedes was armored, and shooting at it would be a waste of time. Ramming it with the truck would cause the bomb to go off, and damage their own vehicle. Until the bomb was disarmed, Waring couldn't start the car and pursue them.

With the dash control, he unlocked the back door allowing Weisenburg to get out. Waring quickly crawled beneath the chassis of the Mercedes to get a look at the device.

"What was all that about?" Weisenburg wanted to know.

While Waring examined the package, he briefly explained to the old man about the bomb. Like Schreck had said, the explosive device wasn't fancy. Two receiver leads ran from the battery to a timed detonator. The smaller of the wires belonged to the telephone recharging pack.

To be on the safe side, Waring crawled back out, raised the hood and disconnected the clamp from the positive terminal before he pulled the receiver from the detonator. He simply yanked the telephone lead from it. The package itself was wrapped in woven fiberglass and attached to the undercarriage by a pair of thin tin straps bolted to the frame. Judging by the crooked bolts, Darren hadn't completely affixed it to the chassis when Waring came upon him in the garage.

With the blade of his pocketknife, Waring easily sawed through the straps and carefully slid the package out from beneath the car. Though he was impatient to get started after Schreck, he couldn't leave the bomb lying around for someone to stumble over.

Gingerly, as though he were walking on eggshells, Waring carried the package over to the bank of the canal, both hands gripping the edges. When he reached the lip of the waterway, Waring gently heaved the bomb up and away from him. Then, he dropped flat, covering his head with both arms.

The package struck the water with a splash, floated for a second, then tipped onto one end. It started to sink.

A geyser of water twenty feet high suddenly appeared where the package had been, and the slamming concussion nearly rolled Waring over. Echoes of the explosion rolled back from the factory buildings like the thunder of distant artillery. Water, muck and a few fish rained down.

It was still raining when Waring sprang to his feet and dashed back to the Mercedes. He quickly reconnected the battery, slammed down the hood and jumped in behind the wheel. He told Weisenburg to get in beside him.

The Mercedes roared through the industrial district, Waring paying no heed to speed limit signs.

"Where would Schreck be going, Professor?," he asked.

Weisenburg shook his head miserably. "I don't know."

"To Eicke's home or office?"

"Perhaps. I doubt it." Weisenburg massaged his temples. "Ulrich must have gone mad. Or senile."

"Why do you doubt it?"

Weisenburg started to say something, then clamped his mouth shut.

Waring turned to face him, eyes shining with a hell-light, lips drawn back from his teeth. "Answer me, goddammit! I just saved your life and I'm calling in the marker!"

Weisenburg was shaken by the sudden blast of fury, unexpected from a man who seemed to practice an icy self-control.

"The only thing at Eicke's office is the telemetry box," Weisenburg said, speaking so rapidly his words tumbled over each other. "But only Julius can get to it."

"Why?"

"It's in a safe, electronically keyed to open by his fingertips."

"The telemetry box would trigger the launch of the missiles?"

"Ja, but that wasn't our plan. That would have been foolish, because of the limited range."

"You were running a bluff, is that it?"

"A bluff? I don't understand—oh, ja. We never intended to launch the things."

"Even though you could."

"Ja, but it was simply a fulcrum, a way to impose a balance of terror—"

The cellular phone on the dashboard rang. Waring snatched it off the hook, wondering if it might be Schreck again.

"Who is this?" Jacobs' voice.

"Waring."

"Where the fuck is Darren?"

Waring didn't respond to the question. He said, "I'm with Jorg Weisenburg—"

"I know," said Jacobs acidly. "I've already received the report about the shootout in front of his home. You'd better get your ass back here, Waring. Solezer is ready to have your balls removed, bronzed and used as a paperweight."

"Find Julius Eicke. Weisenburg tells me that the telemetry box controlling the birds is at Hauser and Hochbach."

"Eicke has been found," replied Jacobs. "At his home. Shot through the brain and mutilated."

"Mutilated? How?"

"Some sick sonofabitch cut off his right hand."

Pressing the receiver to his chest, Waring asked Weisenburg, "The fingertips of which of Eicke's hands opens the safe?"

Weisenburg's brow furrowed. "I believe it is his right hand."

Waring put the receiver to his ear again. "Major, I don't have time to explain, but if you can reach Solezer, tell him to get a unit to Hauser and Hochbach and be on the lookout for an olive-green delivery truck."

"Why?"

"And while you're at it, see if Solezer knows anything about a Ulrich Schreck."

"Goddammit, Waring—"

Waring hung up.

Under his steady questioning, Weisenburg told Waring the most direct route to Hauser and Hochbach, and admitted there was a secret entrance from an alley through a basement, though he had never used it. He seemed confused, disoriented, and would occasionally mutter the name "Inga."

Waring sent the Mercedes flashing through the traffic, running as many red lights as he dared. After about 20 minutes, they reached Wilhelmstrasse.

"There it is," said Weisenburg, pointing to an old, three-story building with a gabled roof.

It was something of an oddity on the street, surrounded as it was by trendy boutiques and eight-story apartment buildings. There was no sign of the armored truck.

Waring circled the block and slowly passed the mouths of several alleys, most of which were service entrances to the shops and stores. Then he saw the truck, parked facing away from the street, but butted up against a wrought-iron fence between the side of the Hauser and Hochbach building and an apartment complex.

Waring cruised down the street and parked. He inserted a full clip into the Ruger and chambered a round. Weisenburg gave him vague directions to the secret basement entrance, apologizing that he didn't know more.

"I do not understand," he said. "Why is Ulrich here? Julius wouldn't give him the telemetry box, and even Ulrich isn't foolish enough to start something in full view of the employees and clients."

Grimly, Waring said, "Julius is dead. Ulrich or one of his Hitler Youth cut off his right hand. If what you've told me is true, he's sneaking in the back way, into the conference room, using Eicke's hand to open the safe, take the box and sneak out again. No one would be the wiser—until a lot of your countrymen are vaporized by a thermonuclear blast."

Weisenburg's mouth gaped open. He stared at Waring uncomprehendingly.

"I suggest you phone and your secret service and give yourself up. Otherwise, Ulrich will only try to have you killed again. And the next time, I may not be around."

Waring got out of the car and walked quickly to the alley. The truck's engine was idling, so someone had been left behind. Making sure he was positioned in such a way that a man in the cab could not spot him in the rear or side-view mirrors, Waring reached the rear bumper and belly-crawled beneath it. It was a tight fit, and the diesel fumes nearly made him cough, but he navigated the length of the vehicle until he was directly beneath the cab.

Turning over onto his back, he listened for a moment, straining to catch any sound. He heard a muffled cough.

Waring inched out from beneath the truck. The driver's side door was directly above him. With his left hand, he reached up and rapped very loudly on the door, in the "shave-and-a-haircut" rhythm.

Scuffling and a voice cursing in surprise sounded above him. The shocks creaked and the door was flung open. A hard-faced man with bushy eyebrows looked around, a Glock 17 in his hand.

Waring shot him through the underside of the jaw. He fell down across the seats. He wasn't worried about the gunshot being heard, since the traffic noise was so heavy, the sound would probably be attributed to a backfire.

Getting to his feet, Waring reached in and turned the ignition key off. The motor stopped, and he removed the keys, putting them in his pocket.

Stepping into the cab, he thrust open the small hatch separating it from the cargo compartment, hoping that Schreck would be there.

He wasn't, no one was. He saw blood stains on the walls and metal flooring, but then Schreck had told him he had wounded a man named Otto.

He went to the fence, found an unlocked gate and pushed it open. Set flush with the facade of the Hauser and Hochbach building he saw a short set of stone steps leading down to a cellar door.

Waring had no idea how many men he was facing. Not counting Schreck, he had seen four of the mercenaries leaving the clinic. He had just now accounted for another, so that left only three to contend with—assuming that no more mercenaries had escaped the raid and joined up with them.

There was only one way to find out. Waring went down the steps on the balls of his feet and tried the knob. It was unlocked.

He inched the door open.

His eyes roved over the maze of rusting pipes running at all angles about the room. A large, cracked porcelain sink was attached to a wall. The flagstones on the floor all seemed undisturbed.

Waring walked in warily, senses alert. He heard nothing but the sounds from the street outside. Weisenburg did not know where the concealed door to the passage leading to the conference room was located, but Waring made an educated guess.

He reached the sink, tugged and twisted at the faucet handles and a section of wall behind the sink swiveled open with a crunch of hidden pivots.

Waring wasn't surprised. It stood to reason that the designers of the hidden doors at the clinic were the same people and would lean toward standardized specs.

Peering around the edge of the panel, Waring saw only a narrow flight of wooden steps leading up into musty darkness. He put one foot into the passageway and onto the second step. It creaked slightly.

Over his head came a faint whoosh, a glint of some dark metal, and a stinging force ripped the Ruger from his hand.

SIXTEEN

WARING FLUNG himself backward, trying to shake some feeling back into his numbed hand. He heard his pistol skidding across the rough floor somewhere behind him.

A large red-haired man sprang from the narrow stairwell, whirling a kind metal flail or whip around in his right hand. It was a series of iron rods, linked together by metal rings. The handle was wrapped around with leather, and at the end was a heavy iron weight with beveled edges. It was about five feet long.

Waring recognized the contraption as a kau sin ke, a Chinese hand weapon which could deliver a lethal, bone-crushing blow. He recognized the man using it as one of the guests at Eicke's party.

The man smiled with genuine enjoyment. "I've been waiting for you. The men you shot down were my friends."

Waring backed away, keeping his eyes on the man's feet. The whirling pieces of metal hummed through the air in a blurry circle. He knew better than to stare at it, because the spinning motion induced a mild hypnotic effect.

"What's your name?" he asked.

"What difference does that make, Amerikanner?"

"I always want to know the names of every asshole I kill."

This man's reaction was different from that of Xauz. He was a professional. He merely grinned in appreciation.

"The name I go by is Ernst. It's not my real name, but it'll do until I come up with a better one."

Waring nodded. "I can relate to that."

He feinted to the left, then leaped to the right, pivoted and swung his left leg up and around in a perfect crescent kick.

Ernst surged forward in the opposite direction. Waring's boot grazed his head, but the weighted end of the kau sin ke slapped into Waring's ribs, smashing all the wind out of him and knocking him backward.

Trying to ignore the needles of intense pain lancing up his rib-cage, fighting for breath, Waring recovered his balance. His eyes searched the cellar floor for the Ruger.

Ernst snapped the jointed lengths of iron at him like a bullwhip. Waring ducked, and the weighted end crashed into the wall, knocking a fist-sized chunk of stone out of it.

While Ernst reeled in the kau sin ke, Waring launched himself forward. Doubling the metal rods, the German met Waring's attack by whacking him across the midsection. Dazed and nauseated, Waring managed to shift the weight of his body, and he caromed against Ernst, grabbing a handful of shirt as he went down. Both men fell heavily, Ernst striking his head against the flagstones.

Waring struggled and heaved and achieved a kneeling position atop the German. He pinioned Ernst's right wrist under his knee. With his free hand, Ernst gouged savagely at Waring's eyes. Batting aside the hand, Waring dashed a straight right into the snarling face under him and started a flow of blood from the lips.

With a twist and sidewise wrench of his whole body, Ernst managed to shove Waring to one side and club at him with the doubled kau sin ke. The blow glanced off Waring's raised forearm. He rolled and came swiftly to his feet and planted a boot on the side of Ernst's neck as he tried to rise.

The man went over on his back, but he unleashed the full length of the kau sin ke in a snake-like strike directly at Waring's head. Waring leaned backward, and the weighted end only brushed the collar of his jacket. Arcing past him, it crashed to the floor, fracturing a flagstone.

Thrown off-balance, Ernst tried to lift the heavy rods for a back-hand blow, but Waring took a quick step forward and kicked hard at his hand.

Ernst yelled with pain, and his fingers slackened around the leather-bound handle. Waring kicked the kau sin ke out of the way.

Ernst hugged his broken wrist, and his left hand groped for some-thing on his right hip. He yelled again, raising his voice. "In dieser Richtung, der Amerikanner—"

Waring slashed down with a stiffened palm, his right arm like a pile driver. The edge of his hand chopped into the base of Ernst's neck. With a liquid gurgle, Ernst sagged to the floor and made no further motion.

Waring wasn't sure if he was breathing or not, and at the moment he didn't give much of a damn. Patting him down, he found a Glock holstered behind his right hip. He removed it, made sure there was a round in the chamber, looked around the basement and found the Ru-ger in a dim corner.

Checking to make sure it hadn't picked up any dirt or grit, Waring squeezed into the passage behind the sink and climbed the stairs as quickly but as quietly as he could.

It was very dark, but ahead and above he saw a thread-thin, rectangular outline of light. Reaching the panel at the top of the stairs, Waring put his ear against the wood. He heard a distant murmur of voices. He pushed against it gently. It gave beneath his hand, and he swung it open just enough so he could see where he was.

He saw three mercenaries, standing on one side of a long conference table. Two were armed, one with a sawed-off shotgun under his arm, the other shouldering one of the HK-94 auto carbines. Both had their attention riveted to a broad-shouldered man with long blond hair who faced a square steel safe door set into the wall. There was no sign or sound of Schreck. Apparently, the Germans had just recently arrived at Hauser and Hochbach, even though they had at least a fifteen minute head start on him. He guessed that dropping Schreck off somewhere had delayed them.

As Waring watched, the blond man removed an object from beneath his coat. It was wrapped in cloth, and it was soaked through with rust-red stains. The man undid the wrappings. revealing a human hand, severed at the wrist. Blood still dripped sluggishly from the ragged stump of the wrist.

The mercenary pressed four fingers of the amputated hand against a dark strip of glass running the width of door. The safe swung open smoothly. The men exchanged grins and words in German.

The blond man dropped the hand carelessly on the floor, reached in and removed a black box. He held it carefully, almost reverently.

Waring kicked the panel open.

All hell broke loose, which he had expected.

What he didn't expect was a fourth man in position against the opposite wall, armed with an auto carbine. He fired first, a steel-jacketed spray that ruined the old and artfully carved oak-paneling.

Waring went to his knees behind a chair at the end of the table, and his two automatics began to roar in a beautifully synchronized rhythm.

A pair of slugs hit the man holding the shotgun with a one-two punch, knocking him backward and forcing the sawed barrels up into the air. They blasted thunderously.

As plaster dribbled down from the ceiling like a heavy snowfall, a burst of autofire splintered the panel behind Waring, and he fell flat to the floor, lunging beneath the table. His tender rib-cage twinged, but he crawled forward, pistols blazing, pushing himself along with his knees and the sides of his feet.

A line of bullets spewed from an HK-94, thudding into the table, but not penetrating the thick slab of mahogany. Waring kept crawling and kept firing. The walls of the conference room beat the thunder of gunfire back and magnified it.

He saw one of the men jerk and double over. He fell face down barely four feet from Waring, rendered unconscious by the shock of triple shots fired at such close quarters.

Waring watched two pairs of feet and legs rush through the big carved door at the end of the room. Waring fired the Glock, and the bullet dug into the wall by the door frame, barely missing one leg by a fraction.

Waring rolled out from beneath the table and came to his feet in the same, lithe motion. He rushed through the door and almost came to a halt.

He found himself in a huge office suite, holding perhaps fifty desks, some enclosed by partitions, all with computer terminals. Word processing clerks, telephone salespeople, all gaped at the men racing through the room. At the far end Waring saw a glassed-in row of offices where a group of surprised executives sat.

Most of the people, men and women, had stopped working and stared at Waring and the men he was pursuing. They shrank away from them as they pounded past.

A uniformed guard wearing a Sam Browne belt with a holstered revolver walked through the far door. When he saw the three running men, two nearly atop him and one wielding an automatic rifle, he went for his sidearm. The auto carbine chattered, punching several holes in the man's shirtfront.

Immediately, screaming pandemonium exploded in the busy office. Women began to shriek, men shouted and took shelter beneath their desks, computer terminals toppled. More than a few ran in heedless, panicked flight between Waring and the mercenaries.

He wasn't about to witness a repetition of innocent people being caught in a crossfire as had happened at the clinic, so Waring held his fire and allowed the men to run through the office. He lost precious seconds dodging people, guns held in both hands.

When he reached the main corridor, he leaped left and forward on his stomach, sliding on the slick marble floor like a baseball player on his way to home plate. The impulsive move saved his life.

Before he had quite hit the floor, he heard the stuttering of the auto carbine, and the clanging impact of the bullets striking the bronze frame of the door behind him.

The man with the HK-94 had been laying for him, covering his companion with the black box.

The slide took Waring fifteen feet down the smooth surface of the floor. As he slid, he fired, working the triggers of both automatics. Ejected shells clattered on the marble in his wake.

Every bullet Waring fired pierced the body of the mercenary. He slammed backward into a decorative pillar. Bouncing from it, he staggered forward, right into a final shot that hammered him between the eyes and emptied the Glock.

Waring didn't wait to see the mercenary fall. Dropping the Glock, he was up and sprinting down the wide corridor toward a rear window, high up from the floor. He could see that the window was open and could also see the blond man scrambling frantically to get through it and out, encumbered as he was with the black box tucked under one arm. It seemed heavier than it looked.

Waring got there just in time to catch the tail of the man's coat as it slid outside onto a fire escape. That would have been enough if the coat had held, but it didn't.

Waring heard the ripping of fabric, an angry cry in German, and he staggered backward from the force of his pull. He had almost the complete coat in his hands, but he saw no one in the window or the fire escape beyond. He heard running steps on the metal steps.

Waring jumped the five feet up to the window sill and swung his body over and out onto the fire escape. He heard police sirens and the squeal of tires from the front of the building and he hoped it was Solezer's people.

Breathing hard, he ran down the fire escape, pausing at each landing to see if he could get a clean shot at the mercenary. The crisscrossing steel beams and walkways blocked him. He knew the man was probably armed, and he also suspected that he had an escape route already plotted, one that didn't include the truck. That vehicle was too easy to spot and too cumbersome to maneuver.

Weisenburg had described Schreck as a brilliant strategist, and that seemed true. The man had anticipated almost every other contingency, so Waring assumed such a crucial mission as recovering the telemetry box wouldn't be left to chance, even it was an eleventh hour plan.

Between the metal slats, Waring glimpsed the German dropping the last few feet from the fire escape to an enclosed courtyard below. He saw him run a few feet, and whirl, the inevitable Glock in his right hand.

It spat noise and flame. Just as he fired, Waring vaulted over the rail of the landing and dropped beneath the shot.

He took a hard fall onto the cement, one that brought a sharp pain to his ribs. He heard men shouting urgently on the other side of the courtyard.

Climbing to his feet, he raced after the mercenary who continued to fire at him without aiming. No bullets came anywhere near him, but when an amplified voice bellowed from behind him through a bull horn, Waring realized the shots served as an alarm to the polizei converging around the Hauser and Hochbach building.

A shot sounded from behind him and the bullet slashed a long white scar on the cement a few feet in front of him. He cast a quick glance over his shoulder, and saw men in black uniforms climbing over the wall of the courtyard. One drew a bead on him with his service pistol.

As far as the Berlin police officers knew, Waring was one of the men who had shot and killed the security guard upstairs. If Solezer had enlisted their aid, he had told them that the intruders would be armed and dangerous. The events at the clinic were only a few hours old, and no one could really blame the police for subscribing, even temporarily, to the "shoot first and get a statement later" school.

Deliberately or by happenstance, matters had been arranged to put Waring at odds with the local law, odds which very well could prove fatal.

He saw the mercenary reach the low wall encircling the courtyard, bound to the top and roll over it, automatic in one hand, the black box in the other. Waring put on speed, but another shot from behind him struck the wall and sprayed stinging grains of stone into his face.

Whirling, Waring fired three rounds, shooting over the heads of the police. The shots were close, for he wanted them to duck or seek cover—which they did. Waring was able to get over the wall without another shot coming from them.

Waring found himself in a narrow alley. Buildings reared around him for an unbroken block. The blond man raced down the alley as if he knew exactly where he was going.

Waring went after him, ejecting the spent clip from the Ruger and sliding in a full load on the run.

He saw his quarry turn right upon leaving the alley. Waring followed him, then was forced to duck into a sheltering doorway.

The blond mercenary crouched behind the open the passenger door of a late model, battleship grey Volvo. He pointed his automatic at the mouth of the alley. He pumped the trigger four times, random shots that served no purpose other than to keep Waring pinned down.

With a high-pitched engine roar, the Volvo leapt away from the curb. Waring didn't shoot at it. He saw the back of a dark head on the driver's side. He realized he was on the street at the rear of Hauser and Hochbach. The Mercedes was still parked at the curb only a few hundred feet away.

Running toward it, he hoped the men in the Volvo wouldn't spray the tires with gunfire as they passed. Fortunately, the car turned left down another side-street before they came abreast of it.

To Waring's surprise, Weisenburg still sat in the car. As he started it and threw it into reverse, he asked, "Why are you here, Professor?"

"I did what you said. I called the secret service. They're sending a representative to meet me."

"The meeting may have to be postponed."

It didn't occur to Waring that the old physicist may have experienced enough violence and fast action for one day. He was far too valuable as a source of information to let him out of his sight. Waring simply told him to make sure his seat belt was secure and wheeled the Mercedes down the side street after the Volvo.

Waring took the turn just as a group of police officers raced around the corner of the Hauser and Hochbach building, blaring their whistles and waving at him.

His foot jammed the accelerator pedal, and the Mercedes whipped away from the angry cluster of police and took the next corner just as their guns began to blast.

The Volvo was several car lengths ahead on a broad avenue. The noontime traffic was heavy, but not particularly slow. Official vehicles were appearing at almost every intersection. A quick glance in the mirror showed another in the rear.

The Volvo turned right, back in the direction of Wilhelmstrasse. Waring followed, knowing that the men he pursued were intimately familiar with the maze of back alleys and side-streets. They could afford to engage in a cat-and-mouse chase with Waring, but he realized it was one he would lose, particularly with the police added to the mix of players.

Trying to imitate every move of the Volvo took Waring in a zigzag, pretzel course, circling the same blocks over and over.

As the Volvo turned at another corner, a police car rolled into sight, spotting Waring just as he made the swing.

Sirens screamed from the next block, and were answered from the side street.

The men in the Volvo had led Waring into the opposite end of the cordon, which the police formed around the blocks and streets bordering Wilhelmstrasse and the Hauser and Hochbach building.

A police car lunged from the curb and Waring slammed on the brakes. Police leaped from it, brandishing automatics, shouting commands. Waring's hands gripped the wheel, knowing that he might succeed in running the blockade, but not without people dying.

Waring put the car in neutral, placed the Ruger on the dashboard and locked his hands behind his head. Automatics thrust in through the windows, voices growled threats. The doors were jerked open, Weisenburg was hauled out by the collar, Waring by the arms.

He was slapped against the side of the car, frisked roughly, and then spun back around. Solezer stood there, staring at him with bleak grey eyes.

"Cuff him," he said quietly. He spoke in English so Waring would be sure to understand him.

SEVENTEEN

WARING WASN'T in the cuffs for very long, maybe twenty minutes. That was as long as it took for a pair of neatly-dressed men to drive him to a non-descript building not too far from the Europa Centre.

Ushered in through a back entrance, the cuffs were removed just before he was shoved into a small holding cell.

Waring didn't resist the treatment. Little was to be gained by arguing or struggling. Even though he knew Solezer intended to do nothing more than flex his authority as the Verfassungschutz section chief, Waring was only concerned about the delay in getting back to the battle.

Using his jacket as a pillow, Waring lay down on the narrow bunk and waited. He had a pretty good idea of what would happen during the rest of the afternoon.

When Jacobs found out about his detention, he would notify his superior, who would notify someone in Washington, who in turn would notify Herne. After a couple of hours of international telephone calls, some high official in the German government would notify Solezer to stop playing power games and release the American specialist and let him get back to business.

Though not particularly comforted by this scenario, Waring was able to relax enough to fall asleep.

The sound of the door bolt being thrown back awoke him. He didn't know what time it was, but he was sure several hours had passed. One of the neatly-dressed men gestured for him to come out and follow him down a corridor to a frosted glass door.

He opened it, gestured for Waring to enter, then closed it behind him. Waring stood in a busy and crowded room.

Phones rang, fax machines were spewing paper, and cigarette smoke filled the air. Men and women were talking, studying maps, jogging back and forth with sheaves of paper in their hands.

Waring had been in enough war rooms to recognize one when he saw it. Obviously this division of the secret service was coordinating their activities with other local law-enforcement and intelligence agencies.

Seeing an open office door, Waring jostled through the crowd toward it. Inside he saw Solezer, Abendroth, Jacobs and Weisenburg. They were seated at a table and glanced up when he entered. All of them looked tense, worried, and in Weisenburg's case, exhausted.

On a desktop against the far wall, Waring saw his equipment cases and his Ruger, snug inside its shoulder holster. He took a chair at the table, asking, "Have you been waiting for me?"

Jacobs cleared his throat. "Yes. There were a few diplomatic feathers that needed to be smoothed first. It's under control."

Solezer's pursed his lips, as though he tasted something extremely sour. "Do not expect an apology from me, Herr Waring."

"I don't. And don't expect one from me."

"Your cowboy tactics could not be tolerated," Solezer said, ignoring Waring's response. "As it is, the news media is harassing the police and my agency unmercifully. They demand answers."

"That's why I made contact with Professor Weisenburg. He may be able to supply some."

All eyes turned toward the old man. His hands were flat on the table and he was staring at them unblinkingly.

"What do you want to know?" Weisenburg's voice was barely above a whisper.

"Some background, first," said Solezer. "How long have you been a member of the Brotherhood of the Black Sun"

"Since the end of the war. Helmut Eicke, who had been my father's S.S. superior at the Reinickendorf West research station, contacted me. I was very angry, very upset by my father's death, by the destruction of Germany. I met Ulrich, Julius, Goetz, Hito and a few others who have since passed away. I was initiated in January, 1947.

"The Brotherhood was explained to me as a society that would isolate the true Aryan race from the rest of substandard humanity. It was a dream that would live on beyond the death of Hitler, which superseded the Third Reich. We would become the true rulers of the earth."

"How was this to come to pass?" Waring asked. He was trying very hard not to be sarcastic.

Weisenburg shrugged. "Through the slow infiltration of decadent political systems, through the use of higher technologies, through cleverness, through simple Aryan superiority."

"What about the higher technologies?" Abendroth asked.

"The German scientific establishment worked exclusively for the military, for the Luftwaffe, the Wehrmacht, the Kriegmarine," Weisenburg replied. "Almost all of that work was concerned with producing advanced weaponry, the so-called 'Nazi secret weapons' that so obsessed the Allies toward the end of the war. One of the major breakthroughs was in the field of electromagnetism, specifically microwaves, building on the work of Tesla and Marconi. My father designed and built an emitter that short-circuited the ignition systems of aircraft engines at a hundred meters. Another emitter was built to ignite flammable materials from a distance.

"My father's intention, aborted by his death in Dresden, was to expand the effective radius of the emitters and at the same time reduce their size. His successors did not have access to his notes, so when the Reinickendorf facility was evacuated and transferred to an underground complex in the Alpine redoubt, most of his research, his prototypes were lost. Helmut Eicke retrieved them and gave them to me."

"And you were so grateful to receive your father's legacy," said Solezer, "you agreed to build on his work for the greater glory of the Brotherhood."

Weisenburg was silent for a moment, then nodded. "That is essentially it, ja."

"That was nearly seventy years ago," said Waring. "Other industries must have made your father's achievements in solid-state physics obsolete."

Anger flickered in Weisenburg's eyes. "Many of his discoveries were duplicated. Some were realized, but never acted upon. Most were employed in a very pedestrian fashion, such as in radar, communications and ovens. Other of my father's discoveries were stumbled across by accident and classified as Top Secret. Your own Navy has experimented with MASER weapons, which are nothing more than microwave emitters."

"How many of these things did you build?" Jacobs asked.

"Ten, twenty, maybe thirty."

"There weren't that many found at the clinic," said Abendroth.

"I wasn't responsible for the storage of the devices," Weisenburg replied. "It would have been unforgivably foolish to keep them all in the same place."

"They weren't all of the same type," she said.

"Quite a few were modifications of my father's prototypes. Others were built using the principles discovered by others."

"Like the Gunn oscillator," said Abendroth.

"Ja."

"Tell us about Ulrich Schreck," Waring said.

A visible shudder shook Weisenburg. "He held the rank of Standartenfuhrer, but he really served as a high priest. As a young man, I idolized him. Later, I feared him. As should you."

"Explain."

"The common assumption is that the true power of the Third Reich was held by Hitler, Himmler, Goering, Bormann and a handful of others. In many ways, the true guiding force behind Germany's war was Ulrich Schreck. I was truly astonished by the extent of the power and influence he wielded.

"Ulrich was regarded as a demigod by both Hitler and Himmler. He was cold and brilliant and relentless, and nearly inhuman. He designed a new world order based on ancient occult principles. He saw the war as not just a struggle for territory or even power, but to restore the planet to its true superhuman rulers."

"What kind of bullshit is this?" Jacobs demanded.

Weisenburg smirked. "The truth was hidden by German technology, German science and German organization. The great innovation of the Third Reich was to mix occultism with technology. Your own government wanted that mix. Why else were so many Nazi scientists imported into America after the war?"

"What did Schreck do after Hitler died?" Waring asked.

"After he executed Hitler, you mean?"

Weisenburg seemed to enjoy the expressions of shock and disbelief on the faces of the people around the table.

"According to Ulrich, he killed him, sacrificed him on April 30, Walpurgis Night, one of the major mystical dates in the old Teutonic religions. He chose that date to restore some balance to the powers Hitler had misused.

"In any event, Ulrich lived in many places around the world. He acted as a liaison between S.S. officers seeking asylum and U.S. and British intelligence, advised the Odessa and as far as I know, helped Josef Mengele stay hidden when all of Israeli intelligence was scouring South America for him."

"Was he the mastermind of this scheme?" Solezer asked.

"Nein, that was Julius. It has been in the planning stages for nearly five years."

"Why so long?"

"Ulrich insisted on waiting until the most favorable time before implementing the project."

"Why was this the most favorable time?" Waring asked.

"Seventy years ago last month, Ulrich, Eric Eicke and Gustav Goetz buried a casket containing the holiest relics of The Brotherhood in a glacier on Hochfeiler peak. The casket was exhumed, but one of the relics was missing, and Ulrich believed our project might not succeed unless it was recovered."

"The Dag," said Waring.

"Ja." Weisenburg stared at him steadily. "He fears its power, fears you because you now wield it."

Impatiently, Jacobs demanded, "Was Avery Simmons a member of this Brotherhood of yours?"

Weisenburg snorted. "Don't be ridiculous. He was simply a pawn. An important one, but a pawn nonetheless."

"Did he cooperate with you willingly?" Solezer asked.

"After a fashion. He was a business and occasional social associate of Julius, you see. During his visits to Julius's office and home, Simmons was subjected to low-level microwave fields, which made him extremely susceptible not only to suggestion, but to behavior modification.

"It required several months of treatment in order to be undetectable, and was not a permanent alteration. That is why Julius more or less overruled Ulrich's objections to implementing the project before the Dag was recovered."

"Who else is involved in this?" Waring asked.

"Aside from me, only Hito and Julius, and a man named deMilteer, who Ulrich killed three days ago. And another man we called Achmet."

"Achmet?" echoed Jacobs.

With a smile, Weisenburg told them Achmet's true name.

"Bullshit!" Jacobs snarled, thumping his fist on the tabletop. "Bullshit!"

"He was very enthusiastic about the project," Weisenburg said, still smiling. "He contributed many millions of dollars to it. However, he may be dead already, since Ulrich is obviously liquidating everyone he considers a security risk."

"Which seems to be everyone but himself," Waring pointed out. "What about the soldiers and the skinheads? How many of them are there?"

Weisenburg shrugged. "The soldiers were Ulrich's province, Julius recruited the young toughs. I don't know the actual numbers."

"Does Schreck understand the workings of the telemetry box?" Abendroth asked.

"There is no reason why he shouldn't. He knows the missiles' rewritten transmission code, and the box is keyed to it."

"How do you think he will employ it?"

Weisenburg shook his head. "I have no idea. The simplest method would be a motorized vehicle equipped with a microwave emitter that could be driven to the general area of the missile site. However, the emitter could just as easily be mounted on an aircraft."

"Do you have any idea where Schreck might be?" Solezer inquired.

"Nein. He could be anywhere in or outside of Berlin. Though I am unaware of its actual location, I was led to believe The Brotherhood maintains a place where aircraft and vehicles are stored."

"I see." Solezer sighed heavily. "Unless you have something to add, Professor, you will be returned to detention."

"Sehr Gut. I am very tired. And hungry."

"I will make sure you are fed."

As he stood up, Abendroth reached out and grabbed his hand. "You're not the slightest bit sorry about any of this, are you?" She sounded more puzzled than angry.

Weisenburg gently pulled away from her. "Iselda, I am too old, too dead inside to be sorry about much of anything."

Solezer walked Weisenburg to the door and turned him over to one of the neatly-dressed men.

Jacobs pinched the bridge of his nose, then massaged his temples. "This is crazy. Just fucking nuts. How the hell do we deal with something like this? This isn't terrorism. This isn't the action of a hostile government. This is insanity."

"At least we have some solid information to go on," Waring said. "And we know the target is Site 611."

Jacobs pulled an attaché case from beneath the table and took a large aerial map from it.

"This is a view of the Site 611 grounds," he said, tapping it. "It's in a pretty inaccessible place. Only one road in and out to the silo itself."

"Where's the main highway?" Waring asked.

"There isn't one. Just a lot of country lanes, cow paths, things like that. The nearest people, dairy farmers, are about six miles away."

"Should be an easy area to stake out," said Waring, studying the map. "With such little traffic, strange vehicles will be easy to stop. Assuming Schreck doesn't come by air."

"The air-space is restricted."

"I doubt he'll let a little thing like that stop him," Waring replied wryly.

"Won't they want to wait for a response to their demands before they take action?" Jacobs asked.

"Nuclear blackmail isn't the plan any longer," Waring said. "It would take too long for results and leaves too much to chance. Government officials can retire, new leaders with different ideas can emerge. Not to mention Schreck isn't getting any younger. He can't afford to wait. He wants to put the show on the road right now."

"You don't think Schreck will try to extract a price?" Solezer asked.

Waring shook his head. "His psychology is fairly simple. My country and yours cares very much about what even one nuclear warhead would do to Germany's population. Schreck could care less. He isn't going to risk a change in the political climate by waiting. The sooner he strikes, the better for him."

"But what can he possibly gain?" Abendroth asked, her eyes shining with fright. "Even the most ardent neo-Nazi wouldn't agree with killing thousands, perhaps hundreds of thousands of our own people and contaminating our Fatherland!"

Solezer ran the tip of his tongue over his very dry lips. "Remember, when Hitler realized that the war was lost, he pursued a scorched earth policy. Three hundred thousand Germans perished when the Berlin U-Bahn, the subway, was flooded on his orders. He required German citizens to raze their own towns, farmers to destroy their stock, bridges to be blown up."

"What was it he said?" Waring asked. " 'Losses can never be too high'?"

"What's that got to do with anything?" Jacobs demanded.

Taking a deep breath, Solezer replied, "Herr Waring said that Schreck's psychology is simple. That it is, but it is also crazed. Ulrich Schreck, with his devotion to occult principles, intends to make Germany and its people a blood sacrifice of truly monstrous proportions."

Waring said grimly, "Like the demigod he believes he is, Schreck wants to be sent with human sacrifices to his grave."

EIGHTEEN

ISELDA UNLOCKED the door to her flat on the second floor. She paused at the threshold, looking around anxiously. A table lamp cast a comforting glow over the living room furniture.

"Clean," she announced to Waring.

He followed her in, his eyes sweeping over the simple but tasteful furnishings. A yellow tabby cat lounging on the arm of the sofa stirred, blinking at the two people incuriously, then went back to sleep.

Iselda laughed with relief touched by nervousness. "If Tesla is this relaxed, then I suppose no ninja assassin is waiting for us."

Waring smiled, "A cat is good barometer of intentions."

"Since he hasn't arched his back and hissed at you," observed Iselda, "I suppose Tesla thinks your intentions are honorable."

"Thanks again for putting me up," Waring said.

"Solezer put you in my custody," Iselda replied. "And it didn't seem like you were welcome at the embassy any longer, either."

"No," admitted Waring. "I tend to wear those out wherever I go."

"A man as charming as you? I find that hard to believe." She grinned to let him know she meant no offense. "Take off your coat—and gun—and relax…if that's something you're able to do. Would you like something to drink?"

"A beer will be fine, thanks."

Waring slipped out of his jacket and shoulder holster, wrapping them all loosely together. Sitting down on the sofa next to Tesla, he absently rubbed the cat between the ears. The animal tolerated the caress.

Iselda returned carrying two mugs of beer, "It's a local brew…a little strong, I'm told."

Waring took the mug, clinked it against hers and took an experimental swallow. He managed to conceal his reaction to the bitter taste.

Sitting down beside him, Iselda sipped tentatively, shuddered and made a face. "Yuck."

"Too strong?"

"Too nasty. Guess I'm not as German as I thought. I suppose I'm more of the orange juice type of German."

Waring grinned. "I'm not much of a drinker myself. It's a liability in my line of work."

Iselda took off her glasses and arched an eyebrow at him. "Sanitation expert?"

"More or less."

Iselda's temper suddenly flared. "Stop being so damned mysterious! You don't always have to be in character!"

"I'm not quite sure what you mean, doctor—"

"—Iselda!" she snapped. "That's my name. Is Michael really yours?"

He hesitated before answering. "More or less."

"Is it more or is it less?"

Waring placed the mug on the coffee table. "You want to know who I am, is that it?"

"Of course, dammit."

After a moment of thoughtful silence, Waring intoned, "Iselda, there are people in the world who actually aren't anyone—they have no family, no past, no genuine connections with anyone, anything or anywhere. They have to invent identities and construct lives."

Iselda frowned. "Faux people?"

He shook his head. "Not necessarily. Their constructions may be bits and pieces they've found along the way, but they're not total fabrications. These people have no choice but to develop their own survival-skill set…and sometimes those skills can be useful to others."

Sympathy softened Iselda's green eyes—then she regarded him distrustfully. "How do I know you're not making that up? For all I know, you could have a wife and six kids in New Jersey."

Waring chuckled. "True…for all8- you know. So it's best we stay strangers. Safer that way."

Iselda's mood suddenly changed. She put her mug on the table and leaned against him. "Why do you have to be this way?" she asked quietly.

"What way?" he asked, adopting her low tone.

"An infuriating bastard."

She tilted her head toward his and her hands linked at the back of his neck. Their lips met with demanding passion. After a long kiss, Iselda stood up, took him by the hand and led him into the bedroom.

Waring carried his gun rolled up in his jacket—just in case ninja assassins came calling.

BY EIGHT PM, Dolf and Veit had changed clothes and cars twice and they were driving along the Reichsautobahn, the National Expressway that covers Germany.

Dolf drove a late model BMW and took an exit that led to the suburb of Spandau. Although the home of the infamous prison, it was also a section of abandoned manufacturing plants, schools and churches. The faces of many of the older buildings were still pockmarked with bullet scars from the house-to-house fighting that had taken place there over a half-century before.

Dolf had several relatives in the area who could still point to the precise spots where invading Russian soldiers had been dropped in their tracks.

Although both Dolf and Veit were fairly young men, they missed the glories of the Third Reich as though they had participated in them. While growing up, they had talked to a number of older Army officers who claimed to have been in the thick of things.

When they were forced out of their careers as internal security agents, they quickly discovered that they were pariahs—not even the polizei wanted them. Even private organizations weren't interested in them. When they were contacted by a mysterious group that had a need for their skills, they asked no questions. Veit, Dolf and many others like them simply joined it.

It was a schizophrenic relationship. Dolf enjoyed his time in the clinic, since he and his comrades were provided with every comfort, even women. He didn't even object to being sent to Brazil, since he had never been out of Germany before.

But the old man, Schreck, frightened and awed him at the same time. Dolf had never heard of the Brotherhood of the Black Sun , but he received the distinct impression of some massive, shadowy wheel in which he served as a simple, expendable spoke.

Schreck demanded complete unquestioning obedience and Dolf cooperated. But now he seriously questioned the wisdom of not only what Schreck was doing, but why he was doing it.

He had lost many comrades at the clinic. Only a few, less than fifteen, had managed to escape. He could not imagine what such a decimated force could accomplish. Any kind of frontal assault was out of the question.

But Schreck had felt that any risks were acceptable to retrieve the black box from the Hauser and Hochbach office. Though the mission had been successful, Dolf had lost even more comrades, and a certain amount of faith to the cause and the man to whom he had pledged his loyalty.

Dolf turned the BMW down a dark side street, away from the business section of Spandau,. He drove four blocks, parked, and he and Veit got out. The night seemed peaceful. A cool breeze, what citizens called the Berliner Luft , stirred the branches of a few trees along the street.

Dolf carried the box inside a suitcase. It felt far heavier than it looked for its size. The two men went three blocks on foot, and came to a group of deserted buildings which sprawled across the space of a city block. A high barbed-wire fence encircled the lot. It was a group of factory buildings formerly housing an automobile manufacturing plant, but abandoned for the last ten years.

Posted signs warned trespassers off and gave notice that the property was in the hands of a real estate concern. The concern had been owned by Julius Eicke.

Although Dolf had only visited the place once, he knew the main building was but a false front concealing a fortress. It generated its own power and housed storerooms, living quarters and a garage containing a fleet of powerful, armor-plated vehicles of every type. Beneath a rooftop bay, two helicopters stood fueled and ready.

God only knew how much money had been devoted to constructing this base over the years, not that Dolf had ever been inclined to ask.

He and Veit walked quickly along the opposite side of the street, parallel to the factory site. They paused when they reached the storefront of a small tobacco shop. The lights were still shining behind the dust-streaked window.

The front of the store faced the fenced-in main entrance of the factory. Dolf and Veit strolled into the store.

The overweight proprietor sat behind a counter, glancing up dully from a German-language edition of Penthouse. His face was covered by leathery warts. He gave a barely perceptible nod and grunted, "Wait."

He waddled around the counter, to the door of the shop and turned a CLOSED sign around in the window. He jerked a greasy thumb over his shoulder.

"Go," he said.

Dolf and Veit walked to the rear of the shop. They opened a door, walked straight along a short hallway, entered a small storeroom and walked directly to a shelf of cigarette cartons and cigar boxes.

Veit, his hands free, reached under the shelf, seized a concealed handle and pushed to the left, then pulled straight back. The section of the wall moved outward. Behind it lay a landing, and a flight of stairs leading down some twenty feet to another door at the bottom.

Veit tugged the wall panel back into place. A latch clicked and a bulb over the door below lit up.

When Dolf had first learned of his employers' fondness for hidden doors and secret passages, he had been amused, then enthralled. It all seemed like some kind of game. Now there was a sinister significance to all the precautions.

Veit mumbled, "This is all so much crap, like something out of some stupid spy movie."

With a surge of fear, Dolf raised a finger to his lips and hushed him. He mouthed, "This place may be wired. He may hear you."

Veit gave him a disgusted look with one raised eyebrow. His "So?" was deliberately loud.

Taking the finger from his lips, Dolf made a gun from it and his thumb and pressed it to Veit's forehead. Leaning forward, he whispered, "Bang. That's why 'so'."

The disgusted look didn't vanish from Veit's face, but he nodded silently in assent.

When they reached the bottom of the stairway, the door swung open automatically at their approach and closed after them. They turned sharply to the left, then right, then walked straight along a passage below street level.

In the dim light, they passed under the street and into the grounds occupied by the factory buildings. Another door loomed before them. This one was set in a concrete wall, reinforced with riveted steel cleats.

Inset into the very center of the door was a small speaker grid. Dolf spoke into it in clear tones, saying precisely, "Schaeffer. One. Two. Peenemunde."

Solenoids clicked behind the door, then the whine of an electric motor as the door swung slowly inward, hinged on the right.

Veit and Dolf passed through it, and the door closed behind them.

They walked along another corridor, entered a wooden door and into a large common room, filled with cots, chairs and a couple of tables.

One man was in the room, lying on a cot. He wore only underwear, his T-shirt pulled up to make room for a blood-spotted bandage.

Dolf walked over to him, murmuring, "Otto. How are you feeling?"

Feeble words came from Otto's mouth. "Like I've been shot, how the fuck do you think I'm feeling?"

"Where are the others?"

"Standing guard duty. Leaving me here to die or get better." Otto tried to raise himself on his elbow. "Maybe dying would be better."

"How many of us made it back here?" Veit asked.

"With you and Dolf, it makes an even fifteen. Including me, that is."

"Fuck," Veit said in a fierce whisper. "We aren't even a decent gang, much less any kind of fighting force!"

Ignoring Veit's remark, Dolf asked, "Where is he?"

"I don't know. I don't care," Otto croaked. "He's out of his mind, thinks he's the devil or God or something."

Otto's voice trailed off into a hacking rattle and he collapsed back on the cot. Blood worked its way out of his mouth. His eyes closed.

Dolf looked at him, realizing the bright red blood indicated a punctured lung, and he also caught a whiff of a perforated bowel. Otto wasn't dead yet, but death was probably only a short time away.

As he left the bedside, Veit said softly, "We'll probably end up like that, you know. All this crap about a new and stronger Germany, making America kiss our ass, is getting us killed off piecemeal."

Dolf said, equally quietly, "He has a plan."

Veit sneered. "Yeah, right. And I've got an asshole. I think my asshole functions better."

They walked down a carpeted corridor and reached a black door, made of polished walnut. Two mercenaries stood outside it, shouldering carbines. They nodded to Dolf and Veit.

"How long has he been here?" Dolf asked one of them in a whisper.

"We got him here about two hours ago. He's Visualizing, but he gave orders that we were to let you in as soon as you arrived. Just you, Dolf"

Veit sighed in relief and walked back down the corridor. Dolf took a deep breath and then rapped on the door.

"Come," said Ulrich Schreck's voice from the other side of it.

Dolf walked into a wide, square room that he had been in once before, and had hoped he would never be forced to enter again.

The only comparison Dolf could make was to a shrine, but it was unlike any church or place of worship he'd ventured into.

Rough-hewn granite blocks lined the room. In the center rose a massive stone altar supported by three boulders. All around the walls hung bronze plaques bearing the Reich eagle and Black Sun symbol. On granite pedestals rested a variety of regalia—swords, daggers, shields, jeweled crowns, a human skull, gem-encrusted crucifixes, a spear-point, and even a heavy diamond pendant. The room was dimly lit by torches flickering in wall brackets.

Schreck stood at the altar. He wore a jet-black ensemble that resembled an S.S. officer's uniform, but with its silver Black Sun emblem worn like a badge.

A pair of blood-red sashes crossed his chest like ammunition bandoliers. The sashes were decorated with symbols, swastikas, sunbursts and jagged marks Dolf had heard called "runes."

Schreck's blue-veined hands rested on a collection of black-and-white photographs scattered across the altar. His eyes were closed, his head tilted back. His lips moved, but he made no sound.

Ulrich Schreck should have looked ridiculous, but he didn't.

Dolf stood silently, feeling a dew of sweat break out on his upper lip. He didn't dare wipe it away. Though the weight of the telemetry box in the suitcase strained at his arm, he didn't set it down.

Schreck tipped his head forward, but he didn't open his eyes. "Dolf."

"Yes, sir."

"Do you understand the purpose of Visualization?"

"No, sir. Not really."

"Come here, Dolf."

Dolf slowly approached the altar. He saw the photographs were of concentration and death-camp victims— men, women and children reduced to creatures barely recognizable as human beings, naked and stacked atop each other in mass graves like cordwood.

"Reality yields to the pressure of an iron will, visualizing a precise reality," Schreck said. "An ancient technique that can turn physical conditions inside out. That explains Hitler's early successes. He had the power, then. But he lost it, and left Germany in ruins."

Schreck opened his eyes. They were calm, not raging or bright. He seemed relaxed, confident, and even fatherly. "I taught the techniques to him, Dolf. I had the power then, and I have it now. Destiny can be controlled, shaped, molded. That is what our undertaking is all about."

Pressing the photographs with his fingertips, Schreck said, "I visualize a reality where all non-Aryans are reduced to the condition of these sacrifices. We can accomplish this, Dolf, though our measures may seem extreme."

Schreck stared at him unblinkingly. "Does that disturb you, my boy?"

"No, sir. It does not. Losses can never be too high." Dolf meant what he said. For some reason, all his apprehension, his fear, was fading away.

"Good boy. I am relying on you. You accomplished your mission?"

Dolf heaved the suitcase up, but he didn't rest it atop the altar. That seemed discourteous, if not blasphemous. "Yes, sir. The American tried to stop us, and we lost five men, but your plan to confuse pursuit by having different vehicles along the escape route worked perfectly."

Schreck nodded. "Sometimes the old tricks are the best. What of the American warrior?"

Dolf shook his head. "I don't know. He could not have followed us here, to our holy ground."

Schreck chuckled. "This is only a replica of the original Black Sun shrine on the sacred island of Rugen. That was a stronghold of the first Aryan race. I had this room built for initiations."

Smiling at him fondly, Schreck tapped his chest. "The true holy ground is in here, Dolf. In our Aryan hearts, in our Aryan blood."

Dolf smiled. "I understand, sir."

"I know you do. Assemble the others. We have plans to make, and we must move tomorrow."

Dolf turned to leave, but Schreck called him back.

"If Otto hasn't yet died, please help him along. His constant complaints are a nuisance. I cannot be distracted."

"You won't be, sir. I swear."

Schreck watched as Dolf marched out of the room, head thrown back, shoulders square, a chest swelling with pride thrust out. He knew that Dolf had walked in consumed with doubts and fears, and was leaving with the conviction that he would die before he shirked his responsibility to the Aryan people.

His influence on Dolf wasn't hypnotism. It was the control and direction of a subtle energy, training the powers of concentration until they could be focused like a laser. The driving force behind the technique was heightened emotion.

Hitler had possessed this ability in latent form until Schreck found him, educated him and trained him to make conscious use of it. It was a power which persuaded an entire nation black was white.

Schreck could recall many instances when Hitler's officers would at one and the same time accept a situation as hopeless, yet remain convinced Der Fuhrer would find a solution.

But Hitler's raw egotism, combined with the powers awakened in him, drove him insane, and he dragged Germany down into ruin.

He was Schreck's greatest disappointment, and he accepted the responsibility of righting the Austrian's wrongs. Sacrificing him had not been enough.

The muffled crack of a gunshot reached Schreck's ears and he smiled. He had commanded Dolf to kill Otto for two reasons—first, because caring for a wounded man in such a critical situation was an unnecessary distraction. Second, he wanted to test the extent of his influence over the man. Otto was his friend, and if Dolf would kill a friend on command, then his grip on him was strong.

And through Dolf, that grip would tighten on the others, who he knew were uneasy and afraid.

Schreck himself was afraid. He feared the American warrior would find some way to tip the scales of probabilities in his favor. The power of the Dag made it possible, and though the warrior could not focus his will through it, the ancient icon still spread its power over him like a protective cloak.

The door opened and the soldiers trooped in, eyeing their surroundings warily. A few bore bandages covering superficial wounds inflicted during the raid on the clinic, but most were in excellent shape, though physically and mentally drained.

That would make Schreck's task much easier.

They stood in a ragged semi-circle around the altar and Schreck stared at each man in turn, keeping his eyes on him until that man either glanced away or ducked his head.

"Greetings, warriors. Your work over the past few weeks has been gratifying. You have done well by your Fatherland, and the shades of the ancient Aryan kings smile upon you with favor."

There were a few smiles, but Schreck wasn't sure if they were amused or impressed. It didn't matter.

"This is only the beginning of your struggle. The power you will eventually control will be unlimited. But there is a little matter of seeing our undertaking through to fruition, first."

Schreck paused. The men shifted uneasily. There was something calculated, ominous, about the man's sharp voice.

"Though we suffered a setback, it was only an inconvenience, not a tragedy. But there may be some of you who believe it is a tragedy and wish to dissolve our association. I urge those who hold to this belief to step forward and speak up."

No one did.

WARING CLIMBED quietly out of bed. He looked down at the sleeping Iselda and repressed a sigh and the urge to kiss her. Their love-making had been alternately tender and fierce. Both of them had reached release at the same moment.

Unlike Iselda, Waring found sleep elusive even though he knew he would have to be on the road well before dawn. He stood at the bedroom window, studying the Berlin skyline without really seeing it. Lines of concentration marked his hawklike face as he replayed Iselda's "faux people" question.

He wondered if her casually spoken query might not be the literal truth. He had always been a loner. The first thing he could remember was the drab green walls of the orphanage. He also remembered the constant dull ache of wondering who his parents had been and who he really was, other than the name the Welfare Department gave him. He had left behind that name the day he left the orphanage.

Waring thought of all those lonely nights spent in prison for a crime he hadn't committed—until he escaped and made his way under an assumed identity to England. There had been so many identities since then, including the one known in certain circles as The Falcon. He had hoped the so-called Falcon legend would fade and allow the man beneath to finally have a life of his own. But he suspected—feared—that the legend and the man were too intertwined to ever be fully separated.

He slammed the mental file drawer shut. He couldn't afford the luxury of brooding about himself so he concentrated on Ulrich Schreck. Waring knew from experience that it was always poor tactics to underrate the power of a fanatic. A dedicated madman could always attract followers and not all of those followers belonged to the lunatic fringe.

Schreck could potentially have plenty of supporters both openly and behind the scenes. Solezer had implied as much. Extremism could always be mass-sold as patriotism.

It was clear the old man wasn't merely a deranged Nazi, romantically dreaming of resurrecting the Thousand Year Reich. He planned a hell of a lot more than that—a countryful of human sacrifices was only the first step.

A faint sound caused Waring to turn his head. Throwing aside the sheet, Iselda rose from the bed, her eyes clouded with sleep. Her tan nude body gleamed with satiny highlights from the dim illumination

peeping in through the window.

She laid her head against his right shoulder. Drowsily, she asked, "What are you doing, Mike? You should be resting."

"I was thinking. I didn't want to disturb you."

With a fingernail, she lightly traced the small outline of the stylized bird of prey tattooed on his deltoid. "What's this…? One of your American eagles?"

"It's a falcon, actually."

"A hunting bird…is it significant?"

"It used to be. I think it will be again."

"Is that what you're thinking about?"

A faint smile lifted the corners of Waring's mouth. "I suppose."

Iselda kissed the side of his neck and his face. She murmured, "Thinking can be such a waste of time."

Waring turned took her into his arms."You're right…so can sleeping."

NINETEEN
June 6

The battered little pickup was parked just off the gravel lane, hidden by thick bushes.

Waring sat at the wheel and tried to enjoy the warm air, rich with the smell of growing things. Part of his mind appreciated the beauty of a summer morning in the German countryside, but most of his attention was focused on hearing or sighting anything the slightest bit out of place.

The ten miles surrounding Site 611 was on full alert, but unless someone knew it there was no way to tell. The woods, the fields, the footpaths crawled with armed men—watchposts had been established in an ever-widening radius around the missile site.

People with binoculars scanned the skies for approaching aircraft—secret service specialists disguised as farmers, berry-pickers and fishermen walked, picked and stooped all over the hills and meadows.

Waring wore tinted glasses, and the brim of a Fedora was tilted to shade his face from the sun. He wore a lightweight tweed jacket and faded jeans. To a passerby, he would've appeared to be either a fisherman or a farmer. Beneath the jacket was his combat harness. From it hung four V40 mini-grenades and six clips of ammo.

A radio dangled on its strap from the rear-view mirror.

In the bed of the truck, covered by a tarp, sat the radiation detector. Only the antenna was visible. A thin wire crawled from the device through the oval window in the cab to a tiny amplifier in his right ear. Every watchpost had a similar instrument.

Waring had been sitting in the truck since dawn, checking in every ten minutes with other watchposts. Beyond cows, a few rabbits and an inquisitive hedgehog, nothing had been seen by anyone.

Jacobs was stationed in the bunker of the site, coordinating and monitoring all the communications. He had spoken very little to Waring and hadn't seemed very interested in hearing about Darren's betrayal or its implications. He was either too ashamed or paranoid to discuss it.

Waring reviewed everything that had been agreed upon during the last meeting. He had studied maps of the vicinity, until he knew every way in and out of the area by heart.

A vehicle or aircraft would be the most efficient way of transmitting the code that would kill a lot of people, but Abendroth claimed a portable electric generator was required to power the emitter up to the proper voltage. Just hooking it into the battery of a car or airplane wouldn't be sufficient.

Since they had no idea of the resources the Brotherhood could call upon, Waring raised the possibility of multiple vehicles and multiple aircraft being employed as decoys.

According to Weisenburg, there was only one telemetry box, but by the time anyone figured out which car, truck, van, plane or chopper carried it, a large portion of Eastern Germany could be radioactive slag.

Neither Jacobs nor Solezer had disagreed, but they were concerned with maintaining a cloak of secrecy over the threat and the operation to thwart it.

Waring understood the diplomatic concerns, but he had no patience with them. He had flown the night skies as a lone hunter for too long to worry about international incidents or hurt feelings. He remembered an old saying: "Defend me from my friends—I can take care of my enemies myself."

The passenger door opened and Iselda Abendroth climbed in. She was dressed as casually as he was. With a great deal of dignity, she pushed the roll of toilet paper under the seat.

"I hate nature," she announced grimly.

Waring didn't say anything but he silently noted her chipper mood had steadily degraded since they had left her apartment at 4AM. The radio crackled with a request to check in. He complied. Iselda started to pour herself a cup of coffee from the thermos, then thought better of it. "That's what got me into trouble in the first place."

She glanced over at Waring as he replaced the radio on the mirror. "How can you be so bloody patient?"

"I'm not."

"You could have fooled me. We've been sitting here for hours, and you haven't moved."

"Sometimes the enemy brings the war to you. All you can do then is wait."

"You're military, aren't you?" She made it sound like an accusation.

"I've already told you what I am, Iselda."

"Oh, right," she said sarcastically. "Do you have a different name today?"

"Later, maybe."

She looked at him expectantly. "Have you chosen a good one?"

When the answer she wanted wasn't forthcoming, she started to speak, but Waring suddenly stiffened and waved her into silence. He cocked his head to the left, out the window of the cab.

Removing the amplifier from his ear, he opened the door and stepped out, scanning the clear sky.

He spied a speck on the horizon, and heard chugging sound of vanes beating the air. The approaching helicopter was new and white, and it looked like it was going to pass right over their position.

Waring reached in for the radio, but it was already squawking. Iselda plugged the amplifier into her ear.

"I see it," Waring said into the radio. "It's a Messerschmitt, a two-seater. It's reducing altitude like it's looking for a place to land."

He kept his eyes on the chopper, and he saw the call letters and logo of a Berlin television station. He called in the description.

The voice at the watchpost said, "Oh, shit! How'd they get wind of this?"

"They couldn't have."

The chopper chugged almost directly overhead. Because of the overhanging tree limbs, Waring couldn't see who or how many sat in the cockpit. Over the booming beat of the blades, he heard a low, irregular sputter, and a sudden hesitation in the engine noise, as if it had lost some power.

Iselda snatched the amplifier out of her ear. "We've got a signal," she cried. "Oh my God—!"

The helicopter banked, lowered, and skimmed the crests of two hills, then sank out of sight.

"It's a decoy," Waring snapped. "That chopper's too light to carry a generator, and we're at least four miles from the site."

Some of the panic went out of Iselda's face. "How can you be so sure?"

"I can't be, so I'm going to check it out. I won't waste my breath ordering you to stay behind. Do what you want."

Grabbing the radio and a leather satchel, Waring set out at a run through the bushes, not waiting to see what Iselda was doing. He slung the satchel over his left shoulder by the strap.

When he heard the snapping of twigs behind him, he glanced back and saw her following him.

Waring set a ground-eating lope, and he wasn't worried about whether Iselda could keep the pace. He pushed through the perimeter of the brush and was in fairly open pastureland, though the countryside was hilly.

The heat of the sun became oppressive, but Waring kept running. He looked back and saw that Iselda was not too far behind, falling into the rhythm of the pace. She was as athletic as she looked—but he had learned that the night before.

Waring went up a slope swiftly, down the other side, splashed through a stream then hit a thicket of pine scrub that slowed him down. He lost his footing for a moment and tripped, going down on one knee by a bush. Iselda Abendroth caught up with him, panting.

They didn't speak, but pushed on through the thicket. Thorns and briars tore their clothes and scratched their faces and hands. They saw the helicopter sitting in a small hollow between two hillocks. The blades were motionless. There was no one in or around it.

Waring drew the Ruger and scanned the area. High, thick grass moved with the breeze, but he didn't see anyone. He reported in to the watchpost and was told a unit was on its way and to sit tight.

Waring acknowledged the message, but didn't say he would comply with it. Whispering to Iselda to stay behind, he moved out into the hollow, the .45 held with both hands.

He crept up to the helicopter from behind, and peered through the Plexiglas canopy into the cockpit. Both seats were empty.

Gesturing for Iselda to come forward, Waring opened the hatch and examined the controls. There wasn't anything unusual about them.

"Maybe it's legitimate, and the pilot was forced to make an emergency landing and walked off to find help," she said.

"It would have been easier to radio for help," Waring replied. "Besides, your radiation detector registered a microwave signal as it passed over, remember?"

Iselda nodded, as if a little annoyed by the reminder. She began working on the latches of the emergency maintenance hatch on the craft's fuselage.

"There's no sign of an emitter in the cockpit," she said. "So if there's one aboard, it has be in here."

Waring let her work on it. He kept his eyes and gun sweeping the area. He didn't turn around until her heard her say, "Right again."

She pointed to the battery. A coaxial cable attached to the positive terminus ran to a small metal-walled box with perforated sides.

"There it is," she said. "Hooked up to the battery. An emitter with a very limited effect radius, but strong enough to register on my instrument."

"You're right again and we're foxed again," said Waring. "Weisenburg must have told Schreck about these detectors you're so proud of."

Angrily, she said, "Well, of course he would have. He's not a fool. Not only did he probably tell Schreck about the detectors, he probably built a few in his time."

Waring turned away, not wanting his temper to fray any further. Not even the most deranged terrorist chief had ever displayed such a cheerful willingness to sacrifice men and materiel to gain an objective as Ulrich Schreck. He grudgingly admitted the man was a brilliant military strategist, as well as one of the most evil sons-of- bitches he had ever pitted himself against.

Waring hated it when the two went hand-in-hand.

He called the watchpost. "Call off the units. It was a diversionary tactic. There probably will be more. The chopper is unoccupied and it doesn't have the telemetry box. I'm going to track the pilot. He has to have some destination in mind."

Waring cut off the watchpost's protests, reached in and yanked the power lead from the battery. He began circling the helicopter, his eyes on the ground.

"You're going to track the pilot?" asked Iselda. "Who do you think you are—Daniel Boone?"

"Go back to the truck, Iselda."

"Why should I?'

Waring bent over grass that had been stamped down and was now rising back up. "One reason is I was told you were to have minimal contact with the field operations. Primarily, I want you to go back be- cause someone has to monitor and operate the detector."

Iselda wanted to argue, but she really couldn't. Mike Waring was right, and it was only discomfort and stinging briar scratches that made her so short with his manner. She watched him stand up and begin walking toward another slope, pausing every few moments to stare at the ground, scan the terrain, then move on again.

"Be careful," she called to him.

He didn't respond.

"Mike," she called, louder this time.

He turned to look at her. "What?"

With a grin, she asked, "Your new name. You never told me."

"You guessed it yourself, Iselda. The name is Boone. Daniel Boone."

She laughed, and went on away from him, walking back in the direction she had come. She glanced back once, and saw the man jogging toward the face of the slope.

Rather than force herself through the thorn-infested thicket again, Iselda detoured up a steep embankment, figuring to walk along its top until she reached open ground again.

She tramped along the crest of the embankment, looking at the wildflowers and enjoying the music of the songbirds. As a lifelong resident of the city, she rarely heard it. As she walked, she slowly caught got up in the warmth of the sun and the sense of tranquility.

Subsequently, Iselda lost her way.

When she realized the embankment had dipped down and curved gently away from the direction she wanted to go, she didn't become upset or panicky. She stopped and looked around, shielding her eyes and tried to reorient herself.

A line of trees less than a quarter-kilometer away bordered a green fenced-in pasture. Cows grazed off to one side. Beyond the pasture stood a two-story farmhouse and a long barn. She was too far away to see anyone, but she remembered Jacobs mentioning a dairy farm in the vicinity. If nothing else, she would make for that and find the lane again.

It was a rougher walk than she estimated, full of foot-bruising stones, briars and muddy patches. Before she reached the line of trees at the edge of the pasture, she regretted her decision.

She snagged her shirt and jeans in the sharp points of the barbed wire fence when she slid between the strands, and before she straightened up, she stepped in a very fresh, very thick cow flop.

Iselda cursed herself steadily as she crossed the pasture and climbed the fence on the opposite side. Following Waring had been an impulsive, childish act, like the ingénue heroine in a young adult novel.

Approaching the farmyard, she noted with appreciation the quaint style of the house, with its gabled roof, rooster-topped weather vane and old-fashioned lightning rod with tiny iron cherubs welded all along its length.

She also noted the metal parabolic dish positioned at an eave but she didn't find it unusual. Satellite dishes were common in Europe, especially in isolated villages where TV reception was blocked by mountains and valleys.

Chickens clucked and scratched in the yard, hunting between a tractor equipped with a six-disc plow and an old Volkswagen panel truck.

Iselda walked toward the back door, cupping her mouth with her hands. "Hello? I need directions back to the lane."

"How the fuck did you get here?" a voice snarled from behind her.

Iselda spun and saw a heavy-set, thick shouldered man in overalls emerging from the barn. He carried a three-tined pitchfork in one beefy, but very clean hand.

The farmer glared at her darkly, not reacting to the smile she turned on him.

"I came across your pasture," she said, gesturing to it.

"What the hell for?"

"I lost my way."

"Your way from what? There's nothing out there."

Iselda started to feel a tingle of fear and danger, so she told him a very sincere story about getting separated from her church group during a bird-watching expedition.

The farmer's flat face did not change expression, but he slowly moved toward her, gazing at her intently. His eyes suddenly widened.

"Goddammit!" he hissed. "I don't fucking believe it. You!"

With a surprising lightness of foot, the farmer leaped forward, thrusting the pitchfork like a spear.

Iselda just managed to fall backward as a tine punctured her shirt and ripped a bleeding furrow just above her waist. She cried out in fear, in anger, in pain.

"You son of a bitch! Are you crazy?"

The farmer pressed forward and swept the pitchfork at her. Iselda ducked beneath it, and her fingers scooped up a handful of dirt thick with chicken droppings. She flung it upward, into the man's eyes.

As he spat and cursed and pawed at his face, Iselda kicked him between the legs. The farmer coughed out a strangled call for help and bent at the waist, dropping the pitchfork. Iselda turned and ran.

She ran right into the muscular arms of a big man wearing a checked flannel shirt and faded jeans. His long blond hair was tied in a knot at the back of his head.

Wrestling her around, he hooked an arm up under her chin and bent her right wrist at an angle that brought a cry of pain from her.

"Dr. Abendroth," he breathed into her ear. "You're much more attractive in the flesh than on video. Welcome to the Brotherhood."

TWENTY

OVER THE years, Waring had tracked human prey across terrain far more inhospitable than the German countryside. He had trailed the spoor of enemies through jungles, deserts, and more often than not, city streets.

Though his target was taking pains to cover his tracks keeping to rocks and hard-packed earth, he might as well as have been leaving a trail of bread crumbs for Waring to follow.

He had figured out the timing—the pilot of the chopper had maybe a fifteen minutes head-start, and no more than twenty. He had no idea where the man was going, but at least he was well on his way to someplace.

At five minute intervals, Waring listened to the watchpost frequency on the radio. There were reports of feints on several fronts—a man in a truck with a microwave transmitter had driven blithely past an observation team. When chased down, he had meekly given himself up. An emitter transmitting a weak signal had been discovered less than two miles from the entrance road to Site 611.

None of the diversions could be ignored, even though Jacobs and Solezer's people were scrambling all over hell and gone. This kind of cat-and-mousing was a new kind of terrorism in their experience.

The sole purpose seemed to be generating fear. He was morally certain that Schreck was somewhere close, enjoying it all immensely.

After about half-an-hour, Waring reached the outer limits of the watchpost's communication parameters so he turned it off to conserve the battery power.

At the edge of a bog, Waring stopped. The long reeds and marsh grass waved in the breeze. A few birds flapped up, and he heard the quack of ducks.

Here and there, rising out of the shallow water, he saw grassy humped hillocks, like stepping stones.

Waring walked along the water's edge and found a place where the mud had been recently disturbed. It was small indentation, already half-filled with dark water. He waded into the marsh at that point, carefully eyeing the reeds and cattails he pushed aside. He noted several of the stalks had been broken.

When he reached the first of the overgrown hillocks, he saw snapped-off stalks and uprooted weeds piled up over something, and then stomped flat.

Kicking the stuff aside, he found a folded white jumpsuit, the right sleeve bearing the same insignia as on the helicopter.

Waring waded back into the marsh, heading for a low range of hills overlooking the bog. His prey had stripped off the jumpsuit for only one reason—he was too conspicuous in it, so he had changed to clothes that would make it easier for him to blend in with his surroundings. Changing clothes would have cost him some time, so the gap between hunter and the hunted narrowed.

Although he'd seen no one so far, Waring assumed there had to be a few people around, farmers, fishermen or sheep-herders. A man in white jumpsuit would be noticed.

At the far edge of the marsh, Waring found more tracks, and he followed them up the face of the hill. When he topped it, he saw a wide pasture spread out below. Grazing cows moved sluggishly across it. In the distance, he saw a barn and farmhouse. They were about a quarter of a mile away, so he guessed it was the dairy farm Jacobs had described as the site's nearest neighbors.

A strip of woodland ran off to his left, bordering the farm property on its west side. Waring made for the trees, assuming his quarry would choose that route rather than exposing himself in open expanse of pastureland.

The woods smelled fresh and clean after the heavy humidity of the bog. He found more and more signs of a man's recent passing, tracks and scuff marks, stepped on tufts of grass, leaves dangling from broken stems.

The pilot appeared to be less concerned about throwing off pursuit, and the only reason for his confidence was he was closing on his destination. The only possible safe haven was the dairy farm.

Rather than spend more time looking for signs, Waring increased his pace, heading through the woods in the direction of the farm. He pushed through bushes and stepped over logs and slipped between tree trunks. The chirp of birds and the lowing of cattle covered most of the noise he made, which was not much louder than an infrequent rustle of leaves.

He reached a narrow footpath, angled away from it, dropped flat behind a tree and belly-crawled forward until he reached a screen of shrubbery. Beyond the bushes, less than an eighth of a mile away, was the farmhouse and barn.

From his coat pocket, he pulled out small, powerful binoculars and put them to his eyes.

On the back steps of the farmhouse stood two men. One was fair haired, the other dark. Both were dressed in work clothes. He brought their faces into sharp focus. He recognized the blond man as the one who had escaped him at the Hauser and Hochbach building.

Anticipation tingled through Waring's blood. Step by step, he had followed the pilot to the main dark site. Scanning the house, he saw something that made him unconsciously tense his muscles.

A parabolic dish protruded from the corner of the building—at first glance nothing more frightening than a large satellite television receiver. Waring estimated it to be about three feet in diameter.

Another man walked from the barn and spoke with the pair standing on the steps. He wore overalls and shouldered a pitchfork, but Waring read his pedigree just the same.

He had no idea of the number of hardmen in the place, but it had to be increased by one. The pilot had led him on a long, circuitous route to the site, and was probably already inside, downing a congratulatory Heinneken.

Under other circumstances, Waring would have opted for a soft probe, to draw out the hardmen, so he could get an estimate of the opposition. There was no time for that now, not even time to get back into communication range of the watchposts. Everything depended on stealth and strategy until he was sure of the killzone.

He heard a soft crunch of leaves behind him. Waring whirled, hand streaking for the Ruger, but not quickly enough.

ISELDA ABENDROTH struggled, bit and kicked, but the big blond man dragged her into the house, through the kitchen and then pushed her up a narrow stairwell.

She tried to claw his eyes and put an elbow in his throat, but he outweighed her by at least eighty pounds. He wrestled her up the steps, putting a knee against her rear and lifting.

He forced her up to the second floor, and shoved her toward another flight of stairs, these leading up to a square opening in the ceiling. Iselda managed to sink her teeth into the man's wrist, the bite going to the bone.

He cursed and spun her around. "You mongrel bitch!"

With one fist, he backhanded her across the face. The blow made a thousand multi-colored stars flash before her eyes. She sagged in his grip, and he roughly dragged her up the steps, one hand tangled in her hair and the other holding her by the collar.

He flung her down on the rough floorboards of a small attic room, a garret with only two windows, one at either end.

"What have we here, Dolf?" said a voice from the shadows.

"It's that American's half-breed whore," Dolf replied. "He must really be desperate if he sends her on a suicide mission."

Iselda pushed herself into a sitting position and looked groggily around. An old man sat in a chair in front of one of the windows. Backlit by the sunshine streaming in, his features were indistinct, but she knew who he was, who he had to be.

"Schreck," she muttered.

"Dr. Abendroth," Schreck said politely. "Since Dolf tends to jump to conclusions, I don't accept his thesis of a suicide mission. So, what are you doing here?"

Iselda didn't reply. Dolf prodded her in the side with a foot, right on the pitchfork wound. She cried out and struck at his leg with both fists.

"Enough!" Schreck barked. "She is here, she is helpless, and so there is no need for further violence. At least for the moment. Go and bring up the first-aid kit."

Dolf hesitated, and then turned left. Iselda stiffly climbed to her feet, one hand covering the bleeding cut in her side.

"I apologize for him," Schreck said. "Dolf can be a bit over-zealous and a little single-minded."

Iselda got a closer look at the man. Her first impression was of intensely penetrating blue eyes—intelligent eyes, all-seeing eyes, the eyes of a visionary. Or a demon.

"What have you done to the real owner of this place?" she demanded.

"Not a thing. You stand in his presence. I foreclosed on the mortgage of the tenants, which is my right. Though the Brotherhood's real estate portfolio is not vast, it is diverse. We even own beachfront property in Miami. Rather ironic, is it not, owning the very buildings in which ancient Jews come to spend their waning years?"

Schreck laughed softly, then said, "However, the question of what you are doing here has yet to be answered."

"We're on to you, Schreck," Iselda said with an exaggerated calm. "You can't escape. The authorities are closing in even as we speak."

"Don't waste my time with such an obvious bluff, young woman. The authorities would not use an academic as a stalking horse, no matter how desperate their situation. No, I believe it is more likely you stumbled into my sphere, directed by the forces swirling around the American warrior and myself."

As he spoke, Iselda looked around the room. At the end nearest Schreck was a small table. On it rested a laptop computer. It was connected by a pair of leads to a square, black metal box.

Her eyes followed a cable stretching from the box to the base of an input port in the wall.

Her heart gave a great lurch when she saw the port was connected to the base of satellite receiver at the window. The dish itself was mounted on the exterior of the house.

Another cable, one much thicker and coated with a heavier insulation, ran from the base of the computer and disappeared down a hole drilled in the floor.

Schreck had followed her visual inventory and smiled at the show of anxiety on her face.

"Yes," he said calmly. "That is the telemetry box built by Weisenburg, connected to a simple laptop computer. The dish itself is powered by a large generator in the cellar. Disabuse yourself of any doubt that the emitter doesn't have sufficient power to transmit the appropriate signals to the missile silo."

Iselda met his gaze, asking, "You haven't done it yet?"

"No."

"Why not?"

"Young woman, though your abilities and exotic looks intrigue me, you do not have the capacity to understand why I am doing anything."

Iselda backed away a step, breaking eye contact. She had the sense of a more-than-human power about this man, as old as he was. He radiated an aura of a deep inner strength. The total effect was chilling, as if she were in the company of an alien.

"You're an evil bastard," she said hoarsely.

Schreck shook his head. "Good and evil have no real existence as anything but mental or societal concepts. Have you ever known a totally good or totally evil person? Of course not. Angels may not be my allies, but neither are they yours. At any rate, I do not deal in philosophical abstracts, but in necessities."

"Necessities," she echoed sarcastically. "What sort of necessities can you see in planning the deaths of so many people?"

Dolf chose that moment to return, carrying a small white case. Schreck gestured. "Lift up your shirt. Let Dolf treat you. A cut like that could easily become infected out here."

Iselda hesitated, glancing from the old man to Dolf and raised the blood-soaked shirt to just beneath her breasts. Dolf, with a surprisingly gentle touch, began swabbing the wound.

Schreck spoke, in a low, patient, almost kindly tone.

"The forces that control the world are dangerously unbalanced. My former pupil began the slide, and others continued it. I do what I do to restore the balance before I leave this incarnation. When I return, in a new vessel, Brotherhood will be restored to the world. It will be at peace."

"A world of masters and slaves," Iselda said.

"You disapprove?"

"Goddamn right I disapprove! So would anyone who was sane."

"Young woman, I am the sanest man you have ever met. The forces flowing through me are not what you could call sane, insane, good or evil. Those are human concepts."

"Are you telling me you're not human?"

"Oh, the flesh I wear is certainly human enough, though it is failing me. I'm not concerned. I've had a long life in this incarnation, a full one, but I knew it couldn't last forever."

Dolf smeared a stinging antiseptic onto her wound, and she bit back a curse of pain.

"I don't know about incarnations," she said, "but I know you're full of shit. People won't stand for your kind of world. It's been tried before and it never works."

Schreck chuckled. "Every government in existence wants my kind of world. Liberty, freedom, democracy – all are no more than labels to keep the sheep content. What do you think will happen after the missiles are launched? The course of world events will be changed forever. New laws of suppression will be enacted, and no one will object because they will think they are in place for their own protection. The mass of humanity will be guided through various channels, and they won't even be aware of it. And even if a few do realize they are being manipulated, they won't care."

"What's in all of this for you, Schreck? What's your reward?"

"Do you have a thousand years for me to explain? No, so let me put it in a very simplistic fashion. I am arresting the tide, changing the flow of destiny. In my next incarnation, all the rules will be my rules."

Iselda's mind reeled. The man was a raving psychotic, he had to be, but there was such a ring of unshakable certainty in his tone, his bearing, she felt blind terror filling her.

"All the people you'll kill to achieve this," she stammered, "how can that help you?"

"Sacrifices." Schreck leaned forward. "What do you think the purpose was of all the concentration camps, the motivation behind the so-called Final Solution? Blood and souls rendered to the forces I serve."

Dolf bandaged the wound on her waist. Iselda trembled now, clenching her fists, her nails biting into her palms.

"Then why wait, you deranged son of a bitch?" she asked, pitching her voice low to disguise the quaver. "Get it over with."

Schreck waved his hands through the air, as if moving them in time to some melody only he could hear. "The terror must rise, the fear must build to a crescendo. I feel it out there, pulsing in the wind, building like a pyramid. You'll feel it, too. When the capstone of terror is put into place, then—"

Schreck reached out and dragged a forefinger along the computer keyboard like a pianist running through the scales.

"When it finally happens, it will be almost a relief. Also, I must wait for the American warrior to return the Dag to me."

"What? You can't really expect him to do that!"

"I do indeed. I realize now the Dag was destined to go to him."

He tilted his head back, closed his eyes and sighed. "And it is his destiny to die with me."

Iselda stared at Ulrich Schreck. She knew, without really knowing how she knew, that the old man was speaking the truth.

Addressing Dolf, he said, "When the American arrives, do not molest him. Allow him to enter."

From below came a rumble and the high-pitched whine of a turbine warming up.

Dolf smiled. "The generator is on-line, sir."

Schreck nodded, and made a dismissive gesture with one hand. "Take her away, Dolf. Put her with the others."

TWENTY-ONE

THE MAN with the gun was dressed in old, baggy trousers, a shapeless cotton work shirt and a grey cap. He held a small Titan automatic, deadly at such close range, leveled at Waring's head. He stood about three feet away.

"Come on, asshole," he said. "Go for it."

Slowly, Waring moved his hand away from the butt of the Ruger.

The man grinned, showing teeth like yellowed bricks. "You've got good sense."

His English was impeccable, touched with an Aussie accent. "Stand up. Slowly. And I do mean slowly."

Waring did as he was told, rising to his feet in stages. As he did, he turned his back to the man.

"Turn around, asshole."

Waring didn't move.

"I said turn around, you Yank bastard!"

The man took a step forward and grabbed the left shoulder of Waring's coat. He allowed himself to be pulled in that direction and then he whirled with blinding speed.

The edge of his stiffened left hand slashed down hard on the clump of ganglia on the inner wrist of the man's gun hand. The man cried out in surprised pain.

He tried to turn away, to bring the little gun into play, but Waring turned with him, locking the man's right wrist under his left arm and heaving up on it with all his upper body strength.

The arm broke at the elbow with a wet crunching sound.

The pain was so sudden, so overwhelming, the man couldn't even scream.

As the Titan dropped from nerve-numbed fingers, Waring maintained the pressure on the captured arm. He forced the man down on the ground, onto his back.

Disengaging the grip, Waring pulled the Ruger in a lightning-fast draw. He had the silenced barrel on a direct line with the man's head, just in case he regained enough presence of mind to scream.

The man didn't. He gaped up at Waring in terror, lips writhing over his discolored teeth in silent agony. Waring looked him over, saw that his shoes and pants were wet and realized he was the pilot he had been trailing for the last hour.

Though he'd carried a gun, he obviously wasn't an experienced hardman. Otherwise he never would have gotten close enough for Waring to execute a standard frontal handgun disarm. He should have stuck with playing with his joystick.

"Tell me what I want to know, " Waring said quietly. "Just a few things, that's all."

Supporting his broken arm with his left hand, holding it out straight, the pilot's face was filmed with sweat. "Like what?"

"How many men are at the farm?"

The man looked away. "Come on, mate, you know I can't—"

The Ruger coughed, and a round kicked up dirt between the man's thighs, barely a quarter of an inch from the crotch of his trousers.

"Tell me," said Waring, "or next shot, you're a eunuch."

The pilot told. "Maybe a dozen, maybe a little more. Some blokes have been deployed around the area."

"And the emitter?"

"I don't know, I just fly."

"Is Schreck there?"

"I don't know that, either. I'm not paid to take a roll call."

Waring walked around behind him. The man tried to follow him with his eyes.

"Face front," Waring commanded.

The Ruger came down sharply, denting the crown of the pilot's cap. He fell over sidewise, unconscious.

Waring made a quick examination of his head, found no sign of a fracture, and stripped off his belt and shoes. He bound and gagged him with his belt, shoelaces and socks, then dragged him beneath a clump of bushes.

Glancing at his watch, Waring wondered if the pilot was allotted a certain period of time to ditch the chopper and make his way to the farm, and if he didn't show up at that time, if a contingency plan would go into effect.

He doubted a search party would be sent out looking for the pilot, but the hardmen could very well assume he'd been captured and disclose the location of their base and make a pre-emptive move.

Waring figured the mercenaries wouldn't become overly concerned if the pilot hadn't appeared within an hour. Much more over that might make them fear a pending raid, and they would either move out, or transmit the launch-enabling code ahead of schedule.

There were no answers to any of these questions, and Waring

couldn't afford the luxury of second-guessing them.

Peering through the binoculars again, Waring watched the movements of the men in the farmyard. Unlike the pilot, these men were disciplined and combat-worthy soldiers, equal to any he had encountered before.

Though they pretended to be casual, they were watchful and wary. He considered changing clothes with the pilot and trying to bluff his way into the compound, but he instantly discarded the notion. The hardmen were too alert, too suspicious.

Scanning the house again, he saw movement between the front and rear doors. Two wide wooden covers slanted out from the foundation and formed a pair of trap doors. It was an old-fashioned storm cellar. As he watched, a man pushed one cover aside and climbed out.

He held a toolbox one hand and he shut the cover behind him, leaning over and latching it shut. Waring moved the glasses to the right and studied the barn.

It was a long, rambling building, several hundred yards from the house, but there appeared to be decent cover until within a few feet of a rear corner.

Taking off his jacket and hat, he moved off an angle through the woods, quickly crossing the footpath and entering the undergrowth again.

He was certain guards had been posted, so his progress was slow and silent, despite a quiver of impatience shivering along his spine.

Yet another long flight of the Falcon, he reflected, once more against unknown odds, against time, against death.

In similar infiltration missions in the past, he had executed diversionary thrusts, but those tactics wouldn't work here. There were far too many X factors to contend with. As far as he knew, Schreck was in the house with the telemetry box, finger poised over a button. He could be one second or one hour away from transmitting the launch code.

A full-out, frontal attack could be the motivation he needed to hit all the right buttons.

Waring crept through the woods carefully, calling on all his experience and expertise in wilderness warfare. Whenever he reached an open area, he crouched behind a tree or a bush, watching, waiting, listening. Every muscle tensed in anticipation of being discovered.

It hadn't happened by the time he belly-crawled through the undergrowth directly opposite the back corner of the barn, and rather than being relieved, his senses were even more alert.

He waited a long moment, straining his ears and eyes in search of anyone who might come between him and his target. He heard and saw nothing, then eased himself up and around, and slipped smoothly inside the barn.

A long cement-floored breezeway ran its entire length. Stalls were on either side, but there were only a few cows in them. They paid no attention to him as he walked through the barn, keeping his body to one side of the breezeway.

Reaching a wooden ladder that led to the hayloft, Waring considered climbing it, then his eyes rested on a shape covered by a sheet of mildewed canvas, pushed up against the wall.

Waring tugged away the canvas. Encased in a large transparent plastic bag were a man and a woman, pressed together face to face. The woman was middle-aged, with a gentle face. She wore a dirndl skirt and a deep blue blouse.

The man looked to be a few years older, dressed like a farmer. Both of them bore knife slashes across their throats.

Waring didn't know who they were, but he was sure they were owners of the farm, simple, decent folk who had something The Brotherhood wanted, and it had been taken from them in one, swift, ruthless move.

He had seen too many innocent dead all over the world to feel much anger or horror. He was saddened by the waste, by the casual, almost contemptuous way two people's lives had been snuffed out.

Waring's metabolism was still running at red alert, so when the man dropped from the hay loft, he wasn't caught completely off-guard.

Waring let himself collapse beneath the weight of the man, then twisted sideways. The pitchfork thrust in the man's hand barely missed him.

He was the big, powerful man in overalls he'd glimpsed through the binoculars. The man hefted the pitchfork and made a stabbing motion again. Waring didn't dare end it with the Ruger. Even a silenced shot might be heard in the quiet of the farmyard.

Waring dived under the tines, catching the man at the knees and toppling him like a tree. He jumped atop him, driving a knee to his stomach and raising the Ruger for a clubbing blow to the man's head.

The man's hand darted out with the speed of a striking snake and closed around Waring's right wrist, immobilizing it.

He was strong, and he struggled with a savage ferocity. He opened his mouth to shout. Waring didn't waste time trying to out-muscle him.

Stiffening his left hand, he curled the fingers inward toward the palm, locked his wrist and forearm, and delivered a leopard's paw strike to the thick tip of the man's nose.

His head snapped back, his nose smashed flat and spewing crimson. His eyes rolled up, showing only the whites, as bone chips were impelled past the sinus cavities and into the brain's frontal lobes. He went limp beneath Waring, faint gargling sounds issuing from his open mouth.

Patting the man down quickly, he found no other weapon. He presumed an order had been issued to avoid gunfire, since it might be heard by any authorities in the area. Noise traveled far over the meadows and pastures.

Around the man's neck was a small walkie-talkie. Judging by its size, the range was extremely limited, probably just to the farmhouse.

Waring doubted the man had time to make a report before jumping him, but that didn't mean he didn't make regular check-in calls. The time for the check-in could be thirty seconds or thirty minutes away.

Dragging him by the back-straps of his overalls, Waring laid him next to the bodies of the middle-aged couple and spread out the canvas to cover him up. Then he turned his attention back to the house.

He studied it from just inside the barn door and heard and saw nothing from within it. Satisfied that the yard was unobserved, Waring moved out. He crossed the expanse of the ground between the barn and the house in a semi-crouch, sacrificing stealth for the greater speed of long strides.

He reached the cellar door. It was secured by an outside hasp and padlock. He leaned close to the door before touching the lock. He heard nothing on the other side.

With a hooked pick taken from his pocket, Waring probed the lock. It opened with a faint click. He froze, listening again. Then he lifted one door panel and slid beneath it, onto a short flight of rough-hewn stone steps.

If someone lurked down there with a gun, he knew he was presenting a perfect target, outlined by the brief flash of sunlight flooding the cellar. Nothing happened.

Waring risked the needle beam from his penlight. All he saw was a typical farmhouse cellar—free-standing shelves holding jars of pickled vegetables, a few tools, an old washing machine and various odds and ends.

He moved across the cellar, his feet making no noise on the hard-packed earth. A rickety wooden stairway stretched up to a closed door.

Waring heard people moving above him, the muted murmur of male voices, and the creak of floorboards.

The penlight showed him the junction box on the wall, a cluster of electrical cables with frayed insulation running down from above, feeding into a metal sleeve. All the cables looked old.

He also saw a flexible conduit of bright, shiny aluminum snaking along the rafters, over to the wall, and terminating at a circuit box attached to the cast-iron casing of an electric generator.

The generator was bolted to a pair of two-by-fours. The two-by-fours were sunk into a clean, whitish-grey concrete slab. The generator looked brand new.

Looking it over, Waring saw it possessed considerable amperage. The lever on the fuse box was up, in the Off position. The generator wasn't connected to the main junction box. It was hooked to a separate line entirely, so it hadn't been installed simply for emergencies.

The door at the top of the stairs suddenly opened and a naked light bulb overhead blazed with light.

Waring glided swiftly behind a shelf. Peering between dusty jars of pickled herring and rutabagas, he watched a squat, crew-cut man tramp down the steps, speaking to someone in a room above.

The man walked over to the generator and opened the panel to the fuse box. He worked a priming handle up and down for a few seconds. Then, shutting the panel, he threw the lever down and the generator rumbled to life.

The loud, high-pitched whine of the turbine filled the cellar and vibrations set the jars on the shelves to vibrating.

The man moved to the foot of the stairs and he and someone Waring couldn't see exchanged shouts.

The man stood at the foot of the stairs, looking up at them. Another shout from above elicited a thumbs-up reaction, and he turned back to the throbbing generator.

A jar fell from a high shelf. The sound of glass shattering was audible even over the steady whine. The man's head snapped around. His eyes widened as he glimpsed the dark figure crouching behind the jars.

The light from the overhead bulb gleamed on polished gunmetal as he brought an automatic from behind his back.

The Ruger spat out a pair of .45 slugs, punching twin paths through the man's chest, barely a finger's width apart. He went down heavily, striking the back of his head against the hard metal surface of the generator.

Waring crossed the cellar quickly, examining the man in the rough work clothes. The Glock was still in his hand.

There was another shout from the head of the stairs, only one word: "Gunter!"

Waring had no choice but to gamble. Stepping to the generator, he nudged a numbered knob to a lower setting and the rumbling whine decreased in volume.

From above came, *"Di bist kommen heraus."*

Waring understood that simple command, and counting on the softening noise of the generator to muffle his voice, mumbled, *"Ich wiess nicht."*

His response evidently satisfied the man, because he heard footsteps going away from the cellar, then the opening and shutting of a door. Waring started up the steps, touching the wooden risers with only the balls of his feet.

Waring walked into a spacious, rustic kitchen. He saw a table with a setting for two and an old natural gas stove.

The door leading to the outside was closed—he stepped over and locked it. He went to the window over the sink and parted the chintz curtains.

At first he saw no one and then a mercenary moved into his field of vision from around the corner of the house. He held a radio to his ear and spoke into it.

The hardman had his back turned to him, so Waring couldn't hear what he was saying, but he appeared to grow agitated. He stared at the barn, and continued to speak into the walkie-talkie.

The man cast a glance toward the house, and Waring moved back from the window a bit. He watched as the hardman pocketed the radio, pulled a Glock from his waistband, and began a quick walk toward the barn.

Waring knew what was going to happen to next. The curtain was about to rise on the last act of the nightmare.

TWENTY-TWO

A CLATTER of feet descending the stairs from the second floor drew Waring away from the window.

He heard two voices, a man's and a woman's. He recognized Iselda's voice, and rather than devoting time to wondering how the hell she'd ended up in the farmhouse, Waring ducked back into the cellar, standing on the top step and closing the door behind him. He left it open a crack.

The tall blond mercenary and Iselda appeared in the kitchen. The weed of suspicion growing in Waring's mind wilted when he saw the hardman had the woman's right arm crooked painfully behind her back. He manhandled her to the door, and ordered her to open it.

Iselda had trouble unlocking it and the mercenary applied more pressure to her arm, dragging a cry of pain and protest from her.

Waring's finger tensed on the Ruger's trigger, but a shot now would endanger Iselda. The round that accounted for the hardman could easily strike the woman as well.

Iselda got the door open and was propelled through it, down the steps. She stumbled, nearly went to her knees, but the blond man yanked her to her feet by a hand tangled in her hair.

Waring watched, teeth clenched in anger. He drifted into the kitchen. The back door hung open, and he peered around the frame.

The hardman who'd been on the way to the barn stopped midway at a shout from the mercenary. The two exchanged words, then the man walked back and grabbed Iselda's left arm. They began dragging her to the barn.

Waring thought of the throat-slit couple locked in cold embrace inside the plastic shroud and left the house in a sprint. He couldn't ignore the possibility that a watcher from another floor could see him, but he disregarded it. Reaching the tractor attached to the six-disc plow, he climbed into the saddle.

The pair of mercenaries had reached the barn entrance and struggled with Iselda. She kicked and shouted. The man put a hand over her mouth and dragged her out of sight.

Waring turned the ignition key and pressed the starter button. The engine caught on the first try. Putting it into gear, the tractor roared toward the barn.

The two hardmen appeared at the open barn door, gaping in astonishment. Both drew automatics from behind their backs, but held their fire. As Waring had figured, they were under orders to avoid gunplay.

Crouching down behind the wheel, Waring turned the disc plows on high speed, and the whirling motion set up a hum. Pressing down a lever, he lifted the blades about a foot from the ground and floored the accelerator.

The tractor roared into the barn, and the pair of mercenaries raced ahead of it. The metal framework of the plow was so wide, the tractor had to be kept on a straight course. If bullets were flung Waring's way, there was no leeway for evasive maneuvering.

However, its width prevented the men from getting out of the tractor's path by putting their backs against the wall or the stall doors.

Waring threaded the tractor through the breezeway, and by the time the mercenaries had managed to run to the rear of the barn, they decided to disobey the no-gunplay edict.

The blond man turned and aimed his automatic. Waring ducked as low as he could, steering more by instinct than sight.

The sound of the Glock firing was less loud than the *whang* of a bullet ricocheting off the front of the tractor. Waring jerked the wheel in the hardman's direction and raised his head and gun hand just enough to find and acquire a target.

He brought the blond man into the Ruger's sights, but the tractor jounced just as he squeezed the trigger.

The bullet caught the mercenary high on the right shoulder. It wasn't a serious wound, or even incapacitating, but he staggered, legs tangling. He fell in the tractor's path.

Waring tried to navigate around him. The tractor's fat tires missed him by a fractional margin, but the plow swung wide on the coupling. He felt the tractor shudder as the blades struck flesh and bone. The crunching, grinding sound was sickening, but he thought about the patients in the clinic used as human shields and the middle-aged couple sheathed in plastic.

A bullet bounced off the hood of the tractor, only a few inches from Waring's face, and metal slivers stung his cheek. Yanking the wheel, he turned the tractor in the opposite direction from which the shot had come.

Manipulating the plow handle, he lowered the blades, and the whirling discs bit into the ground, sending up plumes of dust.

Waring leaped from the saddle, rolled and came to his feet, keeping the tractor between him and the second gunman. He glimpsed him crouching about fifty feet away, peering through the shifting planes of dust.

He also glimpsed Iselda Abendroth, racing full-tilt from the barn, the pitchfork held in both hands.

The roar of the tractor's engine and the clatter of the plow covered the sound of her rushing approach. Without breaking stride, Iselda plunged the tines of the pitchfork into the mercenary's upper back, just above his shoulders.

The man howled, fell forward, then struggled to his feet, his left hand reaching behind him. He looked like a pain-crazed insect, transfixed by a giant pin. With the gun in his right hand, he drew a bead on Iselda.

The silenced Ruger snorted out a round. The mercenary staggered backwards, dropping the Glock, trying to stem the flow from a pulsing throat wound.

He fell, but he didn't hit the ground. The blunt end of the pitchfork's shaft dug into the soft earth, and the mercenary hung there, his body poised on the tines at a 45 degree angle.

The tractor continued on its wild course and smashed through a fence. Without the pressure of a foot on the gas pedal, the fence slowed it down, and the tractor came to a slow halt.

Waring glanced around for more opposition and saw no one. The scene around him was not for the sensitive.

He found Iselda standing near the undergrowth. Fright shone fresh in her eyes. He took her in his arms, but he couldn't afford the time to hold her until her trembling ceased.

"It's not over," he said.

He didn't need to say more. Iselda pushed herself away and began talking, telling him about Schreck in the attic room with the transmitter and telemetry box and the generator in the cellar. She had no idea of how many mercenaries might be around.

Waring said, "Ordinarily, I'd send you out of harm's way—"

Nostrils flaring, Iselda said, "Bullshit. You need my help."

He nodded. "I do. Schreck might hit the launch enabling transmission any second. He may have already done it."

"No. He's waiting for you."

Waring's eyebrows rose.

"He's waiting for you to bring the Dag to him," she explained. She took a breath. "He's waiting for you to die with him."

"He's liable to have a long wait."

"He's given orders that you're not be killed when you arrive. To do so would interfere with destiny."

"We can use that. All his men pulling sentry duty will probably be called back to base, if they're not on their way already."

Waring plucked a Glock from the ground and handed it to her. Detaching a grenade from his combat harness, he gave her quick instructions on how to use it. He outlined his plan briefly and tersely.

Iselda's lips compressed in fear, but she gave a grim nod of understanding. She crouched down out of sight, holding the grenade with both hands.

Waring left her and walked through the barn. He was taking a big chance, relying on the help of a civilian, but it was her country and her future at stake. Contacting either Jacobs or Solezer would only make matters worse and add names to a potential casualties list.

Waring always acted independently of the authorities when the circumstances demanded it. That was why he was chosen for this mission, and Aladar Herne knew it, even if the responsibility for its failure fell on his shoulders.

Waring stopped at the open door long enough to put a full load into the Ruger before slipping it into the shoulder holster. He picked up one of the Glocks and put it in his waistband. He removed two of the grenades from the harness, depressed the finger levers and pulled the safety pins.

Gripping them tightly in both hands, he walked out into the farmyard, striding for the back door of the house. He knew he was being watched. He counted on it.

As he walked, he was reminded of the climactic showdown in High Noon. The comparison was apt.

"Freeze!"

"Stop where you are!"

Two pairs of men, one to his left and one to his right stood at the border of the yard. They trained Glocks on him.

Waring kept walking in measured, deliberate strides.

"Stop, you son of a bitch!"

"Get those hands up!"

The shouted commands carried notes of panic.

The men came closer, moving warily, trying to encircle him. When he was abreast of the VW panel truck, Waring raised his hands and then opened them. The levers of the grenades fell.

All four men swore, yelled and stared to retreat.

Waring tossed one of the V40s toward the men on his right and the other beneath the truck.

The double concussions hurled geysers of dirt into the air. Gravel and clods of earth rained.

The detonating grenade beneath the truck raised the rear and split the gas tank. The fuel caught fire and exploded. Orange tongues of fire lapped out, chunks of metal spun across the yard.

A wave of burning gasoline engulfed one of the men, and he screamed in terror and pain. Falling to the ground, he rolled frantically, beating at the flames.

Waring drew the Ruger and the Glock at the same time, crossed his arms over his chest and fired through the smoke and dust and flame. He continued walking toward the house, but his eyes were constantly moving.

The grenades had accounted for one man, his bullets for two others. The man splashed with gasoline still rolled wildly in the dirt.

Waring reached the back steps. A man appeared in the open doorway, aiming a pistol with both hands.

"Drop it!" he shouted.

Waring kept walking.

"Drop it!" the man shouted again. "Or I drop you!"

The Ruger spat out a single round, and the man in the doorway reeled backwards into the kitchen.

Waring walked up the steps and looked around the kitchen. The man lay on the floor near a garbage pail, leaking fluids. His eyes were wide-open and glassy.

The command Schreck had given not to have him shot down could be pushed only so far. Whatever obedience the hardmen gave Schreck wouldn't supersede their survival instinct. Only a man too dumb to live would stand making threats to an armed intruder that he wasn't allowed to carry through. Waring doubted the next mercenary he encountered would order him to drop his weapon first.

A dark man-shape appeared in the hallway off the kitchen and the staccato beat of an auto carbine filled the house. Waring rolled to the floor and to one side. The steel-jacketed volley raked the kitchen, disintegrating glass, smashing woodwork, ripping wall boards to splinters. The mercenary was good, tracking his target with a continuous stream of lead.

Waring gave him a triple burst from the Ruger. He went down, firing the last few rounds into the ceiling. Plaster dust showered down and mixed with the blood flowing from his chest.

Climbing to his feet, Waring stepped over the body and continued through the house. He came to a flight of stairs stretching up to the second floor. He was tempted to toss a grenade up there, but that would overplay his hand.

With his back to the wall, Waring sidled up the stairwell, the Ruger held in front of him. Several of the steps creaked beneath his weight.

Before he set foot on the second floor, he went down prone on the steps and simply listened.

He heard nothing for what felt like a very long time, then came the almost imperceptible rustle of cloth.

A man lurked on the other side of a wall, a wall he would have to pass to get to the second floor. Waring took aim with the Ruger, gauging where a man would stand in order to stage an ambush.

Waring squeezed the trigger of the .45, and sent three rounds blasting through the wall. He heard wood shredding and splitting as the bullets sought their targets on the other side of the barrier.

By the time he heard the grunt of pain and surprise, he was up and moving.

A man lay on his face, an auto carbine cradled in lifeless hands.

Easing back into the hallway, Waring checked his watch. The time he'd allotted for Iselda to make her move was almost up. Soft-shoeing along the floor, he saw a short flight of steps reaching up to a closed door panel in the ceiling. Waring put his foot on the first step. It creaked, and he waited for a reaction. It was not long in coming.

The panel opened about three inches. A gun barrel appeared and a rattling blast of sound and orange flame erupted from it. Pieces of wood and carpet rose into the air.

Waring ducked back, toward a window, as the autofire chewed its way toward him. He didn't return the fire.

Fitting his fingers beneath the window sash, he slid it up. There was a small, shingled overhang below, and he climbed out, using a drain pipe as a handhold.

The edge of the roof was level with his chin, and he heaved himself up, using only the strength in his legs and the levering power of one arm.

The roof slanted down at a steep angle, so it was impossible to stand. He crawled toward the roof-ridge, hoping the machine-gun in the attic room would continue to chatter and mask the sound of his movements.

He topped the crest of the roof just as the gunfire ceased, and he stopped moving, bending down to listen. He heard voices muttering from below, but he couldn't make out how many or what was being said.

Straddling the ridge, Waring scooted forward, trying to keep his feet from grating against the shingles. When he reached the chimney, he stood up. From his combat harness he took a coil of silken cord and wrapped it around the base of the chimney, affixing it to the bricks with a small grappling hook.

Holding the slack in his left hand, he continued moving along the ridge. His progress felt agonizingly slow.

At the end of the roof, facing the front of the house, Waring leaned forward, looking down at a window tucked between the eaves. An iron lightning rod rose from the juncture. He held onto it as he bent down.

Though it was only a few feet below him, the window was small, barely large enough to admit a man his size. By feel, he looped the rope's slack through a metal ring sewn into the leather at the back of his combat harness. He gave the line an experimental tug, making certain it was secured around the chimney.

It was a dangerous maneuver. He could lose his grip and fall, or not be fast enough and get shot. But rather than stay perched on the roof and go through a litany of things that could go wrong, Waring looped the rope around the lightning rod, flattened out and edged his body forward, allowing his legs to dangle.

He made the assumption that the men in the garret below were on the alert for an attack from the second floor, and felt fairly safe from an assault from above or the outside.

Waring moved carefully, his left hand gripping the lightning rod. Bracing his feet against the top frame of the window, he slowly eased his weight onto the rope.

The line jerked, and one of his feet slipped. For a moment, he kicked empty air. He found his footing again, and he inched further out and down. Using his legs like springs, he pushed himself away from the front of the house. He adjusted the slack on the rope.

Swinging forward, both feet impacted flatly against the window-pane. It smashed inward with a loud clash and jangle. Through the flying splinters and shards of glass, Waring fell to his knees inside a dimly-lit room that ran the length of the house.

A man stood near the far end, whirling at the racket of shattering glass. The auto carbine in his right hand stuttered.

Using the momentum of his fall, Waring somersaulted beneath the stream of slugs, and when he came out of it, his finger was working the Ruger's trigger.

Waring felt a shock of impact against the meat of his left shoulder, and he knew a bullet had gouged a shallow furrow through flesh and muscle. He willed himself to keep pumping the .45's trigger.

The man with the carbine sprouted punctures in his face and head, and he careened backward violently. He slammed against the wall and fell forward, curled around the auto rifle He lay very still.

Waring got to his feet, feeling wet warmth slide down his arm. He saw a man seated in a wheelchair at a computer, his left hand resting lightly on the keyboard. Glancing over at the dead gunman, he said, "Thank you. He needed to be executed for disobeying my orders not to shoot at you."

"Schreck," said Waring.

Ulrich Schreck regarded him with a gracious, almost deferential smile.

"I'm told your name is Waring," he said. "That is no name for such a fierce warrior. I'm sure it's just a nom d' voyage."

Waring approached him cautiously, gun held at arm's length, on a direct line with the man's hairless skull.

"Get away from that keyboard, Schreck."

"At this point in our relationship," the old man said, "there is no harm in confiding your real name to me."

Waring shrugged. "I prefer titles rather than names."

Schreck regarded him skeptically. "And you have such a title?"

"I've been referred to as The Falcon a time or two."

"Ah, so you are the infamous Falcon I've heard about for years." Scheck's mouth twitched in disappointment. "A ridiculous code-name chosen by those you work for."

"I don't work for anyone. I'm not CIA or G2 or Homeland Security. Call what I do a hobby. At times, faced with fanatic fools like you, it's a real pleasure."

"If you're a man of private means, you might consider changing hobbies. I can see you spring from superb Aryan stock."

"I won't tell you again. Get away from that keyboard."

Schreck laughed. "You don't have the stomach to shoot someone in my state."

"No, I don't," Waring admitted. "But if it's a choice between you or hundreds of thousands of people, I'll pull this trigger—several times."

Schreck kept his hand poised, vulture-like, over the keys. He gave

Waring a long, silent, speculative stare.

Waring returned the stare, and he couldn't remember if he'd ever before seen such venomous eyes in a human being. He understood the terrible danger of this man.

He was no posturing bully, no crafty mobster, no deranged terrorist dreamer. Ulrich Schreck was a dedicated man, exuding all the qualities of greatness that bred Alexanders, Napoleons, Caesars—and Hitlers.

There was definitely brilliance about him, but it was warped all out of shape and bent to serve distorted ends. His mind, his imagination were devoted to hate, his sensitivity consecrated to serve twisted cruelty, reason turned to egomaniacal psychosis.

"The manner in which you've outmaneuvered me over the past few days is impressive," Schreck declared. He could have been having a polite conversation in a drawing room. "I should have realized earlier that we were destined to share this moment, and I apologize for tasking you."

Distantly, Waring could hear the generator throbbing in the cellar. He looked at Scheck's left hand. The old man noticed the eye action and smiled.

"Oh, yes. The sequence has already been input into the system. All I need do now is press the enter key."

Waring estimated it would take less than one second for the sequence to be fed from the computer to the telemetry box and another second for the box to send the electronic data to the emitter and transmit the signal. The dish was already powered up, so another three seconds would be required for the microwave beam to travel three miles and talk to the computers on the missiles.

He calculated a total of five seconds would decide the course of history for hundreds of years to come.

"Drop your weapon, Herr Falcon," Schreck said, his voice rising sharply with mockery. "Drop it at your feet and kick it away from you. Now."

Waring let the Ruger fall to the floor.

"Now your satchel."

As Waring slipped the strap of the bag over his head, his hand dipped inside it and closed around a long smooth object. The bag dropped to the floor, but Waring held the Dag in his hand.

He held it up, over his heart. Scheck's body quivered as if he'd received an electric shock. He almost removed his hand from the keyboard, but he checked the motion.

"Give that to me." Shreck's eyes shone brightly, his mouth hung open.

"Like hell," Waring said. "This is my property."

He turned his wrist, and Schreck's eyes followed every motion of the Dag. Fresh blood glistened on its dark grey surface.

"My blood is on it. It's mine now."

Schreck shot him a glare of pure hatred, but there was fear mixed with it. He stretched out a trembling hand, leaning over the armrest of the wheelchair, but he kept his left hand on the keyboard. An aspirated stream of German hissed from between his lips.

Waring smiled. "It was given to me to safeguard. That is a trust I will not betray. Honor is loyalty, remember?"

Schreck snarled, his eyes narrowing to slits. "Ja, I do."

His eyes fixed on Waring's, his right hand dipped inside his coat and came out clutching a Walther P-38.

"You will give me the Dag," he said, speaking slowly and emphasizing each word. "Or I will kill you and wrest it from your dead hands."

"Why not do that in the first place?"

A glimmer of uncertainty flickered in Schreck's eyes.

"You're afraid, aren't you?" Waring asked. "You're afraid that if I have the Dag, there is a reason for it, and if you kill me, you might kill its power."

"You will give it to me, or I will transmit the signal."

"You'll do that anyway. Why should I make things easy for you?"

Lips peeled back from his gums, Schreck spat, *"Schwein!"*

His knuckle whitened on the trigger of the Walther.

The sound of the explosion in the cellar was not overwhelmingly loud, but it was loud enough. Waring felt the shock waves through the soles of his feet, and the concussion shook the foundation of the house. Loose objects in the garret fell over and clattered to the floor.

Schreck punched the keyboard with a triumphant cry, and then he performed a wild-eyed double-take. He hit the keys again—and screamed.

Ulrich Schreck threw his head back and howled, mouthing gibberish. His eyes went wide with panic, with something more than panic. Without aiming, he fired the Walther.

Waring rolled aside, at the same time hurling the Dag in a sweeping side arc of his right arm.

The relic was heavy, poorly balanced, but the point of the cen-

ter blade made a crunching sound as it imbedded itself in Schreck's breastbone.

Schreck stared down at the thing impaling his chest. The Walther thudded to the floor. Shaking hands rose to grasp the hilt.

Schreck didn't try to pull it out. He simply held the Dag, fingers caressing and fondling the stone hilt. He lifted his face and looked at Waring, a silent question in his eyes.

"Iselda Abendroth," Waring told him. "A good person, a good German. She threw a grenade into the cellar where you keep your generator. It cut the power to the transmitter."

Schreck's eyelids drooped. He chuckled, and grimaced in pain. His head bowed and he whispered something in English. Waring leaned down to hear.

"What did you say?"

"I said that perhaps we will meet again, under different circumstances."

"Unlikely, Schreck."

"In our next incarnations. Perhaps we'll even fight on the same side."

"Even more unlikely," said Waring.

Ulrich Schreck didn't hear him. The demigod of the Brotherhood of the Black Sun no longer looked like a man who commanded the forces of destiny.

He looked like a dead old man.

From his wallet, Waring extracted a small white card. It bore no text—only the stylized graphic of a bird-of-prey with back swept wings and outstretched talons, a duplicate of the image tattooed on his right arm. He laid it atop the handle of the Dag, knowing that if the card were found by the German authorities, the signature was too subtle to be understood. But old habits were hard to break.

Waring retrieved the Ruger and before he left the attic room, he expended a single round on the telemetry box, turning it into a mass of split metal and shattered silicon circuitry.

The house was on fire by the time Waring reached the ground floor. The grenade had ignited something flammable in the cellar. Smoke lay in heavy sheets, and flames licked up between the floorboards.

Detecting the metallic odor of propane, he remembered the kitchen had a gas stove. A stray shot must have severed the gas line. He quickly left by the front door.

Iselda waited for him in the yard. He cut off her questions and the noises of sympathy she made over his wound and hustled her away from the house. They had gotten about thirty yards when the gas line ignited.

A thundering column of flame nearly fifty feet high mushroomed from the house. Rolling balls of fire billowed up into the blue sky, and burning debris was hurled in all directions.

Loud, ear-knocking explosions rocked the quiet countryside as ammunition let go somewhere in the wreckage.

Waring looked at the monstrous, crackling pyre roaring into the heavens.

"That ought to attract somebody's attention," he said.

EPILOGUE

THERE WASN't much to do after that.

Verfassungsschutz operatives hunted down the few mercenaries still in the fields around Site 611. There was very little shooting, although a couple had to be clubbed unconscious with gun butts. Most of the mercenaries surrendered gratefully.

Within ninety minutes, all of them had been apprehended and were talking. The identities and locations of all Brotherhood contacts and supply dumps in and around Berlin were turned over to the German intelligence service.

Raiding parties poured out of Verfassungsschutz bureaus all over West Germany. In due course, the innocent dupes, driven by greed rather than politics, would be sorted out from the truly guilty. In the interim, anyone with any connections to the Brotherhood of the Black Sun was suspect.

By sundown, the immediate crisis appeared over.

At the farm, the flames had been doused, and men in oxygen masks and back-tanks kicked through the blackened, smoking debris. There was very little left of the house. Most of it was scattered across several acres.

Mike Waring and Iselda Abendroth watched the search operation, leaning against a Verfassungschutz Land Rover. Both of them were quiet. Waring's shoulder wound had been treated by a medic and no longer throbbed quite as painfully.

The injury was superficial, more unsightly than critical. The bullet had inscribed a painful graze through a few layers of skin and bruised the muscle, but the wound would heal quickly.

That was more than Waring could say for the reunited Germany.

A soot-streaked Solezer approached them, stripping off the oxygen mask.

"I believe we've found Schreck's remains," he said. "At least we think so. There's very little left as a frame of reference for identification."

"And the Dag?" Waring asked.

He shook his head. "No trace yet. It was probably pulverized by the explosions."

"We can only hope so," Waring said.

Solezer eyed Waring sadly and said, "You were right. I was working from the wrong viewpoint. Perhaps I didn't want to admit to myself that the evil of bygone days hadn't died of old age."

"Maybe it did," said Iselda. "But it wasn't interred with the bones of the men who practiced it and so it was resurrected when the time was right."

Solezer didn't reply to that. He went back to directing the search operation. He appeared extremely distressed, and Waring didn't blame him. It probably wasn't the first time Fascist bastards had jeopardized his organization and his job security.

A dark green sedan pulled up in the yard. Jacobs climbed out, looking jubilant.

"We've got the enabling codes at the site changed," he said. "A new set of precautionary measures are in the works. Something like this will never happen again, by God."

"As long as those weapons exist, something like it can happen," said Waring. "Maybe not in our lifetimes, but it will happen again. The only way to stop it is to remove the temptation. Don't just lock the cookie jar, smash the jar and the cookies in them into crumbs."

Jacobs looked sour. "You're an optimistic bastard, Waring."

"I manage."

Jacobs forced a smile to his face. "Thanks to you, I'm going to be as busy as a cat covering up its shit for the next couple of weeks. We've got to sort all this out and file all the intelligence. The Brotherhood has contacts and conduits all over the damn place. Exposing it is a real coup."

"For whom?"

As if he hadn't heard, Jacobs went on. "The Joint Chiefs have notified the White House that they are very pleased with the way we resolved this matter. I'm passing on the congratulations to you. If that makes any kind of difference."

"It doesn't," said Waring.

"I imagine you'll be receiving an official commendation."

"I don't think so, Major. I'm not eligible."

Jacobs scowled and gestured to the sedan. "My driver will take you to the airport. You have a jet waiting, so don't let us keep you."

Waring turned away from him and walked toward the smoldering debris. He stood and studied it from a distance. Iselda came to his side.

"So it's over?" she asked.

"For you, yes. For your country, I don't know."

"What about you? It's never truly over for you, is it?"

When Waring didn't answer, she said softly, "You're wondering what the hell it's all about."

"Yes."

"But you always pick up and go on, don't you? To the next battle, to tilt at another windmill."

She said no more, but pressed up against him and leaned her head against his chest. Slowly, Waring put an arm around her and stroked her hair. He turned Iselda to him, and kissed her tenderly on the lips, cupping her face between his hands.

They stood there in a long embrace, oblivious to the swirling smoke and the men moving around them.

Mike Waring lived for the moments between the windmills, but he knew others always beckoned and always would so long as he lived. But strangely, he felt at peace. He understood that although an evil from seventy years before had been resurrected, so had The Falcon.

That was his true name, and he would be called that until the day he swooped into a hellzone too hot for him to cool down. And even then, that name would be his epitaph.

The Falcon would always spread out both wings and run his prey to ground.

HE WILL BE BACK!

About the Author

MARK ELLIS is a novelist and comics creator whose many credentials include *Doc Savage: The Man of Bronze*, *The Wild, Wild West*, *The Justice Machine*, *Death Hawk*, *The Miskatonic Project*, *Ninja Elite*, *Star Rangers* and *Nosferatu: Plague of Terror*.

In 1996 he created the best-selling *Outlanders* series for Harlequin Enterprise's Gold Eagle imprint, writing under the penname of James Axler. He is the author of over 50 books, and with his wife Melissa Martin-Ellis, co-wrote *The Everything Guide to Writing Graphic Novels*. He has been featured in *Starlog*, *Comics Scene* and *Fangoria* magazines.

He has also been interviewed by Robert Siegel for NPR's *All Things Considered*.

www.MarkEllisInk.com
www.Cryptozoica.com

THE LEGENDARY HERO RETURNS!

THE FALCON
DOCTOR SUN

MARK ELLIS

From Mark Ellis, the Creator of OUTLANDERS & THE SPUR!

"CRYPTOZOICA is a novel for those who really want to sink their teeth into something engrossing to the finish. For a modern take on pulp adventure, you would be hard-pressed to find one that delivers like this!"

-Bookgasm

Available in trade paperback at all online booksellers, and as an ebook exclusively at Amazon.com

As James Axler, cont'd

www.ingramcontent.com/pod-product-compliance
Lightning Source LLC
Chambersburg PA
CBHW050932120626
46552CB00001B/176